The
Reluctant Guardian

by

Jo Manning

Regency Press
Cleveland Heights, Ohio

THE RELUCTANT GUARDIAN

Copyright © 1999 by Jo Manning

Regency Press is a division of
Crack of Noon Enterprises, Incorporated.
The name Regency Press and the Crowned R are registered trademarks of Crack of Noon Enterprises, Incorporated.

ISBN: 1-929085-07-9

First Edition: December, 1999

Printed in the United States of America

0 9 8 7 6 5 4 3 2 1

Regency Press
Cleveland Heights, Ohio

The
Reluctant Guardian

One

London, 1811

Where he is at present, I cannot say, for without giving me the least hint or leaving any Message he went out before I was out of Bed, Dressed very Smart, & I have not seen or heard anything from him since, but I fancy he will not return tonight, for he has taken his Night, and Morning Cap, & has left one hundred guineas in a little Bag in the Harpsichord Drawer...

❖

Bloody hell!

Colonel Sir Isaac Rebow threw the letter onto his dressing room table, sending his hairbrushes skittering and causing his standing mirror to lose its footing and come down with a loud thud. The sound brought him back to his senses. For the moment.

Blast! He was beyond annoyance and frustration. He was most thoroughly vexed!

He reread the missive from his young cousin Mary, dated Sunday last, that had been enclosed in his mother's urgent packet from Wivenhoe Park. His simpleton of an uncle had deserted his daughters; and Madam, Isaac's mother, was summoning him to take immediate action in the disgraceful matter.

Bloody hell! Madam be damned, he did not want this bother.

He tore the mangled cravat from his throat and muttered another mighty oath. Hopeless! His cravat and

1

the situation both. Robbins, his valet, could deal with the former, but the burden for the latter sat firmly on his shoulders. His strong-featured face twisted into an ugly grimace, frightening his timid valet, who just walked into the dressing room.

Ignoring Robbins, Isaac swore, slamming his hand against the dressing table. The resultant pain hadn't a hope of registering into his consciousness; he was too angry. His uncle was a bloody fool. What kind of caperwit would wander off, going God knew where, to do God knew what, and leave his daughters without protection in the middle of London?

Robbins, a thin, anxious man of indeterminate age and diminutive size, hovered near the door of the dressing room, reluctant to enter. Isaac turned. "Well, don't just stand there, man! Do something with this. I'm eager to go out." He gestured to the creased white lawn cravat hanging in hopeless disarray about his neck.

Timorously, Robbins took several mincing footsteps toward his enraged master, carefully unwrapped the ruined piece and replaced it with a clean, crisp swath of cloth. Adroitly, Robbins's nimble fingers fashioned the fabric into an unobtrusive shape.

Not for Sir Isaac Rebow were those flamboyant styles favored by the dandies about town. Rebow looked down his fine Roman nose at the voguish contraptions fancifully named Oriental or Mathematical. A former military man, a country gentleman, now a successful politician and businessman, he was yet a man of simple tastes.

His younger friend Fraser could ape the Corinthian crowd and aim for the desirable appellation *'top o' the trees,'* but he was content with being simply what he was.

As if conjured up by Isaac's random musings, the sound of rapid footfalls was heard on the stairs, and handsome Jamie Fraser himself appeared, in full flower.

Isaac smiled, crinkling the slightly tanned skin at the corners of his dark blue eyes. "What ho, Fraser? Up, out and about before noon? Have you adjusted your usual regimen?"

Fraser suffered his friend's good-natured teasing as he basked in the undisguised glow of admiration from Rebow's valet. Breathless, he sat down in the small dressing room and fanned himself briskly with the sheaf of documents he held in his hands.

Fraser was tall and slim, and took pride in his exquisitely tailored wardrobe. Today he was clad in Weston's finest close-fitting buff inexpressibles and sported a trim Bath superfine coat almost the robin's-egg blue of his eyes. His thick fair curls, cut *à la* Brutus, tumbled over his forehead.

"Sale at Tattersall's, Isaac. Heard about it at Stephen's Hotel last night from two Corinthians in their cups. Baron Derwent's landed himself in River Tick again and is forced to part with his prime cattle. I've a mind to look them over before they go under the gavel." He waved the papers advertising the sale.

He hunched forward, propping one muscular leg over the other, laying a shined-to-a-turn, tasselled brown leather Hessian on his knee. His blue eyes sparkled with excitement and his voice took on a cajoling tone. "You've a deuced fine eye for horseflesh, Isaac. Care to join me?"

Isaac was tempted.

Perhaps this affair of his henwitted uncle could wait. It looked to be a fine day, and any day that roused Fraser before 4 p.m. *had* to be special. It had been a long winter, but spring had arrived at last, bringing with it gloriously sunny weather. And Fraser was correct, the unfortunate gamester Derwent owned excellent bloodstock. Tempting, indeed...

Country-bred and reared, Rebows were mad for horses. The sharp, saddlesoapy smell of the stables on a fine spring morning, the freshness of newly mown hay stacked high for feed, the warm, sweet smell of the nervous, high-strung stallions... Ah, mused Isaac, it was a wonderful way to pass one's time, amongst prime horseflesh: the salvation of his troubled youth. He liked, too, the gentlemen-only atmosphere of Tatt's. It was a private club, like his club, Brooks's, but better.

He had to admit spending the morning with Fraser at Tatt's was preferable even to dancing attendance on the beauteous Sophia, Lady Rowley, his *chère amie*. Fraser was probably slightly better company, too, than Sophia, if truth were told. Yes, he would...

No, of course, he couldn't!

This sunny day was ruined by Madam's preemptive summons. He had gone so far as to take his bad temper out on his valet; he was usually more considerate, sensitive to Robbins's timid nature. It wasn't his valet's fault that Madam was a virago. No, unfortunately, Duty had reared its ugly, many-tentacled head and called clearly, in ringing tones, from Wivenhoe Park in far-off Essex, echoing all the way to his Duke Street abode in Westminster.

Blast!

Isaac shook his head, unfortunately just as poor Robbins was attempting to tie back his master's long dark hair with a silk riband, the old-fashioned style his late, beloved father had favored. The valet pitched forward, bumping his nose against his master's broad, unpadded shoulder. Isaac frowned at Robbins' clumsiness but forebore making the caustic comment at the tip of his tongue. He turned his attention to his visitor.

"Sorry, Jamie. Family matter in Chelsea. My young cousins... perhaps some other time."

Fraser was puzzled. *Cousins?* A naturally inquisitive young man, he was intrigued by this sudden call to family duty.

"Cousins in Chelsea, Isaac? I've not heard you speak of them before," he commented, absently looking away from his friend and twisting an already perfectly centered cufflink into place.

Isaac shrugged his shoulders into the nondescript gray coat Robbins was holding for him, while behind his back, his valet's lips thinned in mute disdain at the lackluster tailoring and style of the offending article. Fraser smiled at the valet's look and winked conspiratorially in acknowledgement. Both Robbins and Fraser had tried, with no success, to interest Isaac in current fashion.

Isaac favored a former military tailor on Conduit Street patronized by no one else of consequence, and had, moreover, refused to style his hair in one of the new short cuts. Fraser was forced to admit the bygone hairstyle of the previous Georges suited his friend's manly appearance, so perhaps that cause was lost, but...

Soon, Fraser promised himself, soon, he would drag him bodily to the fashionable Weston's establishment on Old Bond Street. His friend dressed far too old for his years; who would guess he was scarcely thirty?

Deeply ironical to Fraser, and a cause for amusement, was that both Beau Brummell and Isaac Rebow hailed from sleepy little Wivenhoe, a village tucked away into an inconspicuous corner of Essex. Wivenhoe, incongruously, the birthplace of one man who lived only for setting fashion and of another who concerned himself not at all with what was considered fashionable.

"So, Isaac...what are they like, these cousins?" Fraser persisted, continuing to feign nonchalance as he picked at an imaginary thread on his impeccably clean striped waistcoat, but with ears perked, burning to hear this story.

Canny Isaac wasn't about to reveal his family secrets. Though Jamie wasn't a gossip, the fewer people who knew of his maternal uncle's cabbage-headed antics, the better. Isaac wasn't fond of airing personal matters.

"Not much to tell, Jamie. My cousins are two simple country girls, daughters of my mother's only brother, my uncle Matthew Martin, of Alresford Hall."

There was no need to pretend a lack of interest in the Martin girls; Isaac had no use at all for young girls. He was comfortable only with women, experienced women. Widows. Unhappily married women. Bored women. So long as they were beautiful, witty, and not interested in legshackling him. Sophia, Lady Rowley, beautiful, witty enough, married to a much older man, and bored, admirably fit his bill of particulars.

He smoothed back the hair at his temples and shot his cuffs smartly. "I'm truly sorry, Jamie, we shall have to visit Tattersall's at another time. I wish you good luck on your purchases."

Now, Fraser's curiosity was fully roused. Matthew Martin! He remembered Isaac grumbling about the old gentleman. The fellow was a pest, albeit a seemingly harmless one, who constantly harassed Isaac with his frequent requests for already-franked envelopes—which privilege was Isaac's as a member of Parliament—and who managed on frequent, unannounced visits to Duke Street to poach, unabashedly, the better vintages from his nephew's excellent wine cellar.

"Uncle Matthew? The che—the one with the envelopes and the wine?" Fraser ventured innocently. He had been about to call Matthew "the cheeseparer," but caught himself.

Isaac's responding smile was mirthless. "To be sure, I'm thankful I've so few relatives! Truly, Uncle Matthew creates enough mischief for—"

He bit his tongue. It wouldn't do to speak this way outside the family. It wasn't the Rebow way, nor Isaac's way. Uncle Matthew was an annoying gnat, a pest who had forced him to lock his wine cellars and desks when he was from home, but he *was* family.

Fraser said, "Oh, the sale can wait! Really don't need any more cattle. Don't know what I was thinking...especially if I go ahead and buy that army commission. I'd have to leave them all behind. Mind if I accompany you to Chelsea? I've nothing else on my plate, and my curricle and team are tethered outside. Save you the bother of saddling up." He crumpled the papers into a tight ball and tossed them onto the dressing table.

Damn! The young whelp was persistent. He should make it clear he didn't want Jamie's company, but, on the other hand... On the other hand, he was flattered by Fraser's blatant hero-worship, and he did enjoy his company.

Fraser lapped up Isaac's stories of soldiering in India and admired him for buying his own commission

years ago, despite familial objections. He aspired to the
military life with a passion and looked up to ex-officers,
despite open disapproval from his wealthy father.

Jamie had achieved a measure of independence,
however, with a recent unexpected inheritance and now
had the blunt to pay for a commission. It was not likely
his father could stop him, and Isaac's stories of soldiering in India during the Mysore Wars whetted his appetite
for adventure and glory.

Fraser was unaware that jungle fighting in India's
south had been the preferable alternative for Isaac to
living with Madam's constant demands and hectoring in
England, and witnessing his parents' failed marriage at
close hand. Even the threat of losing one's life under the
dark canopy of a treacherous Indian jungle had been
preferable.

Fraser was interested only in the glory and manly
adventure of military life. So, over brandies at his club,
Isaac reminisced about the thrilling battles fought and
won on war's bloody turf and kept the rest of his hard-
earned knowledge of other kinds of warfare to himself.

Back in England, his father gone to his eternal reward, Isaac took over the reins of the Rebow interests.
In due time, he was elected to Parliament—his father's
seat—and was knighted by the king, as his father and
grandfather had been. Some wag remarked at the time
that in the Rebow clan, unlike the usual custom in England, it appeared knighthoods were hereditary!

There was enough to keep him busy. Or so he
thought, until the morning's unwelcome missive from
Madam. He groaned in defeat.

Oh, bloody hell!

Why not take Fraser to Chelsea, closet himself privately with Mary, the letter-writing sister, apprise himself of the deplorable situation, settle matters, and continue on to Tatt's?

"All right, Jamie, you've worn me down. To Chelsea, then, and don't spare your greys!" He took the
young man's elbow and propelled him through the
dressing room door and down the stairs, past the hap-

hazardly positioned ladders and stacked sheets of hand-blocked, flocked wallpaper and bolts of fabric—colorful chintzes, vibrant silks, rich damasks, meant for walls, curtains, and upholstery—scattered around the front hall and propped up against doorways.

There was much interior decoration to be done in the tall, newly acquired town house on Duke Street. It was barely furnished: wooden cabinets from Seddon's in Aldergate Street had been delivered only yesterday and crowded the front hall awaiting the busy lord and master's approval. Isaac soon would be in a position to do the entertaining his status demanded, and he was looking forward to it...as he wasn't at all looking forward to the morning's interview with his country mouse cousins.

An eager Fraser took the ribbons easily; his superb team of matched greys trotted smartly along St. James's Park and the Palace Gardens towards the Chelsea Road and past the Chelsea Physic Garden, following Isaac's instructions.

The Martins leased a modest townhouse on Draycott Terrace, near Chelsea Hospital. They had resided less than a year in London. On hearing of their move from Colchester, Isaac had thought it was Uncle Matthew's intention to bring the girls out, to attend routs and balls, secure vouchers to Almack's, put them on the Marriage Mart and snare them well-to-do husbands.

That hadn't turned out to be the case. There was no attempt by his uncle to participate in the season's social whirl. Like two caged birds, the girls languished in Chelsea while Matthew sipped claret and discussed Whig politics at Brooks's and lingered long at Watier's, dining with new found friends who saw he was plump in the pocket. He passed his time in London as idly as he'd passed it as squire of Alresford Hall, while his capable steward managed the prosperous estate.

Poor girls! Isaac was always much too busy, of course, to look in on them, but Madam never ceased to complain about her younger brother's gross selfishness and lack of proper parental concern for his daughters' unmarried states. Those poor motherless gels! Isaac heard her prattle, on the rare occasions he weathered her presence at Wivenhoe Park.

"Pretty enough, if one likes the country type, with good dowries both! They'd be snapped up quickly if only the old fool brought some attention to bear!"

Madam, however, was always too busy herself to see that her young nieces had a proper come-out; she was content with criticizing her widowed brother from afar, and her son at close range, whenever given the opportunity.

Hopeless! For a proper come-out, the Martin sisters needed the guidance of an older woman, preferably of *le haut ton* or at least gently born, someone well-versed in the social scene's intricacies. They were hopeless on their own. Isaac felt a slight twinge of guilt. One season had gone by, and 'twas almost time for another to commence.

He had the proper connections to help the Martin girls, and the wives of his colleagues might have graciously agreed to help him. But, now, it was all water under Westminster Bridge. The girls would be packed up and sent home if his uncle had truly decamped and abdicated his responsibilities. *None of his affair!* But the twinge of guilt didn't dissipate, adding to his irritability.

He smiled ruefully, idly watching the fashionable West End neighborhood of St. James's and Westminster change to the more modest precincts of outlying Chelsea. Fraser was a fine hand with the ribbons, and the greys were sweet goers. It was almost a pleasure, this sunny morning ride to Chelsea. *Almost...*

To his supreme annoyance, the Martin sisters were from home. He scowled angrily at the Martins' aged butler, Mapps, a morose looking man in dusty black livery, as Fraser tethered his prancing team in the mews at the rear of the town house.

"What d'you mean, man, they aren't home?" Isaac thundered. "At this hour of the morning?" He stopped. What *was* he doing, going on this way, taking his bad temper out on minions like Mapps and Robbins? Country hours. *Of course!* Like himself, the Martin sisters were country-bred, country-reared. It wasn't easy to rid oneself of the habit of keeping country hours.

If they were used to socializing every night, like the *ton*, they could quickly learn to sleep past noon, but they were hardly in that class of society and hadn't the opportunity to learn to keep late hours. Or, so it seemed.

Fraser took the steps from the street to the brass-knockered front door two at a time, more like an eager schoolboy than a young gentleman. He saw Isaac's angry scowl and heard the exchange with the old Friday-faced servant. "No one at home?" he queried, disappointed.

Isaac sighed. "It appears not. All this way for naught! I suppose I should've sent ahead to let them know I was coming. Let me leave a note, then, and we shall go."

He almost rubbed his hands in glee. He had attempted to do his duty, had he not? There was more than enough time now to make that splendid horse auction at Tattersall's.

Mapps invited the two gentlemen into the small black-and-white tiled foyer and wearily shuffled off to secure writing paper, ink, and quill pen.

Isaac looked about him; he had never been in his uncle's house. It looked like a rental, he saw with dismay. Not that it was unclean, just shabby. The furniture was slightly shabby, too. He frowned. Alresford Hall had lovely antique pieces; why hadn't they been brought to Draycott Terrace? The look of the town house was disheartening.

Not a house for entertaining! Certainly not a house leased to bring two young women out for their season. Chelsea was neither fashionable nor convenient for *ton* events. Had Uncle Matthew gone out of his way to see that his daughters would be left on the shelf?

Isaac frowned in annoyance at his uncle's total lack of concern for his daughters' futures. This house, this neighborhood, were not the thing. When he located his uncle, he would have a good deal to say to that old fool.

The sound of slow, heavy footsteps coming up from

downstairs alerted Isaac, and he turned to see the green baize door open to reveal a rotund, jolly-faced older woman wearing a starched linen apron over a black bombazine dress. Her white hair curled in fine wisps out of an oversized mobcap. She bustled over to him and congenially bobbed a curtsy.

"Master Isaac, is it not?" She smiled. "You don't remember me, but I know you, sir...and your mother! I'm Agnes Pepperwit, Molly and Sally's old baby nurse from the Hall. I'm housekeeper here now."

Isaac smiled in return, not minding the over-familiarity of an old and trusted servant. Mrs. Pepperwit! Yes, he remembered the kindly woman well. She had brought up the girls after their mother died delivering a stillborn infant. Matthew had never remarried. It had been jolly Mrs. Pepperwit and a capable young governess who had taken the girls in hand. And Madam also, of course.

Madam, in her style, had issued orders, orders her younger brother had casually ignored, but she had been a formidable presence. Isaac had given Mrs. Pepperwit and that young governess a good deal of credit for the way they had dealt with Madam. He was about to ask the old housekeeper what had become of the governess when the front door opened wide to admit what appeared to be a veritable gaggle of giggling girls.

Fraser's mouth gaped open as he beheld the bevy of beauties overflowing the shabby doorway of Number Four Draycott Terrace. *What ho, Isaac,* he thought, *what have you been keeping from me, my good friend?*

Three pert and saucy young women stared back at him and smiled, dimples and teeth showing prettily, and three bright pairs of eyes—brown, blue and green—flashed. He gulped, straightened his flawless cravat, remembered he was a dashing young man about town, and murmured, "I say, Isaac, do make the introductions."

Isaac was aghast. Serving wenches attired in faded, shapeless muslin gowns, obviously their mistresses' castoffs, using the front entrance! Things had indeed fallen to a sorry state at his uncle's sorry town house.

Throwing his shoulders back and assuming a military posture—all the better for reviewing green troops and setting them quaking in their boots—he was about to open his mouth when a fourth member of the party showed herself: a middle-aged matron, considerably better dressed than the trio of young maidservants, in a morning dress of yellow spotted muslin that even Isaac recognized as the *dernier cri*, wearing a plain bag bonnet on her well-coiffed head.

Confused, Isaac turned to Mrs. Pepperwit. "Ma'am?" he questioned.

The housekeeper bustled over to the girls, ignoring him. "Ah, Miss Molly. What did you catch this fine morning?"

Fixing the girls with a hard look, Isaac saw that they weren't maidservants at all, but gently-bred maidens, maidens who had clearly spent the better part of the sunny morning outdoors: their faces were flushed, attesting to their encounter with nature. Each carried a fishing pole; one sported a battered straw creel over one arm.

The matronly woman held a commodious knitting bag from which protruded a formidable pair of needles and she held the long ribands of three floppy leghorn straw bonnets. The young woman Mrs. Pepperwit addressed as Molly was the one holding the fishing creel. Isaac realized with a start she was his cousin Mary, the elder Martin sister.

She handed the empty creel to the housekeeper. "All for naught, Mrs. P.," she announced cheerfully in a low, husky, mature voice rather at odds with her youthful, disheveled appearance.

Despite that dishevelment, she was quite beautiful, Isaac realized, with fine dark eyes and enticingly full lips. And that voice! *A courtesan,* he thought with a start, *would kill for such a bedroom voice.* For that was quite definitely where it belonged: the bedroom. He felt a pull in his groin and shifted his feet uneasily.

Isaac slanted a glance at his friend. Fraser seemed quite besotted, not knowing upon which young maiden to fix his gaze. Isaac's irritability returned in full force. He was on a mission, he reminded himself, forcing himself back into military mode, a mission that had to be taken care of quickly. First, though, he had to sort out his cousins.

He turned to Mary, gazing at her intently from top to toe. She was glowing, lovely, truly delectable...

She was chuckling with the housekeeper, moving with a good deal of grace in the shapeless faded-blue muslin dress, which gave no outward clue as to her form. "Mapps can return the worms to the garden where they can strive to enrich that poor miserable soil." She laughed.

Before Isaac could speak, Fraser asked, amused, "Where've you young ladies been fishing?" Having overcome his initial surprise, he was his relaxed, charming, young-man-about-town self again.

The pert blue-eyed blonde began to answer him. "Grosvenor Canal." She stopped, blushed prettily under her sun-kissed skin, and turned to the housekeeper for help. "I...I'm sorry, but who may you gentlemen be?"

Isaac stepped forward smartly, with a stiff, curt bow. "Isaac Rebow, ma'am, and this is my friend, James Fraser."

Fraser bowed smartly in turn, a wide grin splitting his fair, handsome face from ear to ear.

"Now," Isaac continued, "which two of you charming ladies are my cousins Martin?"

❖

She guessed it was he, half hoping, but not sure, because she hadn't seen him in such a very long time. When Papa moved them to London for the season, she thought she would see him with regularity, reacquaint herself with him, get him to know her as the adult she now was, rather than as the small, pesky child she had been, the little girl who had followed him so adoringly, so worshipfully. *Isaac*. Isaac Rebow...her older, much-beloved cousin.

He had been so very good looking, so tall, so strong, so self-assured. She had used to hide in the stables early in the mornings when they visited Wivenhoe Park, knowing it was his favorite place, that what he liked to do best in the mornings was to saddle one of his well tended horses and take a fast gallop before breakfast. So breathtakingly handsome he had been, in his tight buckskin breeches and flowing white shirt, whispering to his horses in a soft, caressing voice.

His voice had thrilled her, warmed her; she'd wished she could be one of his animals, to gain the attention he lavished on them, to hear him speak to her as he did to them, in such loving tones.

He was like a prince to her. She was too little to join him, too little to go riding with him, that was for certain. Much too little to interest him in any way. But he had been kind to the small child she was, when he deigned to notice her. And she'd simply worshipped him. *Isaac!* He was her god.

She knew why he was here. Madam must have written that Papa had gone off and left her and Sally in this dreary house so far from home. She had not wanted to inform Madam, but, as the days went by, and there wasn't one word... Dear Papa! He was absentminded to a fault, but...she was worried. There was no one else to turn to but her aunt, to whom she customarily sent weekly news. Madam had acted with alacrity, it seemed, contacting Isaac to see to the matter.

They had been in town six months, half a year, and Isaac had never paid them a call. Papa had dined with him, but not at Draycott Terrace. She knew Isaac was a busy man, but they were blood kin! Surely, he could have spared them a few moments of his precious time.

She, on the other hand, had spent much time on him, on the Duke Street town house, carrying out Madam's instructions. Surely it was only fair that he...but, of course, he had no idea of what she'd done, had never seen her there dealing with suppliers, workmen, and gardeners, hadn't known she was the one who had procured the right and proper servants from the servants' registry office in The Strand, as befitted the household of a rich, important man...

He was unmarried, she knew, and, questioning her father, she also knew he wasn't engaged to be wed, but more than that Papa wouldn't tell her. In fact, he had blushed red, flustered, when she made her innocent inquiries. What did that mean? It was all very confusing. She dared not ask Madam, but she wanted to know. Was someone promised to Isaac? Did she still stand a chance?

Now he was here, in their home, with an exceedingly handsome fair-haired young gentleman at whom Sally and Henny May were making silly sheep's eyes, and, still, he didn't know who she was.

It was disappointing, nay, it was exceedingly aggravating! She should be furious with him.

She extended her hand to Isaac. "I am Mary, and this is Sally," she indicated the shy blonde girl to her right, "and these are our friends, Mrs. May and Miss May.

"What an unexpected pleasure this is, Cousin Isaac. I fear you have caught us unawares. It was such a lovely morning, we imagined ourselves in the country, taking our poles to the River Colne to catch trout for dinner. You must excuse our dreadful appearance, I beg you."

Mary turned to Mrs. Pepperwit and ordered tea in the drawing room. As she spoke, she gathered up the long fishing poles with easy grace and handed them to the tired-looking butler, Mapps, just returned with pen, ink, and paper, now no longer needed.

They filed into the small room to the left of the center stairs, Fraser, ever the gallant, extending his arm to Mrs. May. Isaac took Mary aside. "One moment, please, Cousin Mary. I need to speak to you in private."

Two

Mary hesitated, her expressive face registering surprise. Her straight, dark eyebrows knitted together, her smooth forehead furrowed. "You've news about Papa?" she asked in a low, throaty whisper.

Isaac shook his head and ignored the frisson of desire that snaked up his spine, activated by his cousin's disturbing voice. "No, but we have urgent matters we must discuss privately. Is there a room to which we could retire?"

Mary looked toward Sally and the Mays, making themselves comfortable in the drawing room. Sally caught her sister's eye, raising an eyebrow in silent question.

Mary made up her mind and replied, "Can these matters not wait a few moments, sir? Tea has been ordered, and our friends the Mays must needs get home soon. Cannot our talk be set aside for the while?"

Isaac frowned, unused to having his merest suggestion opposed, much less by a young chit with a tea party on her mind. But who was he to begrudge her and her sister their tea? Out all morning, they were no doubt in need of refreshment. And Fraser, that young whelp! Perhaps it would be best if he kept an eye on him. He was showing himself too pleased by half to be in such charming female company.

"As you wish, Cousin Mary," Isaac agreed, somewhat stiff-lipped. He stood aside, bowing slightly, to allow her to enter the drawing room. He caught a whiff of rosewater as she passed by him. Altogether a light, pleasant, unexceptionable scent, but why, then, did he feel slightly off-balance? He shook his head to clear it, annoyed without precisely knowing the reason.

❖

Mary's knees were weak as she preceded her cousin into the drawing room. He was even more handsome than she remembered. Rather fierce, with his scowls and frowns—what had caused his bad temper?—but his looks and deep voice had caused her pulse to quicken. Would that he could stay awhile! She didn't want him to go.

Mrs. May beamed at Fraser, engaged him in conversation and encouraged her daughter Henny to enter into it. Mary smiled at the tableau. It would be a wonder if dear Henny could bring herself to do more than simper and giggle.

Mary slanted a glance at Sally. "Dearest, will you not play for us?" She gestured towards the French harpsichord in the corner of the room. Sally blushed, shaking her head in shyness.

Mrs. May didn't wish to shut her Henny out of any musical performance. "Henny can play the harpsichord, Mary. Do persuade Sally to sing for us. Her sweet voice is a lovely treat!"

Sally flushed even deeper, casting a quick glance at the handsome Mr. Fraser, but Mrs. May was persistent. "Mary, can you accompany them both on your Spanish guittar?"

"A fine idea, Mrs. May," Mary agreed. "Ah, how lovely, here is tea. Shall we enjoy a cup before our musical interlude?"

❖

Isaac groaned inwardly. *Musical interlude!* Those two, the matron, Mrs. May, and Mary, had nicely orchestrated that piece of business. Isaac had to admit his cousin was more than a little skilled in getting others to do her bidding. A sudden vision sprang forth: Mary, in full martial regalia, albeit sized down to fit her diminutive person, commandeering a battalion of seasoned, war-hardened soldiers. He had no doubt she could handle the situation more than adequately.

The prospects of his making that pleasant visit to Tatt's dwindled considerably. Miss Martin would allow them to leave when she was good and ready, the chit! From the besotted look on Fraser's face, Isaac was sure the horse auction had faded to an old memory. Ah, to be that young and foolish again.

The tea was excellent, a fine Bohea, such as Isaac himself stocked in his kitchens. In fact...Isaac took a long, appraising sip and inhaled the distinctive, full aroma of the beverage. He would be damned! *'Twas* his Bohea! That high quality tea was shipped directly to him from the finest plantations controlled by the East India Company. He would recognize it anywhere.

Time to lock up his tea caddy, too. He would have to warn his housekeeper. *Matthew Martin,* he thought, *you're truly a rascal of the first water. When next I see you*...then he remembered, there mightn't be a next time. Uncle Matthew had disappeared. That was why Isaac was at Draycott Terrace.

True to her word, Mary marshaled her sister and friend to their musical instruments as soon as they finished the first cup of tea.

Sally—or Mary, more likely, Isaac mused—had chosen two romantical old folk ballads to entertain their guests, *The Sprig of Thyme* and *Sweet William.* Sally's sweet voice was a lovely high, clear soprano. Both men were moved by her renditions.

"Oh, I say, Miss Martin, splendid!" Jamie applauded enthusiastically after hearing her trill the melancholy lyrics of *The Sprig of Thyme*, the notes wafting upward in the small, high-ceilinged room like the voice of a nightingale.

Isaac had shut his eyes as Sally sang, silently mouthing the mournful words to the old country ballad, instantly and deeply moved.

"...I used to know the place where my thyme

it did grow, But now it is cover'd with rue,
with rue, But now it is cover'd with rue...
So beware of a young man's flattering tongue,
he will steal your thyme away, away, He will
steal your thyme away..."

Isaac opened his eyes. Lovely, the child had a lovely
voice. He was angry again with his uncle. How could he
shut this flower away in a London backwater? She
should be performing at musicales, showing off her gifts
to her peers. He was going to murder his uncle, if and
when he found him!

❖

Mary, proud of her skill at the guittar, felt quite
locked out into the cold. She shivered. Isaac had eyes
only for Sally. The expression on his face as he listened
to her sing! Henny and she might well have disappeared
from the room. Isaac and his friend were wholly entranced by her pretty young sister.

She, Mary, might well be invisible. Fraser didn't
matter, of course, although she admitted he was quite
handsome. Isaac mattered. But she obviously didn't
matter. That hurt, it hurt terribly.

Mrs. May was effusive at the trio's performance.
Fraser agreed, finally remembering his manners as he
complimented all of them. Only Isaac was oddly silent,
withdrawn, until Fraser turned to him, "What d'you
think, Isaac?"

As if awakening from a dream, Isaac snapped to attention. "Very fine, very fine indeed. Cousin Sally, I've
rarely heard such a good voice, even at the opera houses.
My compliments."

Sally basked in the compliments and smiled shyly.
Her slim fingers nervously kneaded the fabric of her
worn muslin gown. Mary felt an uncharacteristic stab of
jealousy toward her sister. She excused herself to ring
for Mrs. Pepperwit to replenish the tea and bring up
more cakes.

Meeting Isaac's eyes, Mary smiled brightly, a tad too brightly. "Shall we have our private chat now, Cousin? We can retire to the library whilst the others enjoy the rest of their tea." Spine arrow-straight, she led the way.

❖

Mary shut the door to the room she'd designated 'the library,' another small, shabby room similar to that in which they had taken tea. Isaac looked about him with undisguised distaste. The furniture in this room was even shabbier! Anger at his wayward uncle almost choked him.

He sat gingerly on an armchair in deplorable need of re-upholstering. *Threadbare fabric!* This was unacceptable, totally unacceptable, he fumed inwardly, frowning. What was the old fool thinking of, making do with this scandalous furniture? He dragged his mind back to the matter at hand.

"Now, Mary," he began, "I've no news of your father's whereabouts. Madam instructed me to see how you and Sally were faring, and I must tell you I'm most distressed with this situation. My uncle Matthew has been extremely thoughtless."

Hah! That didn't begin to address the situation, he thought. The Martin sisters were treasures, two rare beauties. The younger one, blonde and delicate, with that extraordinary voice! And this one, this incomparably beautiful diamond of the first water, even in shabby clothes...graceful, sylph-like...her every movement fluid, smooth...

He gazed at the country-fresh young woman and caught the faint, tantalizing scent of rosewater again. Her dark, glossy hair shone under the light streaming through the mullioned glass panes. What was she doing, unguarded, in the shabby and less-than-safe environs of Draycott Terrace? How could a father desert such a young woman? Or her sister? What manner of man was his uncle?

Isaac leaned toward Mary, his hands clasped before him on his crossed knee. "Mary, you must tell me everything, if I'm to help you and Sally."

Mary sighed wearily, nervously fingering the frayed arms of the armchair that was a twin, in style and condition, to the one in which Isaac had seated himself. "What do you know?" she asked.

"Only what you conveyed to Madam in your letter." Lud, girl! get on with it, he thought, wishing he had not shut the library door behind him for their *tête-à-tête*. He could laugh...how many such possibly compromising instances had he avoided during the years of his long bachelorhood? How many pushing mamas with nubile daughters had he disappointed?

Yet here he was, right in the midst of a situation fraught with strong temptation. He knew the truth of it, he shouldn't be in such close quarters with this maddeningly attractive young miss, even if she was his near kin, his blood relative.

Mary sat up straighter in the disreputable chair and absently ran a hand through her touseled curls. Isaac's groin muscles tightened at the girl's innocent, careless gesture; he imagined the feel of her fragrant, silken hair in his hands, the look of it, shining and dark, spread over his white linen pillows...

Mary, innocently unaware of the sharp crackle of desire in the air, gave him a questioning look, then repeated what she had related in her letter.

"Well, sir, that's all. Papa left us during the night saying nothing to any of us, not to me, Sally, Mrs. Pepperwit, or Mapps. The harpsichord drawer was left open...that's how we saw the hundred-guinea bag. When we looked into his wardrobe, we saw that his best suit of clothes, his dressing gown, nightshirts, caps, his toiletries, were all gone. We've not seen him since, nor heard of him, and it's been over one week."

"Is there any reason to fear foul play?" Isaac questioned, then could have bitten off his tongue at the stricken look in the young woman's large, dark eyes.

She recovered from the shock of his question, nervously running her pink, cat-like tongue over her deliciously full lower lip. *So kissable,* he thought, then groaned inwardly at the effect her innocent gesture had inflicted on his heightened senses. He reviled himself for the unseemliness of his impure thoughts.

"No, no, I suspect his leaving was well planned. He left us the old coach, but his horse was gone, and Jenkins, his valet, has disappeared. I believe I neglected to mention Jenkins's disappearance to Madam...but, you know, Papa behaved most peculiarly these past weeks."

Isaac interrupted, forcing his errant thoughts back to his uncle's disappearance and away from the tantalizing charms of the daughter. "What do you mean 'peculiarly'?" he asked.

A sweet smile lit Mary's beautiful, heart-shaped face, almost putting an end to Isaac's good intentions. She continued airily, "Oh, but he was in a most happy state of mind, a pure good humor, for several days, singing songs about the house, leaving on mysterious errands, neglecting to say when he would return or where he was going.

"Also, of a sudden, he had begun to take a good deal of care with his appearance, which surprised Jenkins no end." She lowered her voice, "Jenkins confided in Mapps, who told Mrs. Pepperwit, who told me. In point of fact, I think he was behaving much like a man in love."

Isaac sat back in amazement and shock, regarding his cousin severely. What experience, what knowledge, did the young chit have of love? What a strange statement! *Devil a bit!* She didn't really seem at all upset. No, in point of fact, no one in this queer house seemed that put out by this sorry state of affairs. Having a father and head of household abscond mysteriously in the middle of the night had put no one in an uproar.

No, it seemed rather to be life as usual at Number Four Draycott Terrace: worm-gathering in the back garden, fishing in the canals, taking afternoon tea, impromptu musical performances, fathers disappearing without a trace. All one and the same to the Misses

Martin and their household! His ingrained sense of order was deeply disturbed, and he frowned darkly.

This wasn't, he feared, the most normal of domiciles. It needed a strong hand at the helm. A very strong hand. Unconsciously, he flexed his right fist. Yes, it would benefit from a strong hand like his.

Mary stole a furtive glance from under her lowered eyelashes at Isaac's clearly displeased face. He was very angry. He had been angry from the first moment she saw him on her threshold and matters hadn't improved one whit.

Why was he so upset?

This business was alarming, to be sure, but dear Papa had left behind a hundred guineas, a small fortune to most people. She was sure he wouldn't neglect them forever. They were certain to hear from him soon, were they not? Nonetheless, she felt a shiver of fear creep up her backbone. She sat straighter, as if to compensate for the unfamiliar sensation.

While it seemed Cousin Isaac was most concerned, and it was surely kind of him to drop by, it wouldn't do for him to be overly concerned. She and Sally were used to running a household and keeping things orderly. They'd been doing just so for a very long while.

This house could do with refurbishing, that was true—by the looks he cast at their horrid leased furniture she could see Isaac was disturbed—but she did mean to see to it once she finished setting his Duke Street town house to rights. Their furnishings alone didn't indicate their household was poorly run.

Dear, dear Papa was quite sweet but hardly an organizing sort of man; he ran neither Alresford Hall nor Draycott Terrace. It was simply the way he was, but how would Cousin Isaac know? He didn't even know what she'd been doing at his own town house, under Madam's absentee direction. So, how could he know them, or their doings here? He knew nothing about them. Nor, prior to this, had he seemed to care overmuch.

She felt a pang deep in her breast. If the price to be paid for his concern was seeing him more frequently, perhaps it wasn't too high a price?

Should they pretend to need his counsel if that meant he would visit them more often? No, she decided firmly, it would be a sorry trick, indeed, to play for the pleasure of his company. There should be a better reason for him to care than this distressing, but temporary, circumstance. She stole another look at his handsome features and prayed he would discover the better reason soon.

Isaac spoke, breaking into Mary's woolgathering, his voice perhaps a shade too stern. "I shall have to go to Colchester to speak to Samuel Ennew, your family lawyer. He needs to be informed immediately. We shall need his good advice as to how to proceed. Your father, my uncle, has been supremely irresponsible, and—"

He stopped when he saw Mary's fine dark eyes glaring angrily. "Yes, Mary?" he asked.

Those eyes flashed fire as she defended her father. "Papa is *not* irresponsible! He *will* come back home. This is temporary. I write to Madam every week to tell her news, but I didn't mean to dismay her, to trouble her, nor to bring you—or Lawyer Ennew!—into this. We're rubbing along quite well here, Sally and I.

"The lease is paid through July. We've ample monies for food and to pay the servants. If worse does indeed come to worst, we can retire to Alresford Hall..."

"My very dear child," Isaac began, more than a little exasperated. What was wrong with this stubborn little chit? Did she not realize she and her sister were in the direst of straits? They were in a large and dangerous city of over a million people with no protection save an incompetent elderly butler and an equally old and too-doting housekeeper!

No one was in charge: that was the truth of it.

Damn his uncle! He'd willingly strangle the foolish old rascal with his bare hands right now. He fairly itched to have Matthew Martin's scrawny neck between his...

"Cousin Isaac, y-you misjudge me. I'm no child, I can manage very well, I..."

Isaac stared at the stammering young woman. Confound it! The girl was as foolish as her sire. *A man in love, indeed!* She was soft in the head, like Martin. Such things, he knew, ran in families.

"How old are you, Mary?" Isaac's voice, cold and harsh, cut through her protests.

Mary gulped, refusing to be browbeaten by this hateful, domineering stranger. For, yes, that's what he was, a stranger, not anyone she knew, not the princely, soft-voiced figure she eavesdropped upon so long ago, cooing tenderly to his horses at Wivenhoe Park. He was a stranger, trying to take control of their lives, hers and Sally's, trying to impose his considerable will, trying to tell her what to do.

Well, Mary Louisa Catherine Martin wasn't about to let Colonel Sir Isaac bloody Rebow have the final say regarding the disposition of her household. How dare he attempt to take over?

She wasn't about to jump up, salute smartly, and have him issue his odious orders to her. She wasn't a lowly foot soldier in his Indian Army regiment. Nor was her sweet Sally. They would rather die first!

She had run her father's household competently since her governess, Emma Wells, had left Alresford Hall three years ago to wed. She consulted on every aspect of management with their able steward, John Groves, and their farms and properties turned a smart profit every year. They weren't paupers. Even if Papa didn't return—and she refused to think for a moment that he wouldn't—they could surely manage.

There was no question in her mind that they couldn't manage.

"I am nineteen," she answered defiantly, her chin stubbornly up-thrust, "and Sally is nearly eighteen." In actuality, Sally was nearer to seventeen than eighteen, but Mary didn't think Isaac would remember her sister's true age.

Isaac rose to go, terminating what had become an acrimonious interview, slapping his leather gloves smartly against his muscled thigh, and hitting Mary with a sharp parting salvo.

"You're both under age, my dear. A guardian will have to be appointed for you if your father shows no sign that he plans to return. I shall send a message to Samuel Ennew this afternoon apprising him of the situation and letting him know that I intend to see him, to work toward deciding what's to be done.

"For now, consider yourselves under my protection and expect to hear from me soon."

Mary's full lips thinned appreciably as she formed her response. "How very, very kind of you, Cousin Isaac, to be so very, very concerned for our welfare. I had no idea, you see, you knew who we were. We've, after all, been here half a year and not had the pleasure of seeing you even once."

Isaac winced. *The little baggage!* The cutting remarks had been right on target. Yes, he'd been unforgivably remiss, and he now felt the guilt, but he'd make up for it. She wouldn't like it, this high-in-the-instep little miss, she wouldn't like it one bit. But, he thought, smiling grimly, *he* would.

Yes, he'd very much enjoy putting his dear hot-tempered little cousin in her rightful place, under his heel, or, better yet, over his knee!

Miss Mary High-and-Mighty Martin of Alresford Hall would soon learn who was in charge here. *Impudent little baggage!*

"Well, dear cousin, all's not lost. You've shown me where my duty lies, and you and your sister shall be quite safe under my protection and guidance. I fear many aspects of your social education have been sadly neglected—and for that I blame my absent uncle—but that shall soon be corrected, I do assure you, miss. You've my word as a gentleman upon it."

His words were carved in pure ice, his face frozen; his hand, which he longed to apply to her *derrière*, was gripping the doorknob tightly.

"Now, my dear, I would relish another cup of tea before I take my leave...if you would be so kind?" He ushered her out of the library, noting with pleasure the barely controlled fury on her expressive face. Fleetingly, he wondered if she could read his thoughts. He rather hoped she could.

As she flounced her skirts and stomped off ahead of him, her spine rigid, he leaned his forehead briefly, wearily, against the doorjamb. *What, dear Lord, have I just done?* He groaned softly. What manner of unwelcome responsibility have I taken on? And why?

No answers came readily to mind.

Three

"Odious man!" Mary had barely contained herself until their visitors departed. Then, she swore a ferocious oath she had heard the stableboys use freely at Alresford Hall and threw her fine French china teacup at the fireplace, cracking it into fine splinters and splattering the remnants of her tea on the hearth.

"Mary, please! Have you come over queer? What is the matter?" Sally bent down to pick up and mourn over china shards. She rose just in time to see her sister's hand reach for the dainty saucer that was mate to the deceased cup, and with a quick backhanded movement barely restrained Mary from hurling it as well.

"Mary! Why are you so upset?" Sally was the family peacemaker. Her large sky-blue eyes stared worriedly into Mary's storm-dark ones as she took the delicate porcelain dish from Mary's trembling hands and led her agitated sister to the sofa.

Sorely tested by her conversation in the library with her cousin, Mary tried to gain control of her emotions. She acknowledged that she had behaved badly; indeed, she had shown an appalling lack of manners and good breeding during their protracted interview. She had not, however, been able to help herself.

She had come face-to-face with the man of her girlhood dreams, her longed-for fairy-tale prince, and had thoroughly antagonized him. He had barely concealed his contempt for her behavior behind an icy wall of politeness. It hurt. *Badly!* And it was all her fault. She had provoked him, and he was only trying to help. How could he not have taken a disgust of her?

He had further enraged her by markedly ignoring

her afterward. He had eyes for no one but her little sister Sally. Sweet, dear, always-anxious-to-please Sally. But how could she blame Isaac, after the rag-mannered remarks she had addressed to him, if he chose to pay court to the sweeter sister instead? Things had come to a sorry pass. The pang she had felt in her chest earlier was now a dull, throbbing ache.

"We've had a delightful afternoon with two most charming gentlemen, one of them our dear cousin Isaac, whom we've hoped to see this age...I don't understand, Mary, why you're carrying on so."

Sally cradled the broken pieces of teacup in her small hands, tears streaking down her cheeks. "This was from our dear Mama's favorite set, Mary. How could you?"

Wearily, Mary apologized, embracing her sibling and kissing her wet cheeks. Unfair to take her bad humors out on an innocent teacup, much less on dear Sally, whose lovely soprano voice had entertained them so sweetly.

Sally was truly mystified by Mary's unusual behavior. Her sister was strong-willed, opinionated, but hardly ever angry. Wiping away her tears both for the destroyed china and Mary's unhappiness, she pleaded, "Mary, please, you must talk to me. What's wrong?"

Mary allowed Sally's gentle hands to stroke her brow and to brush back unruly strands of dark hair. Turning an anguished look on her sister, she whispered so low that Sally had to strain to hear. "He believes Papa will not come back, Sally."

"Impossible," Sally countered, then paused, troubled. "Why would he think that?"

Mary shrugged, her shoulders moving easily in the too-large dress borrowed from Mrs. May's abigail for the fishing expedition. "I don't know. And how can he know?" She raised her voice passionately. "He doesn't know our Papa as we know him. Papa loves us."

"But, Mary, he did leave us without a word of explanation... Cousin Isaac may have the right of it, whatever we may want to think. He's a man of the world, and knows its ways." Sally stopped at Mary's blank, hard look. Still, troubled, she persisted, "What does he propose to do, Sister?"

Mary crumpled into a small, sad heap on the sofa, hunched her body, and worried the worn fabric at the hem of her dress. "He proposes to see our family's lawyer, Samuel Ennew, in Colchester."

She looked at Sally again, the color bright on her high cheekbones. Her anger rose. "He says we must have a guardian to protect us now that Papa is gone from home."

Sally collapsed next to Mary on the sofa, the breath knocked out of her. She stammered, her words all a-stumble, falling and breaking against each other. "But...who...how...what does he mean?"

"He means *himself*, of course, the horrid, odious man!"

"But, Mary!" Sally, no longer incoherent, attempted to placate her overwrought sibling. "He seems all that's kind and well-mannered. He is a gentleman, our close blood relative."

"*Hah!*" Mary snorted, none too ladylike. "He's a cold-blooded stranger, an interfering nuisance! He cannot, he shall not, take our Papa's place. I shall not allow it! I've a mind to write Madam this instant and tell her." How dare he, she fumed, how dare he order them about? How dare he hold her in such contempt?

How dare he ignore her in favor of Sally?

Sally Martin, unaware that for the first time in their lives her sister harbored jealous feelings toward her, watched, distraught, as Mary stormed into the library and began to slam drawers, making a horrendous racket. Sally shook her head, troubled and uneasy at this distressing turn of events.

Ah, well, she thought, it was a good thing that cold-blooded, interfering, odious Cousin Isaac kept their dear Papa well supplied with pre-franked envelopes. Whatever else this troubling situation cost them, postage, at least, didn't cost a thing.

❖

Isaac Rebow's head hurt.

Jamie Fraser had been sickeningly effusive, fulsome, endlessly complimenting the Martin sisters, all the way back to Duke Street. Isaac had begun to wish himself deaf. The headache throbbed beneath his temples, working its way down to the base of his skull. He never had headaches. It was his first. *Bloody hell!* It would be his last, if he had anything to say about it. He needed a drink.

"Saunders!" he bellowed across the hall to his butler, shocking that correct, prim servant right down to his highly polished shoes. "Brandy, please! In the library!"

As Saunders scurried to do the bidding of his unaccountably out-of-sorts master, Fraser suddenly fell silent. Something was terribly wrong: Isaac wasn't himself. He never barked orders at his servants. What had occurred between his friend and his young cousin at Draycott Terrace? Fraser frowned.

The morning had been amiable, had it not? The young ladies were gracious, quite lovely and talented. Their conversation was genteel, their manners exquisite, and their music! They had played like angels. Sally Martin's voice...

He caught himself up short. Now that he thought back, there was a decided coolness between Isaac and Mary when they rejoined the group for tea. He reflected on their behavior and realized the two had sat apart and neither conversed, addressed, nor looked at each other, for the remainder of the visit. Had they an altercation during their private discussion? How odd...and for what reason?

Was it even remotely any of his business? Perhaps a bit of it was, the bit that concerned Sally, for Fraser realized he was more than a little interested in that charming blonde songbird.

Fraser cleared his throat with a loud harumph. "I say, Isaac, old man," he began tentatively, "is something, that is...er...amiss?"

Something was decidedly amiss. The grim look on Isaac's countenance boded trouble. Fraser cradled the snifter of good French brandy Saunders handed him, and waited for his friend's reply. The dark, clear liquid swirled as he rotated the glass.

Isaac was caught up sharply at his friend's inquiry. He cursed himself for allowing his emotions to show through in this family matter. *It would never do!* He mustn't reveal the roiling feelings buffeting him; he must endeavor to cultivate an outer calm.

Clearly, he had made a mistake taking Fraser to Chelsea. Now he must present an unruffled, bland exterior. He had to recover his equilibrium quickly, and wondered if his acting skills were up to the task.

Accepting the brandy with thanks from a slightly wary Saunders, he waited for the butler to leave before responding. He looked down into the amber-hued spirits as if seeking a sign, then turned to Fraser and smiled. The effort it took to smile was painful, for the hard throbbing in his head hadn't abated one whit.

"No, Jamie, no, not at all. It is only that...well, I find I've a good deal on my plate just now. You're more than welcome to lunch with me, but then I must leave on urgent business, business to do with my holdings in Essex. I'd thought to handle it by messenger, but..." He drained the strong liquor in the glass in one fierce gulp. "I shall be out of town for a few days. Sorry about that sale at Tatt's."

Fraser nodded, not altogether gulled by Isaac's glib assurances that all was well. Something wasn't quite right, but he pretended to be satisfied.

"Oh, there shall be other sales at Tatt's, Isaac. Count on it!" He clapped his hand on Isaac's broad back in a comradely fashion, intrigued no end by the drama he sensed was transpiring in the background. The drama he was absolutely certain starred the lovely Martin sisters. He smiled.

"Ah, Isaac...while you're gone, I would find it a pleasure to call upon your young relatives. Take them riding in the park, perhaps ices at Gunter's, the usual sort of thing. That is—" He paused briefly as the shadow of a grimace seemed to pass over his friend's visage. "That is, if I...ah...if you've no objections to that, old chap? "

Isaac froze. Blast! Fraser nosing about Draycott Terrace? How long would it be before his inquisitive friend discovered there was no *pater familias* on the premises. Should he let the young pup find out for himself?

Isaac shrugged. "I cannot answer for those young misses, Fraser. If their papa knows you're a friend and doesn't mind your kind attentions, and if the girls are agreeable, and properly chaperoned, why should I voice an objection?"

Fraser probed delicately. "Their papa seemed to be from home."

"Temporarily. Uncle Matthew's quite the gadabout, with his clubs and such. The girls would welcome a ride in the park, I'm sure. I fear they don't get about much in society." Isaac placed his emptied snifter on the silver tray Saunders had left behind and slapped his hands together, as if dismissing a very minor question.

Yes, Fraser would soon sniff out the whole story. Isaac had left his cousin Mary in an angry state; he had a strong and troubling feeling that Fraser's empathetic demeanor would encourage her to vent her spleen.

The young man was a charmer, well-practiced in the gentlemanly art of social flattery. A comfortable coze or two with the sisters, a sincere outpouring of sympathy, and soon he would hear the whole sordid story.

Isaac's head ached as he imagined the indiscreet comments Mary might make in an unguarded, impetuous moment...many of them about him, no doubt. *Ah, why should it matter?* The fact remained that it did matter. He couldn't release that thought from his throbbing brain. It mattered very much.

The anger in an extraordinary pair of dark, flashing eyes set in an exquisite, beautiful face mattered.

❖

Halfway through luncheon, Isaac remembered he had pledged attendance at a dinner party and musicale that evening at Sophia Rowley's Mayfair town house. He now had to break his promise to attend and knew she'd not be pleased. It would cost him. *Dearly.* Lady Sophia wasn't a woman to be crossed. He sighed, causing Fraser to dart a sharp glance at him over the asparagus *au gratin*, lamb cutlets, and tomato aspic.

He would have to send a footman to Rundle & Bridge's. There was an ornate pearl brooch in their window that Sophia had admired—volubly—the last time they strolled by that venerable jewelry shop. He grimaced, remembering the pitch and tone of that lady's voice as she voiced her admiration of the brooch. *Less than subtle.* Sometimes, however, one had no choice; one had to pay the price. If he wanted to continue to partake of Sophia's excellent company, not to mention her practiced bedroom skills, he had to pay what it cost, play by her rules.

Reflectively sipping his excellent claret, it dawned on him that lately they always seemed to be *her* rules. Was he becoming too complacent in his dealings with Baron Rowley's beautiful, spoiled wife? A thought to ponder. His natural instincts had always warned him away from manipulative women who displayed latent signs of shrewishness. Was his normal caution slipping?

Later. He'd deal with it later. Currently, there were more important things on his mind than Sophia Rowley's burgeoning acquisitiveness, both of material goods and his person. There were things he must deal with quickly and effectively if he was to have any peace of mind.

He rubbed his temples wearily. Would this tedious headache never go away?

❖

While his groom prepared the best team of horses for his trim, fast curricle, Isaac saw Fraser out. Robbins was busy packing several changes of clothes in a commodious portmanteau Isaac would bring to Colchester, where he would interview Ennew, the Martin family lawyer. Unfortunately, he would also be obliged to pay his respects to his mother at Wivenhoe Park and apprise her of the status of the situation.

With luck, he would return in three days, before all the Martin family secrets were displayed and hung out to dry on Rotten Row for *le haut ton.*

It had been difficult to make small talk with Fraser through the hasty luncheon. Isaac was well aware his friend was no fool; he had undoubtedly felt the tension between him and Mary. He shuddered, remembering that young woman's effect on him.

Only Madam had ever gotten to him in such a manner.

He had reined in his great annoyance, but she'd noted it. Yes, she had noted it, all right, but it hadn't stopped her. She was a headstrong handful...of trouble. Yet, he couldn't help but feel sorry for her and her sister. Their father had landed them in a rare bumblebroth, one from which he had no choice but to try to extricate them. The truth of it was, there was no one else who could step in.

Yes, he felt guilt. She—*the impudent little baggage!*—had seen to that. He had ignored them. No, that was refining upon it a bit too much. To ignore, one has to be aware. His awful guilt lay in the fact that he hadn't even been aware of them. He should've been. He had to assuage his conscience now, make things right. The question was, how far was he prepared to go?

And what would the consequences be?

The brandy prior to luncheon and the claret during luncheon hadn't helped his head. Why had he imagined it would? It still ached. And, as unpleasant as this splitting headache was, he knew for a chilling certainty that far worse was to come.

❖

Lady Rebow, née Martin, known to all and sundry

as Madam, was in high dudgeon. Not a rare state. It occurred with some frequency, most especially when her son was in attendance.

Her son. *The young fool!*

Whatever was he up to? All he was supposed to do was bundle her sorry nieces and their incompetent servants home to Alresford Hall, shut up that miserable rented residence, and wait for Matthew Martin to reappear. For reappear he would, she had no doubt whatsoever of that.

Matthew Martin, the old fool—for all that he was years younger than she—was obviously losing his mind. He had wandered off, and would wander back in due course. When he found Draycott Terrace to let, he would hie himself off to Essex. Then he would hear from her!

Her brother Matthew had always been softheaded. Though he was the male, and she the female, *she* should've been the son and heir, not he. In her opinion, Matthew possessed few manly traits.

Indecisive, absent-minded, weak, that was Matthew Martin. He had fared better during his brief marriage to a strong-minded woman, but afterwards...after his wife's death he had gotten worse. If it weren't for her excellent advice, who knew what would have become of those poor, motherless girls?

The girls, once back into their country routine, she was sure, would be well enough. There were a number of chores awaiting them at Wivenhoe Park when their duties at Alresford Hall were taken care of. The devil made work for idle fingers, 'twas said...well, she would see to it those lively, industrious young fingers were never idle. *She'd make good use of their time!*

Despite her youthful appearance, Madam conceded she was of an age when she had to guard against overtiring herself. She had such trouble securing young women to serve as companions from the servants' registries in London. Her nieces would be fine companions, fetching and carrying at her bidding. *Better still, she wouldn't have to pay them ha'pence!*

Yes, she decided contentedly as she reclined on the

over-stuffed pillows cradling her head on the comfortable green-striped silk chaise longue in her sitting room, and plopped not one, but two, huge chocolate bonbons into her mouth. Yes, she would make excellent use of those girls.

They'd be a succor and a comfort to her in her encroaching old age, reading aloud to her from the novels Mary ordered regularly for her from London's Minerva Press—Madam's preferences ran to Gothic, lurid romances—cosseting her, jumping to her tune, plumping up her pillows, responding to her every whim, and so eager to please. More of a comfort than her infuriating son Isaac, that cold lump of ingratitude, had ever been, or ever would be. She snorted loudly, startling her cowed abigail, Lizzie, and causing the girl to upset a stack of soiled linen she was sorting.

In a sudden fit of bad temper, she threw the empty French chocolates box at Lizzie, surprisingly agile for a self-styled 'old' woman, and berated the girl for her clumsiness as the linens fell further into disorder. In tears, the abigail swooped up the discarded bonbon box with the dirty laundry and ran out of Madam's sitting room. Straight against Sir Isaac's broad chest.

❖

"Here, now, Lizzie!" Isaac caught the thin young maidservant, saving her from falling. He couldn't help but note her reddened nose, watery eyes, and damp cheeks. "What's amiss?" he asked kindly.

The girl was in a hurry to be gone belowstairs. "Naught, Master Isaac, naught! I mus' get these linens into the wash, thankee, Sir." She bobbed a clumsy curtsy, dropped half of the dirty cloths, retrieved them haphazardly, and ran as if all the hounds of hell were at her back and breathing down her neck.

Isaac shook his head; he recognized too well the signs of an unpleasant encounter with Madam.

His mother's cruelty to her servants was legendary and never ceased to unnerve him. *Amazing she kept any servants!* But the servants' registries were full to bursting with applicants for even the most menial positions. A job was a job, even if it meant coping with a monster like Madam. Poor Lizzie! Isaac sighed. *Poor little thing.* He bent to retrieve a wrinkled handkerchief, stuffing it absentmindedly into his pocket. He knocked sharply on his mother's door.

Lady Rebow looked with little favor upon the appearance of her only child, her son Isaac. She had suffered terribly bringing him into the world thirty years ago, and never forgave him for it. She never let him forget it, either. Nor had she ever allowed her late husband to forget it.

Mary Rebow had driven her husband, Isaac's father, a quiet, self-effacing, kindly man, into the arms of other women after deciding she had fulfilled her conjugal duty by providing him with an heir. She had made it clear she no longer had any use for the intimacies of marriage, intimacies that, moreover, had always given her a disgust of him. She lived for herself, having perfected self-centeredness to a unique art form.

"Well? What do you have to say for yourself?" Bristling, her annoyance and contempt evident, she fixed a baleful faded-blue eye on him.

"And good day to you, also, Mother." Isaac smiled as he leaned against the doorjamb, his tall, well-built form dwarfing the entrance.

"I've no time for your sarcasm and nonsense, Isaac. You can save your rhetoric for Parliament," she stated sourly. "Come out with it...what did you discuss with Lawyer Ennew?"

Isaac sighed, moving away from the door and walking to the window. Madam's sitting room faced onto the broad back lawns of Wivenhoe Park, which sloped gently toward a man-made lake. From his vantage point, he could see a small herd of black-and-white Holsteins and two cinnamon-skinned Jerseys chewing their cud at a stile near the outer edge of the Park's extensive, game-filled woods.

A peaceful, pastoral scene, at odds with the dark

drama that had gone on inside this house. The bucolic landscape had been painted by Thomas Constable, then at the beginning of his brilliant career. The work had been commissioned by Isaac's father, builder of Wivenhoe Park.

A stunning portrait of Madam had been painted some time before the erection of Wivenhoe Park, when the Rebows' primary residence had been Colchester proper, in the 17th-century Headgate House. Constable's rival, Thomas Gainsborough, had painted that portrait. It hung downstairs over a white-marble Adam mantelpiece, in an elegant drawing room paneled in rare Congo mahogany.

His mother had been beautiful, Isaac acknowledged. Young bride Mary Martin Rebow had been painted in a stunning panniered formal dress of shining blue satin with embroidered white underskirt. Gainsborough matched the blue of her wide-set, innocent eyes exactly with the shade of her gown. Pretty, with a slender, gently-curved figure, she was not unlike her dainty niece Sally Martin in looks. But Isaac hoped the resemblance ended there.

When seething with barely contained rage at his mother, wondering aloud what his poor, put-upon father had ever seen in her to love, Isaac remembered the Gainsborough likeness and knew. That sweetly pretty face, that lovely figure, obscured for a while the innate meanness of her small mind and unloving heart. The artist had painted an ideal young woman, not the real-life shrew who posed for him.

His father's marriage had been hell. Isaac knew this from sad experience as a young child in a troubled household. Marriage was truly a trap for the unwary. *The parson's mousetrap.* A fitting name, indeed. Woe to the poor, trapped, about-to-be-dispatched mouse!

It would never happen to him.

There was no bait appealing enough. He had come close, but each time was brought to his senses when he remembered Madam. As if stepping into an ice-cold hipbath, the thought of her always cooled down his fervor. No, he would remain a bachelor, a happy, satisfied bachelor. Love was a brief illusion. His poor father had learned that truth.

Madam's sharp, shrill voice sliced into his sad musings and brought him back to the present. "*I said!* What did you and that weasel of a lawyer discuss?" she snarled.

Isaac turned slowly, drawing out his words. "Yes, the esteemed Mr. Ennew, a fine gentleman, a good friend of your late husband, my distinguished father, Madam, if you'll recall..."

Madam snorted.

Isaac continued, ignoring the unladylike sound. "Who, of course, sends you his very best regards, Madam. Yes, Mr. Ennew. We had quite a good talk."

He seated himself on a fragile, lattice-backed Chippendale side chair, facing his mother. He was deliberately drawing this unpleasant encounter out, driving her mad, relishing every moment of her evident discomfiture.

Then he reminded himself sharply to discuss the matter at hand. He had wasted enough time in Essex, not counting the important and altogether necessary discussion with Bertram Staples, his bailiff—a disciple of Turnip Townshend's scientific farming principles—concerning crop rotation. Now, he was eager to return to London to set events in motion.

"Ennew says I'm legal guardian to Mary and Sarah Rebow in their father's absence. It's so stated in Uncle Matthew's will; they can do nothing without my say-so. He agreed with me that the Chelsea lease should not be renewed, and the girls should be settled in a residence nearer to Duke Street so I can supervise them more easily."

Isaac ignored the sudden dark scowl on his mother's face and continued to narrate the discussion with the lawyer, his voice low and clear, his tone calm and reasoned.

"The other possibilities were that they be moved in with me at Duke Street, or return to Alresford Hall, but I think the option we arrived at is by far the best."

Taking a deep breath, he concluded, "Uncle Matthew cheated his daughters out of a season. I shall do my best to give them one before sending them to rusticate at Alresford Hall. And, who knows?" He gave his mother a sly grin. "Mayhap they shall each of them snare a rich husband."

Four

Madam was beside herself.

Choked with rage, her face red, she hurled abuse at her son. "More fool, you! Why," she sputtered, "why go to the expense of a London season for those backward country chits! They'll be a good deal happier here, back home..."

Feigning surprise, Isaac raised his dark eyebrows. "Why, Madam, I thought you were so insistent that Uncle Matthew bring his daughters out into society. You chided him repeatedly and often for failing in his fatherly duties."

Madam's short fingers formed into claws. She fairly itched to throw something harder and sharper than an empty bonbon box into the smug, handsome face of her son, but she wasn't so brave as all that. She feared the potential of his so-far-unleashed rage. Isaac had the capacity to frighten and intimidate her that his weak father never had, though he seemed unaware of his power. She fought for control of her temper and regained it...just barely.

"At his expense! Not yours! *Not ours!* You'll be throwing our good money away, and what for, what for? What shall we get out of this *débâcle*?"

What shall *I* get out of it, that's the important question, she thought, fighting to control her anger at her son's stupidity. Unmarried, the girls were at her beck and call, unpaid handmaidens and companions. Wed, they were under their husbands' thumbs. That was the way of it. They would answer to strange men, men who'd control their dowries, their properties; uncaring men who would not give a thought to their wives' dear aunt and her needs.

Paid companions, she thought, agitated, her mouth pursed sourly. *Paid companions...forevermore.* She couldn't bear it!

Isaac smiled with false indulgence at his mother. She was fit to burst a blood vessel. Her color was dangerously high, the veins standing out in her ropy neck. It pained him to acknowledge what a selfish, greedy, grasping old woman she was.

He knew full well why she wanted the girls in Essex. She didn't fool him; he had read a multitude of letters from her detailing their devotion. Even in London, she had hinted slyly, they'd done her bidding. *Well*, that was over.

He drove the final bolt home. "Why, Madam, to be sure, we are doing this—you and I—out of the goodness of our hearts. The girls shall bless you for it, I assure you. And now—" He rose from his chair, brushing down his well-fitting trousers. "I must bid you *adieu* and hurry back to London. "

Isaac sketched a bow to his mother and kissed the tips of her fingers, fingers now shaking with rage. "I know you want me to stay, dear mother, but...duty calls, you know. Family obligations, and all that. You did train me so well concerning my obligations to my family, to you, dear Madam. I must see to resettling Mary and Sarah as soon as possible."

At her door, a final, mischievous thought occurred to him. He could not resist the wicked temptation to further unnerve her.

"I could settle half our problem"—he stressed the our, drawling it out—"by offering for one of them myself. Who, do you think, Mary or Sarah? Beauties both, and of excellent family background. Mary's the elder, so perhaps she would be more fitting, but Sally's much more demure and tractable, two highly prized qualities in a wife.

"Ah, 'tis a pity I'm not a Musselman, for in that eastern faith, a man's allowed four wives. Then I could wed them both, and yet be entitled to two more..."

He laughed and ducked as Madam, exasperated beyond endurance, threw a plump goosedown pillow at him, missing by a mile. She was losing her touch, no doubt about it. Her aim had been much better in the past.

"*Adieu,* Madam," he grinned, exiting.

Outside her door, his hand gripping the latch hard, the back of his head resting wearily against the paneled wood, all of his jauntiness and cheek evaporated. No longer playing hurtful games with his mother, he closed his eyes and pondered on the second folly to which he had committed himself, compounding his earlier folly in Chelsea.

For Lawyer Ennew had agreed with Madam, a rarity in their strained relationship. Since they never spoke, however, Isaac was secure in the knowledge his mother wouldn't know Ennew had recommended that the Martin girls return to Alresford Hall.

The idea of giving them a season had been his, Isaac's, and his alone. Where the decision had come from, he honestly didn't know, and, in the cold light of reason, he couldn't fathom his mysterious thought processes. In both his heart and mind, he knew it for a mad scheme, utter nonsense, doomed to failure.

What did he know of launching young women into a season? Or into what remained of this one? He had *bona fide* social *entrée*, but the girls needed a female chaperone, a guide to oversee, prepare, and school them. The *ton's* rules were set and rigid; no mistakes could be made, none forgiven.

Further, how could he assume the Martin sisters were interested in a season? Would they entertain, much less agree to, such a plan? He didn't know their minds, their hearts. The sad truth was, he didn't know his young cousins at all.

Ruefully, he shook his head and sighed. What a muddle. Worse, he couldn't go back on his word now, not after he had faced Madam down so confidently and contemptuously, throwing her own neglect of her nieces back at her. Nor could he retract what he had said to

Mary Martin without appearing an utter fool. Madam hadn't liked what he had said, neither had Mary, but he was the one who had taken charge and put himself on record.

He had assumed an awesome responsibility, and he was at a complete loss to know why he had committed himself to such folly.

❖

While Isaac doubted his sanity in Essex, his friend Fraser squired the Martin sisters about town. It was hardly the *tête-à-tête* he'd envisioned, however, as the girls had asked Mrs. May, Henny's mother, to chaperone. Henny, of course, accompanied them.

It could be worse. Jamie chuckled. He could endure Mrs. May and Henrietta to see Sally. And it didn't harm his reputation among his Corinthian peers, the fashionable, sporting crowd, to be seen at Gunter's pastry shop with three such charming young women.

Lord Robin Bradshaw and the Honourable Charles Higginbotham, two old school chums, saw them and sought introductions. Jamie noted that roguish Robin seemed quite taken with Mary, while shyer Charlie positively ogled red-haired Henny.

As the stylish gentlemen pulled up chairs to chat, Jamie had the opportunity to speak with Sally somewhat privately. They sat side by side, with Mrs. May at Jamie's right hand.

"We seem to have amassed a crowd, Miss Martin. But," Jamie commented gallantly, "how can they resist such divine female pulchritude?"

Blushing, Sally noted Mr. Fraser's beautiful smile, showing off a full set of very white, very even teeth. She thought he was the handsomest man she had ever seen, and was beside herself with happiness. At first, though, she wasn't sure to which of them, herself, Mary, or Henny, Mr. Fraser was more partial.

Sally was fond of her dear sister, and wished her the greatest joys and all her heart's desires, but she hoped

Mr. Fraser was not either of those. No, she, Sarah Emily Gertrude Martin, wanted handsome, charming, kind Mr. James Fraser all to herself. She blushed even more hotly at the boldness of her thoughts.

Jamie saw Sally's face go pink and was charmed once more by the young girl's innocence. She was no pampered *ton* miss, all guile and artifice, soliciting compliments as if they were her due. Sally was unused to male attention, and that endeared her to him. She brought out quite unfamiliar urges, the urge to protect, to safeguard from harm, to hold her close to him forever.

He had become so jaded, following his crowd in search of new excitements, that it had taken him fully three days to understand the depth of his feelings toward Sally. When he had babbled on, so irritating Isaac, all the way from Chelsea, he had not been able to help himself.

Not wanting to expose how utterly taken he was with the younger sister, he had heaped praise upon the elder, as well, and had not neglected Miss May, though he thought her rather silly.

Isaac had been strangely silent. True, he wasn't overly talkative, but he was almost sullen that day. *Most odd!* Jamie didn't know his friend well enough to attempt to probe his innermost thoughts, much less his feelings, but...

"So, Miss Martin, how long will you and your family be in town? Do you stay for the remainder of the season?" Jamie directed his probing toward the object of his desires.

Sally raised her blonde head from Gunter's delicious raspberry ice and wondered what to say in response to Mr. Fraser's questions. Mary had cautioned her not to venture a word about Papa's disappearance, but surely there was something she could say that wouldn't compromise her vow to her sister.

"We...we may be returning to Essex within the month, to Alresford Hall. Although," she hastened to add, her eyes sending him a beseeching look, "I wish that mightn't be so." Feeling her cheeks turning hot again at her rather forward remark, she bent her head quickly and dipped her spoon into the ice.

Fraser paled visibly, appalled at the prospect of the Martins' imminent departure from London. "I fervently wish you are incorrect, Miss Martin, *my very dear Miss Martin*, for both our sakes." He dared, then, to reach for her dainty hand and run his index finger over the top of it lightly, oh, so lightly.

Sally thought she would never again take a breath, that she would die right then and there. She placed her spoon on the rim of her dessert dish and closed her eyes for a brief instant, then looked up into Fraser's clear blue eyes and exhaled slowly. Never could she have imagined that such a feather-light caress would set every nerve in her body tingling in sweet anticipation.

"Mr. Fraser," she began, then stopped, not knowing how to continue.

"Forgive me, please, Miss Martin," Fraser begged, his voice lowered so only she could hear. "I didn't mean to be so forward. Excuse me, I beg you."

Sally smiled, a smile that lit up her perfectly oval face, a serene, gentle face with angelic features, rather like seraphim in Renaissance paintings. Her heavenly-blue eyes met his again and held them, and he knew instantly there was nothing to forgive, nothing to excuse. Their two yearning souls met in mid air and embraced.

Fraser shuddered at the force of the emotional impact. He was clearly in love, top hat over Hessians in love...there was no question about it. Nor was there any question in his mind as to how Sally felt. Her beautiful eyes and sweet smile gave it all away. His heart pounded wildly. Was there ever such perfect bliss? He sighed with joy, elated beyond belief.

❖

Mary happened to turn her head at the exact moment the souls of Jamie Fraser and Sally Martin communed over melting fruit ices at Gunter's.

She drew in a sharp breath, then looked away

quickly. It was as if she had witnessed a deeply intimate act. Her heart gave a happy leap and she smiled brightly at Lord Robin, who was regaling her with a series of only mildly amusing anecdotes. Her too bright smile caused that young man to think even more highly of himself than he usually did, and he puffed out his rather concave chest.

Mary's building jealousy of her younger sister evaporated in a flash. Isaac Rebow might prefer Sally to her, but it was obvious where Sally's affections now lodged. Sally and Mr. Fraser had formed a *tendre* for each other, and it appeared to be quite serious. *No room for Isaac there!*

Mary almost simpered at Bradshaw as she encouraged him to relate further anecdotes. Observing flirtatious Henny in action had taught her how to flatter the egos of young, self-centered men, but—who was there to teach her how to capture the heart of a cold, cold, man who barely knew she was alive?

She pushed away her ice and continued her pretense of being utterly enthralled by his young lordship, while the ache she had nursed in her heart for the past three days returned to take up permanent residence.

❖

Mary was on Isaac's mind again on the long trip back from Wivenhoe Park. No, whom was he gulling? She had never left his thoughts. The awful headache had gone, but the other headache, Mary, his impossible young cousin, was still firmly in place. He couldn't dismiss her presence from his life.

Ridiculous! He was a man of the world. He'd enjoyed more women than he could remember; not that they were so numerous and he such a great lover, but most were, frankly, forgettable. Memories of those had faded away, bleached out like colored cloth left too long in the unforgiving Indian sun.

Marry? What brought that repellent idea into his mind? He urged his horses on past a crossroads, cutting

around a hay waggon behind which he had no desire to
trail for the next few miles. Mary...marry...marry
Mary...the waggon's wheels clanked rhythmically as he
sped by. The two words were uncomfortably similar. He
shuddered, remembering it was his mother's name, too.
She had always boasted *'dear Mary'* was her namesake.
What a coil!

He should never have made those offensive comments to Madam about taking multiple brides. What had
gotten into him, joking to her about offering for his
cousins? *For Sally?* She was an infant! And Mary? *Even
worse!* Mary was naught but a rag-mannered, stubborn
child. And that voice! She should do something about
that voice. It was too...

Ah! What was he doing, thinking of that child's utterly inappropriate, unsuitable, disturbing...voice? He
snapped his whip in the air, then regretted it as his team
reacted skittishly in alarm and pulled forward much too
fast, jolting him back in his seat. He set his teeth at his
cowhandedness. Fraser would be appalled to see how he
was handling his prime cattle.

Blast! She would be the death of him yet, perhaps
on this very road. He was in danger, and he knew it, just
as certainly as he knew she could not change one decibel
of that outlandish voice, that seductive, uncalled-for
voice. That voice he couldn't get out of his head. And
that was just the start, for he couldn't get her beautiful
face, all light and dark and expressive, out of his head
either. Nor that lithe, petite, generously-curved body...

He groaned aloud, flustering his team again as they
shied slightly off the road. *Damme, I'm scaring my own
horses!* Ah, brilliant, brilliant, he chastised himself. Get
the chit out of your mind! *You can't marry her,* you fool.
Your only salvation is to marry her *off*...and get back to
your own life. And quickly, man, he added silently and
fervently, quickly!

He turned his team with a deft and practiced hand
and made for the high road to London.

❖

Strong yellow sun streamed through the many-paned windows of the morning room at Duke Street as Isaac sipped a cup of hot black coffee and scanned the morning newspapers. He read through the myriad personal advertisements in the heap of pages strewn over his table, sheets of *The British Gazette*, the *Sunday Monitor*, *The Times*, the *Morning Post*, and the *Observer*, looking for a format he could adapt for his own advertisement. An advertisement requesting the immediate response of a certain Matthew Martin.

Ennew had suggested the wording, a brief, simple message instructing Matthew to respond to a newspaper box number on a matter of utmost urgency. Would it be enough to flush the old rascal out? Isaac wondered, even as he knew Martin was an inveterate reader of newspapers and journals, preferably those bought with someone else's coin. He passed a good deal of time at his clubs and at Duke Street reading the papers.

Unfortunately, he had not been seen at Brooks's lately, nor at the other gentlemen's clubs. Isaac had sent footmen to inquire, but no news turned up. The thought had passed through Isaac's mind that his uncle might suddenly appear on his doorstep when he went to Essex, but his watchful staff hadn't seen him at all.

Isaac instructed his staff to allow Matthew Martin entrance, but to follow when he left and thus ascertain his direction. They were to ignore Matthew's irritating custom of unlocking cabinets, borrowing pre-franked envelopes and tea, and drinking and taking away his wine.

The other issue discussed with Ennew had been the matter of finding a woman to chaperone and advise the Martin sisters if they agreed to stay for the London season. Thanks to the lawyer, he'd received the direction of the former governess, Emma Wells, who had left the Martin household to wed.

Now Emma Davenport, she was the wife of naval captain Michael Davenport. The great good news was her recent move from Portsmouth to London; she was residing close by in Queen Square, alone in a too-large house her husband had lately inherited. Captain Davenport was on duty patrolling the eastern coast of Canada in a brigantine, and not expected home for some time.

Mrs. Davenport appeared delighted to renew her acquaintance with her former charges and help them navigate the hazardous shoals and channels of the London season. She was also fond of Mrs. Pepperwit and Mapps, and agreed to add them to her household.

She shook her short, fashionable mop of chestnut curls and commiserated with Isaac. "Poor, dear Mr. Martin. He's a loving father, Sir Isaac, I do believe that, but he's...oh, I do hate to say these things about a former employer, one who treated me so very kindly."

Mrs. Davenport was pouring tea in her spacious, sunny drawing room. She had been instructing the new kitchen maid when Isaac appeared at the front door. No butler or housekeeper was in evidence; she had answered his knock herself.

Isaac noted she was pretty, in a quiet, intelligent way, with a generous, quick-to-smile mouth. He remembered her remarkably erect carriage from Alresford Hall and chuckled to himself when it brought to mind her former charge's ramrod-stiff spine. He wondered if Miss Wells had made her young pupil sit on a straight chair balancing a large book on her head to achieve that perfect posture.

Mrs. Davenport pursed her lips, reflecting. "Mr. Martin was rather scatterbrained, Sir Isaac. It went beyond simple absentmindedness. The household learned to work around his habits. Mrs. Pepperwit was used to say...oh, dear, this is low servants' gossip."

Isaac encouraged her, and she continued, albeit reluctantly. "The servants said Mr. Martin was never altogether right in the head"—she tapped her temple for emphasis—"after his wife died in childbirth. Mrs. P. was certain he had become unhinged."

Isaac nodded. "A sorry time. I was a youngster at school but came home for the funeral. Everyone was quite distraught. The little girls..." A sudden memory flashed of his two small cousins during that sad time, the death of their young mother.

Toddler Sally was unaware, but Mary had cried and called for her Mama for days. Upon being told her Mama and baby brother were in Heaven, she had stamped her tiny foot and said, *Well, tell Heaven to bring them back home! Now!* The injustice of it all was unacceptable. Even then, she was a force to reckon with.

"I never stopped to think how it affected my uncle. I was too young."

Mrs. Davenport nodded. "Yes, I think the household had great sympathy for Matthew. He was indulged, cossetted, left to go his own way. No one wanted to burden or trouble him, so his responsibilities passed to others. Alresford Hall has an excellent staff. It's probably one of the best-run estates in all of England. Managed rather by default, but, nonetheless, managed well."

Over a second cup of tea, she agreed to take in the Martin sisters and their servants and guide the girls through what was left of the Season. But the recurring image of a tiny girl, stamping her foot imperiously, demanding that Heaven pay attention to her wishes, nearly broke Isaac's heart. He needed every bit of help he could muster to deal with Mary—short of putting a pistol to her stubborn head!—and prayed Emma Davenport would be the ally he desperately sought.

Five

Dorothy Scofield peered anxiously into the dressing-table mirror, searching for signs of age. Though only twenty-six, she was aware 'blondes fade.' She heard it often enough from the jealous dark-haired cats she had encountered in her years at the Covent Garden nunneries.

Pah! Not yet, she reassured herself, *not yet.* There were a few faint—very few, very faint—crow's feet at the corners of her slanting aquamarine eyes, but she had an ointment to take care of that small problem. Dorothy prepared her own cosmetics and was skillful in their use. When she had to augment her income, she found eager buyers for those wares. As to her other wares...

She smiled as she applied a mixture of black frank-incense, resin, and mastic to her arched blond eyebrows, darkened them expertly, and thought of dear Matthew Martin, her brand-new husband of less than a week.

Those other wares, her voluptuous body and masses of spun-gold hair, had reeled him in like a besotted trout, netted him like a stunned turbot. *So easy!* Marriage was the perfect answer to her dilemma, less work than the risky game she was forced to play on the London streets with her disreputable brother.

She leaned back and stretched, her full, heavy bosom lifted by the action and straining against the cheap silk of her worn chemise. She needed new clothes and lingerie. Time to pay a visit to her favorite modiste, the French *émigrée*, Mademoiselle Dumont. It had been an inordinately long time between perusals of the latest fashion plates.

She stared back into her mirror, pleased with the

result of her applications. She and Bart had enacted that piteous routine in front of a right good cove that one last time, she thought.

Matthew had come running to the aid of the lovely young widow robbed by a hulking footpad, a brutish ruffian, and he had been the answer—so to speak—to her prayers. She chuckled. Dorothy was never one to spend much time in church, much less on her perfectly rounded knees *in prayer*...of all things!

Matthew, short, stocky, so earnest, so rich, had been the perfect cove, begging to be gulled. He took her to a nearby teashop, insisting that the hot, strong brew would alleviate her shock. He was solicitous to a fault, pressing sovereigns on her from his capacious purse and insisting she take a hackney to her flat.

The Scofields' game was to convince unsuspecting fools to accompany Dorothy to temporarily hired lodgings, where Bart, blackjack in burly hand, would render them senseless and relieve them of their fat purses and gold watches. Countless numbers had been victims; she had lost track of the number.

With Matthew, however, Dorothy hesitated to play their usual game. She sensed larger possibilities in his person. Much larger.

She discovered in the teashop that he was a well-off widower with two daughters, now living in Chelsea, that he owned a large country estate in Essex, and that he was lonely and extremely gullible.

Ever since being given her *congé* by her last wealthy protector, a Cit in the textile trade who unceremoniously turned her out of an elegant St. Martin's Lane *maisonette* for a young opera dancer, Dorothy had been forced to live by her not very considerable wits.

Enter brother Bart, recently escaped from Newgate Prison, a temporary solution to her immediate financial needs, but not one entirely to her liking. What she really wanted, what she needed, was another protector. Dorothy hated having to take care of herself.

But Matthew Martin had fallen in love. He offered marriage, not simply protection. She was taken completely and breathtakingly by surprise; she'd tried marriage once, at sixteen, and it had not at all been to her liking.

She had left that arrangement and her country village with no qualms and came to London, where she soon found herself in the muslin company. With a natural aptitude for the work, she soon found the first of her long-term lovers, rich men looking for excitement outside their dull, arranged marriages.

The first relationship lasted two years. The man, a London tradesman, died suddenly, not having made a permanent provision for her with his man of business. Turned out of a beautifully appointed town house off Sutherland Street by his vengeful widow—the lease was in her protector's name—she barely managed to take some few clothes and even fewer jewels with her.

She had no choice but to return to her former Covent Garden abbess, Mother Nell, then operating out of a more respectable address in King's Place, St. James's. An empty stretch of time followed in that nunnery, until she caught the eye of a dissolute baronet and was once again set up in style.

By then, she had learned from more experienced Cyprians, and from her friend the abbess, to have other men at the ready when the inevitable happened. When the baronet gave her the not unexpected *congé*, she had an elerly earl waiting in the wings.

So it went, until that last miserable Cit's change of heart. She wasn't with him long, certainly not long enough to have another man interested and waiting. It was quite a blow, a shock to her hard-won confidence.

Now here was this plump little morsel, this lovely prize from the landed gentry, at her well-shaped feet, proposing marriage! She lost no time accepting. They eloped in the early morning to a tiny parish church in Knightsbridge; Matthew had arranged for a special license. He also located and leased a substantial house in the neighborhood.

Dorothy was not concerned or disturbed over Matthew's apparent desertion of his two daughters. Her intelligence, like her morals, was quite low, and she didn't understand that in Matthew's class such lapses from correct behavior were frowned upon.

The Cyprian lived in the here-and-now, and it suited her needs. She didn't realize Matthew and his children were part of a larger Society, quick to condemn and censure. It didn't dawn on her that eventually Matthew would have to reconcile with his daughters and make up for the unconscionable transgression of deserting them to elope with a strange woman decidedly not of their class.

What worried poor, stupid Dorothy now wasn't the travail Matthew's girls might be going through with their father gone, but her murderous brother, Bart, whom she had betrayed. She shivered in the frayed silk of her thin chemise; she didn't want Bart to find her. The possibility that Bart *might* find her made her frantic.

She hoped she would be safe in Knightsbridge, still a small village hunched sleepily on London's broad left shoulder, away from Bart's usual evil haunts in the city's dank slums south of the Thames. He also tended to run to cover in crime-ridden neighborhoods such as Seven Dials, far from the northern suburbs. Nevertheless, she worried.

Bart's temper was foul, and her desertion of him wouldn't be easily forgiven, if at all. Perhaps she and Matthew should retire to their country estate. She liked the sound of that, *their country estate*. And perhaps Bart's dangerous lifestyle would soon do him in.

Then, she'd have no worries at all.

❖

*"Let Fame puff her trumpet, for muffin
and crumpet/They cannot compare with my
dainty hot rolls/When mornings are chilly..."*

❖

The street hawkers were out early, crying their

wares. Mary kept her bedroom window wide open at night, as she was accustomed to doing in the country, and so the London vendors woke her in the morning just as Farmer Whaley's roosters on the home farm woke her at dawn at Alresford Hall. It suited her well; she enjoyed rising with the sun, hearing the soft stirrings of the farm creatures, walking the green lawns with the gentle, ever-present buzzing of the Hall's bees in her ears.

Mary yawned, stretched, and hopped out of bed with the spring of healthy youth, going eagerly to the window for a breath of morning air. Alas, here reality dawned. London's foul air, by no stretch of the imagination could ever smell as wonderfully fresh as Essex country air, all salty fens, woods, and fertile farmlands.

She sighed heavily, elbows resting on the window-sill, fists against her cheeks, the short, pink-flowered chintz curtains wafting in the slight morning breeze over her mop of thick hair. She studied the brilliant white puffy heaps of cumulus clouds on the far horizon. Another fair day in London. But it would be even more beautiful in the country, at Alresford Hall.

She wanted to go home.

Much as she loved her old governess, she didn't want to remain at Queen Square. Mary chafed at Mrs. Davenport's gentle chaperonage and bristled that she was under the thumb of her domineering cousin. She had always been her own mistress and couldn't cope with restrictions. Nor did she want this season.

Sweet Sally had prevailed upon her to do this, to allow herself to be paraded into society, for Isaac's sake. She and Mrs. Davenport had argued persuasively on his behalf and pressed upon her that he was taking his valuable time to see they were properly introduced to society. Mrs. Davenport dwelled on the entertainment and fun they would have in the weeks to come. Cousin Isaac was outfitting them with new wardrobes, treating them to theatre boxes, accompanying them to balls and musicales.

Sally thought the sun rose and set on wonderful cousin Isaac, when she wasn't thinking it rose and set on wonderful Jamie Fraser. She had her own reasons for remaining in town, did Sally! She refused to think ill of Isaac, truly believing he was so kind, so deferential, taking his temporary guardianship so seriously, simply out of the great goodness of his kind heart.

Hah!

Isaac couldn't gull Mary. He wasn't doing this for them. He was making room for them in his busy social calendar because of his terrible guilt. He had ignored them, and trouble had befallen them. Now, as a consequence, they were his responsibility. Yes, he was doing it for himself, as penance. Perhaps he could pull the wool over innocent Sally's eyes, and fool even a matron like Emma Davenport, but Mary knew the truth of it. She had endured that disastrous interview at Draycott Terrace; she had felt the full brunt of his terrible anger.

Her lower lip trembled as she confronted the other truth, that of her great cowardice. She had agreed to stay, to move to Queen Square, to put up with this great farce of an *entrée* into society, because...

She took a deep, shuddering breath. Because this way she could be with him. She needed to see him, even for only short, circumscribed periods of time. The need was real, profound, and diminished her in her own eyes.

She was a coward. He was still her handsome, fairy-tale prince, and she still desired him as much as ever. No longer, however, was that desire a child's innocent desire; she desired him now as a woman grown. The reality, though, was that in Isaac's eyes she was still a little girl...worse, she was a little girl who could do nothing right.

Depressed and feeling altogether too sorry for herself, she turned from the window, wiping at a stray, unbidden, coward's tear, as the street vendors paraded below, their melodic cries wafted upward by the gentle breeze.

❖

"Six bunches a penny, sweet blooming Lavender..."

❖

*"Come buy my fine roses, my myrtles and
stocks/My sweet-smelling balsams and
close-growing box..."*

❖

*"New brooms, green brooms, will you
buy any? Maidens come quickly, let
me take a penny..."*

❖

The young farm wenches passed by the square, their
strong, country-accented musical voices carrying up to
her room as Mary busied herself with her gown, washed
her face with the cold water in the basin, and combed
and braided her long hair.

Before anyone else rose, she usually managed to
take a long walk on the by and large deserted streets of
Westminster and its environs. If she had enough time,
she—clad in boy's buckskin breeches—could take a
canter through St. James's Park, wishing that Bess, her
old mare, were under her, and that she could be riding
astride in the woods near Alresford Hall.

Time was wasting! No woolgathering now. She
brushed her teeth, checked her reflection quickly in the
mirror, and silently opened her door. No one about. She
was free!

Her fast feet took her to Duke Street. She was day-
dreaming, crossing the quiet streets without a thought
where she was headed. How embarrassing! *What if
Cousin Isaac...?* He kept country hours, she knew; he
could be up and about even now. She had better return to
Queen Square before she was found out.

She had been scrupulously avoiding him while carrying out Madam's orders and acting as an intermediary
with suppliers and the servants' registries. Isaac had no

idea she was responsible for the efficient setting up of his new domicile. She, not Madam, deserved full credit on that score. Mary ran back all the way to Queen Square. The run was exhilarating, but her mad rush brought her badly pinned plaits down from her head, and her hair was in frazzled disarray and her face flushed when she made her entrance through the kitchen.

Agnes Pepperwit, putting up the kettle for the servants' tea, looked her over disapprovingly. She shook her head so vigorously that her oversized mobcap threatened to fall onto the hearth's hot coals.

Mary cut off her old nurse's reproofs, laughing as she hugged the ample body to her slender one. "Now, don't scold, Mrs. P., I took a little longer than usual on my walk this morning, no cause for alarm."

Mrs. Pepperwit shook her head again, less agitated. "Mrs. Davenport wouldn't approve, and 'twill be on both our heads!" She clucked softly, taking in Mary's dishevelment. "Will you look at yourself? A young lady coming out into Society does not go around looking the hoyden, Miss Molly!"

"A hoyden? I?" Mary Martin laughed, unbraiding her thick hair and combing it through with her fingers. To the chuckling Mrs. Pepperwit, Mary looked like a lovely young witch, her dark hair flowing in ringlets from the tight braiding.

The housekeeper flicked a white linen cloth at her. "Off with you, minx! You shall be the death of me, I vow."

Mary was still laughing as she came up the backstairs, her fingers working through the tangle of her dark locks. She walked cheerfully through the foyer to the dining room. Sally should be awake by now; she would have company for breakfast.

She had company, indeed.

Cousin Isaac stood at the sideboard helping himself to eggs and devilled kidneys. Emma and Sally were seated at the round oak table. All three looked at her as she entered the room. Mary gulped back the remains of her laughter, almost choking on it.

Six

Emma frowned, Sally looked worried, and Isaac almost dropped his plate at the sight of Mary's unkempt hair and her shapeless drab-printed cotton twill dress. A too-short frock she had clearly outgrown, it exposed far too many inches of trim ankle.

"Good morning!" Mary greeted them, smiling brightly. "What do we have for breakfast this beautiful morning?"

She seated herself nonchalantly and poured a cup of tea. *So far, so good,* she thought. Her nerves hadn't betrayed her; her hands weren't shaking. Inwardly, however, she quivered in anticipation of the peal Emma was sure to ring over her head.

It wasn't long in coming...

"Where were you, Mary?" Emma asked quietly, unsmiling. What had possessed the girl to don a frock even a scullery maid would consider unsuitable. And that wild hair! *Wherever was Clara, the new abigail she had hired?*

Oh, Mary thought, wildly, oh, Lud, why is *he* here? Her voice pitched high, she responded, "It is such a beautiful morning, I thought I would take a fast turn in the park."

Isaac placed his breakfast plate on the table; he fixed Mary with a hard stare. *"Alone?* Are you in the habit of going out alone?"

He was scowling at her. She couldn't stand it; he was angry again. She could do nothing but displease and anger him.

She forced an even brighter smile on her face, a face that felt strangely stiff, as if all the muscles were work-

ing in opposite directions. "I go out every morning,
Cousin Isaac, just as I've always done since we came to
London. At home, I'm used to going riding then.

"I am sorry if I worried you, Mrs. Davenport." Mary
turned to Isaac. "I did a poor job of plaiting my hair. I
was up too early, you see, for our abigail to attend to me.
My hair came undone as I walked briskly through the
park."

Isaac still fixed her with a disapproving look, but
said nothing. She continued, a bit desperately, to explain
further. "No one saw me in the park, Cousin. It was
quite deserted. I've not disgraced you..."

"You've disgraced yourself, Mary," Isaac commented, his voice low, devoid of emotion. He seemed to
be on the point of saying something else, but took up his
fork instead and began to pick at the devilled kidneys.

Emma turned to Isaac. She spoke through thinned,
compressed lips. "I am sorry, Sir Isaac. I didn't realize
Mary was in the habit of taking early morning
walks...alone. In future, if she feels she must take the
morning air, I shall see to it that Clara rises early and
accompanies her."

She fixed a distressed look at Mary and her voice
fell low. "And I shall instruct Clara to dress her mistress's hair before she leaves the house."

Mary couldn't stand it. Emma was visibly upset,
barely in control of her voice. She glanced sideways at
Sally and saw that her sister seemed on the verge of
tears. She gulped in embarrassment for her untoward
behavior and the distress it was causing those dearest to
her.

Isaac waved a hand. "Let us leave off this discussion for now, Mrs. Davenport. We should have our
breakfast. It is becoming cold."

No colder than your tone of voice, Mary thought,
staring at Isaac, *no colder than your cold, cold heart.*

She almost jumped, then, when he began to speak to
her. Had he read her mind? Had he heard what she was
thinking?

But, no, he was saying quite something else.

"You've no doubt worked up a fine appetite with your jaunt about the park, Cousin. Shall I fill a plate for you?"

I'd rather die than have you fill my plate for me, as if I were a child unable to help myself, Mary thought, choking back the reply. He was so unspeakably cruel. She was amazed to find her voice, and that she could still speak. "No, thank you, Cousin Isaac. I can serve myself."

Mary rose hurriedly, too hurriedly, from her chair, scraping it back against the waxed hardwood floor, nearly overturning it. She caught Emma's wince at her uncharacteristic clumsiness, and was shamed. Sally, who seemed to have blinked back tears, looked pained.

Can I do nothing right this morning? Mary asked herself, heaping eggs and toast on her plate with hands that trembled and a fork that clattered loudly against the china in the dead silence of the morning room.

It was a dreadful breakfast.

Mary, usually the heartiest of eaters, took only one helping and thought she was ingesting straw and ashes. Swallowing was difficult, if not almost impossible, with the obstacle of the large lump in the middle of her throat, but she somehow managed. Tears pricked the back of her eyeballs, but she refused to give in to them. She wouldn't, she couldn't, further embarrass herself in front of Isaac.

He would not make her cry. He would not see her cry. *Not ever.*

Isaac broke the silence as they were sipping their second cups of tea. He dismissed Emma and Sally, saying, "If you don't mind, Mrs. Davenport, Cousin Sally... I would like to speak to Mary alone for a few moments."

Mary stole a quick glance at her sister. Poor Sally looked terrified. Did she imagine their loathesome guardian would lock the doors to the morning room and take a birch rod to her back? Mary smiled reassuringly at Sally, whose wide blue eyes betrayed her anxiety.

"I shall be in the drawing room, Sir Isaac," Emma replied.

Isaac nodded coolly.

Mary fiddled with her silver teaspoon, tapping it nervously on the edge of the teacup and stealing a look at her cousin. He looked impossibly handsome today, she thought. She was fascinated by the old-fashioned way he wore his hair, tied at the back of his neck in a queue. The bygone style gave him a piratical look that was especially pleasing to her. He was attired in a well-fitting double-breasted nutmeg-brown coat with a wide-cut collar, and tight buff trousers tucked into high leather boots. His linen, as always, was white and crisp.

Perfect. He was always perfect.

She looked down at herself, at her awful frock, and lifted the heavy hair off the back of her neck. She looked no better than a street urchin. How could he bear to gaze upon her? *He has every right to birch me,* she thought with a start. He was her guardian, and she had behaved badly...not for the first time, and probably not for the last time.

It had finally dawned on her: *Cousin Isaac was in charge.*

❖

Why was she looking at him that way, with those large, frightened eyes? *Does she think I will take a cane to her buttocks for her ill-advised behavior?* Isaac stifled an ironic laugh as he drank the rest of his tea.

He remembered their first meeting, when they had crossed swords, strong will versus strong will, and how his hand had fairly itched to wallop her bottom. That image had been quickly supplanted by other fantasies, much to his discomfort and woe. He wasn't proud of those fantasies. And this constant tension...

Why did it always have to be a clash of wills with Mary? Why was she hell-bent on challenging his authority? Did the child not understand he was concerned for her well-being? That he cared for her? And for her sister, too, of course.

Ah, Mary, why do you make this so difficult? He wearied of this struggle of wills. *Why can you not be*

*like Sally? Sally, so sweet, so tractable, always willing
to please...but if you were Sally, my dear, dear Mary, I
wouldn't care as much. It would, none of it, matter as
much...*

You are a great fool, Isaac Rebow, he told himself,
as he brought the teacup down on its saucer with a re-
sounding clatter. *A great fool!* His dark brows knit in
frustration. What was he going to do with her? What
could he say? Isaac was too engrossed in his own con-
voluted thoughts to note how Mary fairly jumped in her
seat as he banged his cup down and scowled darkly.

"Cousin Isaac?" Her mouth was dry and she was
extremely nervous, but she wanted to get this over with,
whatever it was he was going to do or say to her. Her
hands, clasped tightly in her lap, trembled.

"Yes, Mary?" Did she detect a kindly note in his
tone? No, it was probably her imagination. He sat back
in his chair, elbows on armrests, long fingers steepled
under his chin.

She gulped. "Cousin Isaac..if...if I have distressed
you or Mrs. Davenport, I'm very sorry. I assure you, I
shall try to behave with more decorum and propriety
while under your guardianship."

She breathed a long, ragged sigh. There, it was said.
She had apologized. She was utterly humiliated. It had
cost her dearly to say it, more than he could ever imagine, but she could not bear his anger any more. She simply could not. She was truly a coward, a coward craving
his approval, hopelessly desiring his love...

"Mary," he began gently, so gently she was momentarily startled. She had been steeling herself for his
dark, rich baritone to drill holes through her, to reduce
her to sobs with each diamond-sharp word of reproof.
Ah, but he was beginning much too gently...

"Mary, you are not a child," he continued. "You're a
rare young woman, with many God-given talents and
abilities. I recognize them. Mrs. Davenport, who was
your governess, recognizes them."

Isaac paused, fixing her with a puzzled look. His
fingertips tapped a slow tattoo on the surface of the ta-

ble. "So, why, my dear, do you make it so difficult for us?

"Why do you put yourself in danger by venturing alone into the streets and causing us alarm?" He frowned.

"From this morning forward, Mary, you are not to leave the house unescorted." He looked directly into her eyes and paused, expecting to hear protests. Somewhat surprised at her silence, he continued. "I shall instruct Mrs. Davenport to have Mrs. Pepperwit burn, or give to the poor, if they'll deign to accept them, those miserable frocks you seem to favor for your unchaperoned forays. Mrs. Davenport is about to make an appointment with a dressmaker. I suggest this appointment be undertaken as soon as possible, *for all our sakes.*"

His voice had risen somewhat as he lectured her on her shortcomings, but now he lowered it again, almost to a whisper, an ungentle, slightly menacing whisper, she thought. His lips were set in a tight line.

"Mary," he said, "do I make myself clear?"

Mary didn't reply. She looked away, seeming unable to look him in the eye. She was very still.

"Mary?" Isaac rose from his chair and pulled out the one next to hers. Sitting down, he lifted his hand and tilted her chin toward him. She recoiled at his touch.

Excellent, Isaac, excellent, he berated himself. *She really hates you now. See? She cannot bear your touch...*

Mary thought, *If I look at him I shall cry; I cannot look at him while he continues to tell me how dreadful, how childish I am. Oh, I cannot bear it!*

He touched her. Her senses somersaulted from the heat at the point of contact, suddenly overwhelmed by him. His flesh...on hers. She reeled.

Notwithstanding her jerky movement away from him when his fingers brushed her chin, he suddenly had the mad urge to pull her to him, to hold all of her sweet, curvaceous body tightly against his own, to enfold her in a passionate embrace. He wanted to cover her with kisses, to set his lips against that lovely mouth, those enormous dark eyes, the silken cheeks, that pulsating hollow at the base of her long, white throat.

Isaac was overwhelmed with the ferocity of his passion. He fought for control, before he made a complete idiot of himself with this child who was his ward. This girl who couldn't bear his touch, no more than it seemed she could bear his never-ending lectures.

He removed his fingers from her chin and stood up abruptly. He was going mad, out of his mind. She had cast a spell on him, this witch-child, with that mass of shining black hair standing out from her face like a halo...no, no, not witch, but angel.

She had cast a spell, regardless, whether angel or witch, and he was securely bound and caught in it. He knew he was well and truly doomed. In truth, he had known it for longer than he cared to admit. The country mouse had him in her thrall...

Mary opened her eyes and looked at him, and the sweet, hot rush came over him again. *Madness!* He had to leave, while he was still able to will his strangely reluctant-to-move legs.

"Mary? Please, promise me you'll be more circumspect," he asked. "I do not mean to be harsh, my dear. Forgive me if I seem cruel. I do not want you to think ill of me. Can we not cry friends, Mary?"

He put his hand out and grasped hers, shaking it firmly. Mary didn't draw back, nor did she cringe. She drew a quick breath and nodded, holding on to him. He placed his other hand over hers and they looked at each other for several very long seconds, almost a lifetime. And then he was gone.

❖

He was out the door, breaking the spell. That was what it felt like, she thought, taking several deep breaths, as though time had stopped, and they were spellbound. The anger dissipated, the air cleared, all in a few heart-stopping moments. Why, she had actually thought, in the midst of that intense passage of time, that he was going to kiss her.

Isaac? Kiss her? Hardly likely! What a strange fantasy...

Yet...her mouth felt seared, as if he had truly kissed her there, kissed her with heat and feeling. Her lips were sensitive, quivering. All he did was touch her chin and take her hand in his. She leaned back in the chair and closed her eyes, touched her trembling lips with tentative fingers, and took low, shallow breaths to calm herself. She clutched her arms tightly across her breasts.

They had cried friends, parted on an amicable note...why, then, oh, why, was she so desperately unhappy?

❖

Florette Dumont's modest dressmaking establishment was the second floor of a small building in an elegant Piccadilly enclave. Cutting and sewing for her best customers, the Fashionable Impure, guaranteed her a steady income, but she also counted respectable wives and daughters of the minor aristocracy among her clientele.

The trick was impeccable scheduling.

Florette made sure, to the best of her Gallic sensibility and tact—for she made a point of keeping up with all the latest *on dits* and society gossip—that a man's mistress never ran into his wife and daughters.

There were always the potentially embarrassing unscheduled drop-ins, but Florette wouldn't turn anyone away. She valued each customer, for she had family in France whom she supported by her clever, talented hands and her quickness of mind. She moved fast when she had to, and her staff was trained to move even faster. Mishaps were rare.

Dorothy Scofield went back a long way with Florette's establishment. Dorothy was a charter client when the young Frenchwoman first set up shop in London with the modest amount of seed money raised by the efforts of a kind English clergyman and his family.

Dorothy's protectors might have changed over the

years, and with some frequency, Florette noted, but they had one characteristic in common: tardiness taking care of the beautiful but dimwitted Cyprian's large dress-making bills.

So, it was with some surprise, and not a little pleasure, that Florette Dumont found a wadded handful of large-denomination pound notes pressed into her hands. She recovered quickly, folding the paper money neatly and secreting it securely under the tight, puffed sleeves of her plain muslin frock.

Just as quickly, she had Dorothy seated comfortably on a velvet-upholstered settee, surrounded by the latest fashion plates. In addition to London's own *Gallery of Fashion, Fashions of London & Paris,* and *The Ladies' Monthly Museum,* there were some Parisian fashion periodicals, *Le Journal des Modes et Nouveautés, Costumes Parisiens,* and *La Correspondence des Dames.*

Dorothy's contented sighs, too long repressed, sounded as she settled back on the padded bench. She was in high alt indeed!

Florette signaled a young apprentice to bring down bolts of pale-hued and patterned cloth from the floor-to-ceiling shelves arranged against one side of her bright, airy showroom. She held out her fabrics for Dorothy's approval: soft, thin Indian muslin, stiff, lineny Leno, fine Mull, hard-finished, nearly transparent Swiss muslin, Organdy, soft and opaque, patterned Madras cloth...

Dorothy contemplated each bolt, her mind's eye imagining the finished gowns. She nodded in approval, made several selections, and asked that silks and lace also be brought down for her consideration. She sat like a languid river nymph, colorful material draped and arranged about her like so many flowing, rainbow-hued streams of water, and was oblivious to the entrance of three other women into the modiste's pleasant quarters.

Florette jumped to greet the new visitors, enveloping the oldest of the three in a quick embrace and applying enthusiastic kisses on her cheeks.

"Madame Davenport!" she cried. "It has been an age!" She beamed as she greeted her oldest, dearest,

English friend, daughter of John Wells, the clergyman who had helped her open her business.

A bit breathless from the modiste's genuine show of affection, Emma introduced her to her two charges. "Mary, Sally—Florette will outfit you with complete new wardrobes: morning gowns, evening dress, riding habits, accessories..." To Florette, she explained that they were the Misses Martin, from Essex, about to get their first taste of the season.

The clink of ready money sounded in Florette's brain. Ever the consummate professional, she motioned the three women to one end of the large showroom. "How soon will the young ladies be needing these garments?"

She started to take their measure with her experienced eyes, noting with approval their straight, slender young bodies, excellent coloring and complexions. She contemplated their most flattering shades, mentally laying colors against their hair, eyes, and skin, seeking what would enhance their considerable natural beauty.

Emma settled herself on a side chair, responding to Florette's query with a vague wave of her hand. "Oh, no great rush, except that we're desperately in need of evening dress for Saturday's opera at Drury Lane."

Isaac had sent a message to Queen Square concerning the performance. This would be his wards' first exposure to the *ton* and he wanted it to be an enjoyable event. He had thought they'd be enchanted by the musical entertainment, as they were musicians themselves. Jamie Fraser was also invited.

The unpleasantness of the previous morning, when Mary had disgraced herself, seemed forgotten. Sir Isaac was a kind and generous man, Emma thought. Despite his unhappiness with Mary's hoydenish behavior, he had simply lectured her and extracted a firm promise of improvement. The evident tension between Mary and Sir Isaac, however, had given Emma unease. The atmosphere in the dining room had been highly charged. It was unsettling.

Florette's strongly accented English brought

Emma back to her surroundings. "Two gowns, Madame
Davenport?" she asked, signaling to two of her most capable seamstresses, Jeanne and Alphonsine, to accompany the girls to a dressing room.

"Yes, Florette, if we could have those two immediately, the rest to be sent later, that would be wonderful,"
Emma began.

"Three dresses, Mrs. Davenport," Mary interrupted,
her husky voice taking on a cajoling tone. "For you must
have a new gown also for our splendid evening out."

Emma considered. It had been a long time between
new gowns. She smiled to herself. Yes, a new
gown...Florette would give her an excellent price. The
émigrée and she had known each other a long time!

❖

The exchange between Mlle. Dumont and her other
customers was overheard with great interest by Dorothy.
Her eyes narrowed as she realized that here, in Florette's
establishment, might be Matthew's two daughters!

An unbelievable coincidence, if true. But Martins,
from Essex? She would have to be careful. She hadn't
corrected Florette when she had addressed her as Madame Scofield. The less the modiste knew of her present
circumstances, the better!

The courtesan's practiced eye passed over the girls,
in a way different from the measuring appraisal of a
seamstress. She conceded they were attractive, if one
liked the natural look. They were, however, both in dire
need of an experienced lady's maid to tame those wild
mops of curly hair, and some rouge, artfully applied,
would do wonders for the blonde's pale skin.

The brunette, Dorothy thought, had altogether too
high a coloring for her taste. Dark brown eyes and black
tresses were *not* the thing these days. She sniffed. And
that voice! A Cyprian would have killed for the sensual
timbre of that young woman's tones. Not fair such an
asset was wasted on a young chit! Dorothy felt a quick
stab of envy and resentment.

She assessed the sisters coldly from under her artificially blackened, lowered eyelashes. From the force of long habit judging potential rivals, she dismissed the girls as too slender. Men preferred lush, abundant curves like hers to girlishly lithe bodies, but Dorothy had to acknowledge the brunette's bosom was high and full. Her pouting lips thinned. *Too full.* The girl's rather ordinary morning dress, however, cut high and squarely across her chest, did nothing to flatter that promising part of her anatomy. Their taste in clothes, she thought, made clear their provincial origins.

Smug, satisfied the Martin sisters didn't measure up to her own standards of beauty, pleased they showed no clothes sense, Dorothy returned to contemplate the hand-colored fashion plates in her hands, sighing softly as she pictured herself in each elegant ensemble.

❖

Emma consulted with Florette while Mary and Sally were measured and fitted. Only then did she notice the modiste's other customer...and was shocked. The woman appeared to be a *demi-mondaine*, painted, powdered, and attired in a too-revealing, low-cut garment.

She raised a questioning eyebrow at Florette, conversing in French, explaining she didn't want the woman to overhear. Emma recounted the story of Matthew Martin's abrupt disappearance and Isaac Rebow's determination to introduce the sisters into society before they returned to the country.

"Colonel Sir Isaac Rebow?" Florette inquired. "The Isaac Rebow rumored to be involved with the beautiful wife of the elderly Baron Rowley?"

Surprised, Emma almost replied in English, but remembered the sharp-eared woman seated close by. "What do you know of Sir Isaac?"

"He's rich, a very handsome bachelor," Florette began, rolling her dark, expressive eyes. "Ah, Emma, I've heard my customers describe him! *Oh, la, la,* dark looks, strong jaw... He's said to be a fine-looking gentleman!"

Emma agreed. No argument there; Sir Isaac was

indeed darkly handsome, quite attractive.

"He's been squiring Lady Rowley about town for some time, and there are those who say it is more than mere friendship. The *on dits* are that as soon as her old, sick husband 'sticks his spoon in the wall', as you English so quaintly put it, Lady Rowley will maneuver Sir Isaac to the altar...one hears she is quite open about it, although her husband is still very much alive.

"She's very beautiful, this woman, tall, very blond, sparkling blue eyes like the finest sapphires. A most elegant couple; they are seen everywhere together." Florette gazed expectantly at Emma.

"This is the first I've heard of Sir Isaac having a—" Emma cleared her throat. "A...close...relationship with someone. It comes as a surprise to me that he would be so openly involved with a married woman. Are you quite sure of your information? Perhaps they *are* simply good friends, and he is doing her husband a favor by escorting her..."

"Emma, *ma petite!*" Florette giggled. "Ever the clergyman's daughter." She threw back her head and laughed at her friend's obvious discomfiture.

Emma blushed. She knew she was conventional, but she could not help it. She had rather strong ideas on marital fidelity. Her high opinion of Sir Isaac was shaken.

She shrugged, freely acknowledging her lack of worldliness. "I fear I don't travel in circles where such behavior is considered acceptable."

Emma clearly was uncomfortable discussing Isaac's putative mistress—for what else could the woman be, if this story was true?—with the Frenchwoman. She felt that Mary would be extremely distressed if she heard this story. And what if they encountered the woman in public? Emma was also unsettled about the nature of Mary's relationship with her guardian. Something was not altogether right there, but she hesitated to put her uneasy feeling into words.

She clutched the brightly colored pattern cards in her lap, creasing their edges, and hoped her suspicions were wrong.

❖

Frogs! Dorothy's sharp ears—sharper than her wits—had listened in on the animated conversation between the plain-faced Cit and the French mantua-maker with barely concealed scorn. London was full of spies, spies for Boney, making mischief against honest English men and women like her. What were those two scheming?

She had caught Matthew's name again. Did they suspect that she—? Nay, not possible. She was reminded, nonetheless, of how the jealous demireps at Mother Nell's nunnery had always kept secrets from her, laughing behind her back.

Dorothy sniffed, puffed up by her own secret, her elopement with the girls' father. Well, Matthew would never hear about this encounter. She would keep father and daughters apart as long as possible. As for Florette, well, she was seriously considering taking her custom elsewhere, if this was how she was to be treated! She did not appreciate being neglected for the past half-hour or more by the modiste.

First things first, however, the crafty Cyprian realized. She needed a new wardrobe, but afterwards... Dorothy smiled slyly. Afterwards, she would look for a more stylish dressmaker, one befitting her new and higher station in life as the wife of Matthew Martin, Esquire.

❖

A week passed, but the personal notices in the various newspapers brought no results. Isaac thought that if another seven days passed this way, he would persuade Ennew to undertake another strategy to smoke out his uncle. Setting aside that distressing line of thought, he pondered the coming weekend's pleasures.

One of his favorite singers, Michael Kelly, would be

reprising his role in *The Marriage of Figaro* at the Drury Lane Theatre. Isaac had been present at the very production some years ago, on the eventful night a madman named James Hadfield had shot at the monarch.

It had been extraordinary. King George III had stepped back a few paces upon hearing the report of the pistol, then come forward again to the front of his box, put an opera glass to his eye and looked steadily and calmly about the house.

Isaac had felt a begrudging admiration for old George—only recently shunted aside in favor of his son, the Prince Regent—at this show of personal courage, an admiration he had not felt before nor since. At the finale of the performance, which went on as scheduled at the king's insistence, Michael Kelly stood before the curtain to sing a new verse of *God Save The King* that Sheridan, the playwright-cum-theatre manager, had quickly written to mark the unusual occasion.

"From every latent foe/From the
assassin's blow/God save the King!"

Isaac hoped nothing so dramatic as an attempt to assassinate a monarch would occur on Saturday, but, with Mary, there was always the distinct possibility something untoward might occur. He had very mixed feelings as to the outcome of their evening, but he was also experiencing a rare eagerness to escort his young wards into the social scene.

He wondered what society would make of them, even as he fought the knowledge that it was Mary he couldn't wait to see. After the last intense session between them at Queen Square, Isaac feared seeing her privately. He needed the safety of numbers at their encounters; he didn't trust himself alone with her.

Isaac hoped a full-to-capacity opera house would ensure safety enough for him.

❖

Bart Scofield spotted the old cove, the one he and Dot hadn't fleeced, coming out of the posh men's club at

Number Sixty, St. James's Street. Out of curiosity, or perhaps inbred criminal instinct, he followed him to the end of the street. And what did he see?

No less than his traitorous sister in the brazen flesh, Dot herself, coming out the door of a dressmaker's in an alley off Piccadilly. He whistled softly through his broken front teeth. He couldn't believe his good luck.

The portly, middle-aged swell hailed a coach and helped Dot into it. The little turncoat was jabbering away, all smiles and laughter. Bart's brow furrowed deeply and his big, ham-like hands formed into fists. He'd wipe that smile off her false, ungrateful face soon enough. But now—he hailed another hackney—now he had to find out where that lying bitch was hiding.

Seven

Mary turned before the mahogany-framed cheval mirror in Emma's bedroom, viewing herself with alarm.

"Sally! What have I done?" she cried, frantic, as Sally submitted placidly to Clara's final touches on her toilette. Both saw the distress clouding Mary's pale face.

The abigail laid down her brush. "You look ever so nice, Miss Mary," she ventured.

"My hair!" Mary whimpered, agitated, running her hands through her new, short cut.

Sally sighed, patting her own newly shorn locks into place and dismissing Clara. "Mary, love, you did agree to have Monsieur Charles cut your tresses."

Mary sat down heavily on Emma's bed, making incomprehensible moaning noises. She seemed about to burst into tears.

Sally and Clara exchanged glances. Sally mouthed, *Fetch Emma, please*, and the abigail scurried to do her young mistress's bidding.

Briskly, Sally plumped herself down beside her elder sister. "Mary, dearest, you look lovely. Shorn hair is *all the thing* in Town, Mlle. Dumont says. We cannot embarrass Cousin Isaac with unfashionable hair. This style, *à la victime*, is very French, very chic, according to M. Charles, and he is London's most sought-after hairdresser."

Mary turned large, dark, stricken eyes on her sister. "You look lovely, Sally, but I, oh, I look a veritable quiz!" she wailed.

Emma strode into the bedroom. Her eyes softened: the Martin sisters were beautifully attired. Lovely! She silently thanked Florette for the stylish gowns she had stitched so quickly and for her suggestion that the girls' unfashionably long hair be cut. The country mice had been magically transformed.

Emma clapped her hands and beamed brightly. "Splendid, just splendid!" Sally, in pale pink and white, was an angelic vision, and Mary, in pastel green, was luminous. *Oh, goodness, too luminous,* Emma saw with burgeoning alarm. Her eyes were glinting oddly wet.

Mary burst into tears. Emma looked questioningly at Sally, who shrugged her slight shoulders and decided to leave her watering-pot sister in Emma's soothing hands.

Emma put her arm around Mary. "Dearest, whatever's the matter?" she asked in her most dulcet tones.

"Cousin Isaac will hate this." She grimaced, pointing to the perky, gamine-like cap of thick black curls on her head.

Emma handed Mary a handkerchief and instructed her to wipe her tears. "You will be coming all over blotchy, my dear, and we cannot have that."

"But—!" Mary shrieked.

Emma smoothed the lines of her new gown, a high-cut tunic dress of tissue-thin gold crepe worked in a darker gold Greek key pattern at the hem. An Indian shawl of white, fine Cashmiri wool edged with glittering gold thread was draped over her shoulders. She peered into the cheval mirror and pulled back a stray tendril of hair, purposely ignoring her young charge's hysterics. "We shall be late, Mary. Depend upon it, your cousin will hate that more. Your hair is lovely. You are refining overmuch on the change, which suits you admirably and is most flattering. I shall instruct Clara to rearrange your attire."

She fixed Mary with a quelling, most governessy look. "Mr. James Fraser has been cooling his heels in the withdrawing room this past half-hour, Miss. It would be the height of rudeness to keep him waiting very much longer."

Mary swallowed and obeyed. Tears dried, coiffure re-combed, reticule and shawl in place, she was ready to go. She wondered, briefly, if it was thus that lambs were made to meekly go to their own slaughter.

❖

Sophia Rowley, Isaac Rebow's *chère amie*, was surprised to see him at the opera. She'd asked him if he planned to attend, but his response had been noncommittal. She had assumed he was going to be busy with parliamentary matters. Had she possibly misunderstood him?

Now, it was a bit embarrassing for her, sitting alone in her own box, right next to his, while he also sat by himself. He quickly told her that he had invited several guests, thus forestalling her natural move to his box, where she was so used to sitting. And where the *ton* was so used to seeing her. She frowned at this strange turn of events. His manner was more than slightly off-putting, but she was in a good humor and decided to let it go.

But his behavior was very odd, she thought, for never, in her recollection, had she seen him so nervous. Isaac? Nervous? Yes, he didn't seem to know what to do with himself. He fidgeted with his cravat, tapped the sides of the box with his programme, frowned abstractedly at the audience beginning to fill the theatre, and pulled absentmindedly at his lower lip.

What was wrong with the man?

An evening at the opera was usually what Isaac enjoyed above all things. *A true music lover!* She had never seen his like: he actually listened to the singers and followed the performance, lost in the music. Most amusing, how he was so concentrated on what most of the audience ignored.

The *ton* came to see, to be seen, and above all to see who was with whom, but most certainly not to attend to the actual performance. It was almost embarrassing to be in Isaac's company at these times. *Almost.* He made up for this unfortunate lapse, however, by the cool and aloof way he behaved at other times. Indeed, then he was by far the most sophisticated gentleman of her wide and far-ranging acquaintance.

Sophia smiled and fanned herself languidly with her painted ivory fan—a past gift from Isaac—and self-consciously patted the pearl brooch that was his most recent token of affection. She had privately asked Rundle & Bridge's to appraise it and was awed; Isaac was truly the most generous of lovers.

"Isaac? Is aught amiss, my dear?" she whispered, lowering the fan, reaching over to his box, extending her arm and running her fingers lightly, familiarly, over his tense, muscled thigh.

Isaac's dark blue eyes snapped into focus. "Pardon?"

A slight wave of irritation began to surface from deep within her, but Sophia fought it back. "I wondered, dearest, if something was disturbing you." She removed her hand from his leg; he had regarded her fingers as if they were some repulsive trespassing insect.

He frowned, rolling his programme tightly and tapping it against his knee. "I wonder what is keeping that young pup Fraser. He assured me he would collect Mrs. Davenport and the girls early..."

Isaac took out an ornate gold pocket timepiece, his late father's watch, and frowned. He muttered an oath under his breath as he replaced it in his waistcoat pocket.

Sophia coolly ignored the oath. Aha! So those were his mysterious "guests"—the country chits, his new wards—their governess, and his amusing young friend Fraser. "It is likely a veritable crush outside. I shouldn't worry. If they miss the opening act"—she shrugged her creamy white shoulders—"so be it. There'll certainly be more than enough music left for them to hear."

Sophia shuddered slightly. *More than enough music for her*! She barely tolerated Italian opera, though she made a pretense of enjoyment for Isaac. She smiled reassuringly at her paramour.

The look he gave her was stern, admonishing. "My wards are musical prodigies, Sophia. They have never seen an actual opera performance and so I'm eager they see this one in its entirety. I want this evening to be most pleasurable."

Sophia felt rebuked, as if slapped for her flippant comments. She frowned again, a thin line creasing and marring her brow. "*I see*," she replied, her crisp tones glacial.

Sir Isaac appeared not to take notice of Sophia's obvious annoyance. He stood as if to leave the box, then changed his mind. Turning his back to Sophia, he scanned the faces in the orchestra below.

Sophia seethed. Isaac was too concerned about these country chits by half. He was cutting her out of his life while he attended to their needs. *She* needed him, also! She had been looking forward to accompanying him to the Granthams' ball on Wednesday next, but he had made it clear it would not be proper for her to act as chaperone, or, indeed, to meet his wards at all. He had actually suggested that she stay away from the event!

She fumed inwardly at his overblown-in her opinion-sense of propriety. He was discreet to the point of idiocy about their relationship. Everyone in the *ton* acknowledged it; it was a relationship not at all unusual in their set. Everyone, it seemed, but Isaac Rebow!

She looked forward to the girls' speedy return to the country. This situation was unbearable. She and Isaac could not interact in public while he had this responsibility. Indeed, when they arrived tonight, he would be uncomfortable with her even in the next box. She hoped he would be extremely uncomfortable. He deserved to be made as uncomfortable as she was now.

Her fingers played absently on the smooth, perfect pearls that made up her costly new brooch and she winced. She removed her fingers, as if the pearls had suddenly flashed white fire, burning her with the knowledge of what Isaac had paid for them.

Sophia set her lips purposefully. She wanted Isaac. Her husband George was on his gouty last legs and wouldn't long endure. She should be in dreary Yorkshire attending to him, but she dared not let Isaac out of her sight. There were—thanks to the murdering French—too many widowed Englishwomen on the prowl this season.

Sophia didn't like the way other women looked at Isaac. If George didn't expire soon... Her gaze hardened at the prospect of someone else catching Colonel Sir Isaac Rebow's eye.

Lady Sophia's impoverished father, the Earl of Langford, had bargained her beauty for money to recoup his crushing losses at the gaming tables. She'd been married off quite young to a reckless marquess who broke his neck in a fox-hunting mishap before she had the opportunity to present him with an heir. His estate left her a meager settlement, which her father quickly ran through, and so she found herself once more frequenting the London Marriage Mart on the arm of her dissolute sire when the obligatory year of mourning was done.

Still very young and very beautiful, Sophia managed to secure another titled and even wealthier husband. Unfortunately, her second bridegroom also expired quite suddenly, victim of a chance outbreak of the influenza during their brief winter honeymoon in Scotland. This time, she was left quite a bit more from the estate, but it was hardly enough to keep her in the lavish style to which she and her reprobate father had so quickly and easily become accustomed.

Though the English are not necessarily a superstitious race, the twice-widowed Lady Sophia was being looked at askance by men who would otherwise have been taken in by her beauty. The phrase *"Black Widow"* had been whispered on more than one occasion after her second husband's death. Men were not queuing up eagerly to become husband number three.

Lord Rowley, much older than Sophia's first two husbands, less handsome by any reckoning but a good deal wealthier, unfazed by her bad reputation and able to deal well with her greedy father, had stepped into the breach. He reasoned, and rightly, that it was her poor, unlucky husbands who had suffered misfortune to be thrown from horses and beset by swift, deadly respiratory ailments. She was the lucky one, a young, healthy woman, more than good enough for his purposes.

Baron Rowley was widowed after a long marriage. His wife had been barren, and he had no heirs. He saw Lady Sophia's robust good health as an excellent indication of her breeding potential, and so offered marriage. Running out of prospects, Sophia didn't keep him waiting over long for an answer.

The baron was more than generous. He made it clear that after providing him with an heir—and, hopefully, a spare—she was her own woman. Getting on in years, he wished to retire to his lands in Yorkshire; he also understood that she, still a young and vibrant woman, might have other needs.

Sophia promptly provided George with two sons in the first two years of their marriage. They were now both at Eton, visiting their father on school holidays, rarely seeing their mother, who preferred London life. A most satisfactory, most sophisticated arrangement. So long as Sophia brought no scandal upon the distinguished Rowley name, she was free to do as she liked.

And so she did. Do as she liked, that was, with a series of lusty young aristocrats and others whom she met at balls, dinners, and extended country house visits. Generous with her favors, Sophia demanded no promises of undying love or fidelity from her casual liaisons. It was a delicious game, one she played well and happily, until she met Isaac Rebow.

Isaac was different. He made no promises, but it was clearly understood he expected fidelity. He was not the sort of man to share the favors of a mistress with half the *ton*, and he also demanded the utmost discretion in their relationship. He did not want to flaunt it in the least. Sophia readily acquiesced, for she fell in love with Isaac, madly, passionately in love, a new experience for her. She wanted him for her husband, as she had not wanted the three men with whom she had walked to the altar.

Truly, she didn't wish George Rowley dead, but she could scarcely wait to be thrice widowed. She was aware her looks wouldn't last forever; while they lasted, she knew she had to make the most of them. She was slightly older than Isaac and time was running out. If only dear, sickly George would cooperate!

Sophia was confident she could lead Sir Isaac Rebow to the altar—she could hum and stride to a wedding march by heart—even though he professed no intention of entering the married state. She was aware *he* didn't love *her*, but their physical relationship was more than satisfactory, and, further, she would be an ideal hostess.

He was an up-and-coming politician; she was well-versed in the intricacies of the *ton*. Together, they would be truly formidable. She knew that the betting books at White's and Brooks's had heavy wagers favoring her.

This complication of his young cousins was an annoying wrinkle in her plans, but she would get through it. She fanned herself faster. Irritably, she began to tap an elegantly slippered foot. She could pretend to Isaac that this temporary annoyance was of no consequence, indeed, she would dote on his prattle about the boring chits, if she had to, in order to stay in her paramour's good graces. But she would hate every minute of it.

Where were those brats? It was getting late. The performance would begin soon.

❖

There was a ripple in the audience, a stir, a sudden flash, a glint of quizzing glasses and *lorgnettes* reflecting light off the ornate crystal chandeliers in the theatre ceiling. People in the orchestra pit were turning and looking up to the boxes as if an invisible wire was drawn through their bodies.

Among the many others at the Drury Lane, Sophia turned to look. Someone important has arrived, she thought, a leading politician, a great beauty, a notorious rake... She moved to get a better view. It was so late... Who could it be?

❖

Mary was sure they would be terribly late. Isaac's coach hadn't moved over an inch in half an hour when they decided to leave the carriage and walk the few yards to the theatre. It was slow, indeed, making their way through the throng gathered outside the doors to ogle those entering. To see and to be seen, Emma told them, that was the way of the *ton*. The music was of secondary importance. A poor second.

Emma at the lead, Fraser at the rear, the girls were shepherded expertly through the entrance and up the wide, curving staircase of the opera house. Emma glanced neither right nor left, but marched her charges straight ahead.

Shy Sally sensibly kept her eyes downcast, but Mary, dazzled by the well-dressed crowd and the glittering elegance of the playhouse, looked about her. To her great mortification, she found herself being stared at and whispered about.

A tall, handsome buck in the sporting garb favored by the Corinthian set—so out of place at the theatre!—winked at her outrageously, as his companions, veritable tulips of the *ton*, laughed. A trio of society belles, their scandalously dampened muslin gowns leaving little doubt as to their no-longer-hidden charms, looked her over jealously and raised their thin, haughty eyebrows in disdain.

An elderly, dissipated *roué* licked his carmined lips and made unsavory smacking sounds as she passed him by too closely. The color rose in her face, suffusing her throat and breast. Mightily chagrined, she was thus introduced to the pink of the *ton*.

She didn't raise her eyes until she was safely in her cousin's box and heard introductions being made. She looked at Isaac. He stared at her, and she self-consciously moved a hand to her shorn head. He hated it! *She knew he would.*

❖

If anyone had asked his name, Isaac would have

been hard put to supply it. He gazed at Mary, his ward, and forgot it. Forgot everything, even the stirring speech he recently gave in Parliament. He forgot who he was, where he was, and who were the company surrounding him. He had eyes only for her.

Mary's gown was low-cut silk sarcenet, palest seafoam green, with short, shirred sleeves. The style showed her high, full bosom and fine white shoulders to perfection. The modiste had outdone herself with a gauzy, sleeveless tulle overdress scattered with tiny, embroidered silver seashells. Mary looked to Isaac's mesmerized eyes a veritable marine nymph risen from the sea. Her dark, shiny cap of curls fitted sleekly, seal-like, to her well-shaped head.

She was a woman, not a girl, not a child. *An exquisite, beautiful woman.* It was Mary to whom all eyes turned as Fraser held the curtain open to Isaac's box. Isaac stood as one transfixed, caught in the spell of her beauty, intoxicated by the sweetness of her perfume, that clean, sharp mixture of rosewater and her own delicious scent, and he could not get one word of greeting out of his mouth.

"You do hate it! I thought you would," Mary began, reacting to Isaac's dark, piercing gaze.

"Pardon?" he replied, his voice strangely raspy, not at all his normally deep baritone.

"My hair," she gestured at her head. "I was persuaded to have it cut into the latest fashion, but it was a mistake. I knew you would hate it."

"Hate it?" Isaac took her hand. "You look...my dear Mary, you look ravishing. And I do believe—" He turned and gestured toward the curious opera house crowd below. "I do believe I'm not the only one who thinks so tonight."

Mary took a long step backward, as if trying to fade into the thick red velvet draperies at the rear of the box. She felt like a butterfly impaled on a pin, the cynosure of all eyes. "Oh." She blushed furiously.

Isaac turned to block her body from the gaze of the curious. He smiled encouragingly at her. She noted his voice had lost its initial raspiness. "Take it as a compliment, my dear, the seal of approval upon your entrance into *le beau monde*. I would venture they also approve of your new coiffure."

She smiled back at him tremulously. He hadn't let go of her hand; she held on to it as if to a lifeline. She needed his comforting touch, Mary realized, she needed it badly, as she entered into this new, puzzling world of the *ton*.

❖

From her vantage point in her own box, Sophia looked upon the scene unfolding so close by and feared she would faint. She felt for the *vinaigrette* in her netted reticule, whilst the need to use it diminished. She gritted her teeth and looked at her lover Isaac in disbelief. He seemed so enraptured. What was he whispering? Why could he not forbear from looking at his ward with such...*oh, goodness, such longing*...in his eyes?

The oldest woman of the three who had entered the box spoke up, jumping into the whispery silence that threatened to drown them all. Sophia turned her eyes from Isaac's face to Mrs. Davenport's, who was explaining their tardiness.

"I'm so sorry we are late...the crowds," she began.

Sophia heard Isaac say, "No import, the performance has yet to begin." She could also hear, behind her, the curious buzz of the watchful audience. It seemed that it was their fate tonight to be the farce preceding the opera. Well, she thought grimly, so be it.

Sophia smiled at Isaac's guests, hoping for an introduction, however brief. She was sharply aware that Isaac, standing so close to the lovely, dark-haired girl, still seemed entranced.

Sophia fixed a hard stare on Mary and knew, with a sinking heart, that she was going to have a struggle on her hands, a struggle to the death. A struggle for her lover's heart. *Isaac!* Ignoring them all, he was speaking in a whisper to the girl, but she could not make out the low-murmured words. They were holding hands now and gazing deeply into each other's eyes. *Oh, goodness...*

And still she was not introduced. The governess cast her a worried look. Sophia willed herself to keep smiling, her brain in turmoil, her heart in danger of shattering. Not for anything would she let Isaac note her acute distress.

Finally, he acknowledged her presence with a brief nod toward her. Jamie Fraser smiled at her, nodding his head. The governess's smile was pinched. The girls looked at her curiously and sat down. Sophia smiled brightly, a smile that cost her a good deal to accomplish, but Isaac would never guess at the high price of this pretense at gaiety.

The attention of the fickle crowd waned as another coterie entered the boxes above, a group of notorious high-flyers, courtesans led by the beautiful Cyprian rumored to have caught the eye of one of the monarch's sons. Her extremely immodest gown occasioned several rude whistles and loud remarks, drawing the last straggler's attention from the Rebow party, as the orchestral prelude began and settled the latecomers and rabble rousers in their seats.

❖

Emma darted a quick glance at Isaac and feared that the worst of her suspicions was confirmed. The man seemed dazed, besotted by his young ward, while his beautiful mistress looked on in alarm from the adjoining box where she sat alone. Now, Sir Isaac was leaning back in his seat, his eyes shut, one hand resting on his lap, the other cradling his forehead.

In the midst of the lovely music emanating from the stage, indeed, despite it, it seemed to Emma Davenport that he was deep in the throes of a major headache.

❖

Lust. Pure, unbridled lust. No, not so pure, he corrected himself, unable to allow himself to be lulled by
the beguiling strains of Mozart's exquisite arias as the
curtain rose on *The Marriage of Figaro*. He should be
thoroughly ashamed of himself. Not only for feeling this
way, but for making his feelings clearly known to everyone in his box, to Sophia, who should not have been
there, and to the entire audience at the Drury Lane.

How could they not have missed his reaction to
Mary? One would have to be deaf, dumb, or blind not to
have noticed that his attention had been riveted on her.
He had been strung tight by his baser emotions...for all
to note.

He was attracted to her from the first. Even her
hoydenish attire had not shielded her one whit from his
low desires. Tonight, dressed like this, she was an In-
comparable, a veritable Toast. She set the *ton* on its ear.
He heard the murmurs in the orchestra pit as she made
her entrance. *Phenomenal!* The child—nay, *the woman*—had been dazed by the reactions of the pit.

Isaac groaned inwardly. Sophia...was there no end
to this muddle? Sophia had looked upon him with disbelief writ over her lovely face. What must she be
thinking? He had to establish some modicum of control
over himself before it was too late. What had become of
his military discipline?

That sunburnt country bumpkin with her straw creel
full of wriggling worms... *She had brought him to his
knees.* The victory was hers. He would find his errant
uncle if it killed him! Never more than at that moment
was he so reluctant to continue his guardianship. He saw
his world—a world based on order, discipline, and propriety—crumbling at his feet.

Isaac knew he would have to woo Sophia all over
again if he wanted to keep her, and that he would have
to erase the memory of his foolishness from that lady's
mind. Why had he not simply suggested to Sophia that
she absent herself from the opera, as he had suggested
she absent herself from the upcoming ball? This evening
was a terrible mistake. Now he had to rectify that mis-

take, Lord help him!

❖

During the interval, Fraser's cronies, Lord Robin and the Honourable Charles Higginbotham, made their appearance as Isaac and Fraser rose to secure refreshments. Robin pulled a chair close to Mary's and began to shower her with effusive compliments, unaware of Isaac's dark scowl.

The Honourable Charles, finding himself with the handsome governess and pretty Sally, made the best he could of the situation, while bemoaning the absence of Henny May. He noted the charming blonde peeress, Lady Rowley, in the next box, all by herself. Odd that she was there, he thought; it must have been embarrassing for old Rebow.

Eight

Bart saw his chance. *Now!* he thought, as his faithless sister ventured into the rose garden of her spacious Knightsbridge town house. She was alone, a woven straw garden trug dangling from her arm.

The old man had driven away earlier in his carriage, so he was safely out of the way. Now Bart would face the bitch and hear her feeble excuses. His fingers fairly itched to wring her lovely, lying neck.

He watched as Dorothy reached to clip a full-blown pink rose from a heavily laden bush. Her secateurs grasped the thorny stem and sliced it through. A clean cut. She placed it in the trug and clipped several other big-headed blooms at a leisurely pace, oblivious to the tall, heavyset man spying on her behind the garden's ornate wrought-iron fence.

"Oh!" she screamed, as Bart vaulted the fence and wrestled the sharp shears from her. Before she could raise a further outcry for help, he clasped a big, dirty hand across her mouth, bruising her lips and effectively stifling her cries. Her slanted acquamarine eyes darkened several shades in color and widened in abject terror as she recognized her assailant.

"Keep yer trap shut," Bart growled menacingly. They were face to face. "I'll move me hand, but, not one sound, mind? Make one sound and I wring yer miserable neck!"

Dorothy managed to nod her head in assent. She hadn't seen her brother for weeks, but she saw he still wore his hair long and sported a heavy beard and full mustache. She was among the few who knew the hair hid an ugly, distinctive scar, the result of a particularly brutal knife fight Bart had lost years ago.

Bart shoved her down to a wooden bench set under a budding tulip tree. "Now, me dear sister, what've ye got to say for yerself?" he asked, as he jerked her roughly and sat beside her.

Trembling and shaking, Dorothy whispered, "H-h-h...how did you find me?"

"Never ye mind! What made ye think ye could get away from me? We had an arrangement, us two, or did ye fergit it?"

The scowl on Bart's face was horrendous to behold. Dorothy went pale, almost fainting. Bart shook her none too gently.

She took a deep breath. "Why, brother, this is far better than that dangerous game on the streets. He's married me! He's rich! He has an estate, land, in Essex, and—" She stopped, her eyes flickered uncertainty as Bart raised a hand to silence her torrent of words.

Dorothy quailed, eyes wary; she wondered if what she feared was truly upon her. Bart had killed at least one man—she knew that for a fact—and she'd not be surprised to learn he had killed more than that one. Killing a woman, to him, wouldn't even count; to a murderous felon like Bart, blood—her blood, their blood!—was not thicker than water.

"Ye little fool!" He shook his sister by the shoulders, losing all patience. "Ye're married already! Ye're no widder, free an' easy t'marry a second time. I saw yer miserable, dirt-eating clod of a husband last time I wuz in Tipperhowe. Farmer Smith, he wuz very much alive, he wuz..."

Dorothy's pretty, stupid face showed actual signs of dismay, but only momentarily. She brightened. "But Martin doesn't know that, and Tipperhowe is a long way from London, or Essex. Farmers like Ezekiel Smith, they never leave their home villages."

Bart Scofield nodded, impressed for once with Dorothy's logic. Perhaps she wasn't as stupid as he had always thought. "Mayhap ye're right," he agreed tentatively, stroking the coarse hairs on his chin. "But it's no good taking chances with the gentry. They ain't our kind, ye know that."

"I've been...acquainted...with the gentry a long time, brother. I know my way around them, and, if we're patient, Matthew Martin's money, his estate, his lands, will fall into my waiting lap." Her almond-shaped eyes slanted greedily as she mimed a windfall showering over her plump, pretty thighs.

Bart was thoughtful. He had released the hard pressure he'd been exerting on her wrist, and now the tender skin was purpling fast. "Yet, has he no kin? Have they asked no questions about ye? About yer fambly? Where ye're from? And how does he not know th' kind of woman ye be, Dot? Is he that much of a blind fool, not to know?"

Dot smiled winningly at her brother, warming up to her tale. "He's old, lonely, and besotted with me, brother. He does anything I ask." She gestured expansively about her, indicating her house and grounds. "We have this beautiful home. He's provided me with a splendid new wardrobe, servants, a brand-new carriage. He's assured me I'm in his will..."

Scofield silenced her self-satisfied prattle with an upraised hand. "Answer me, ye little fool! Has the old cove no kin?"

Dorothy's lower lip trembled at the latent menace in Bart's growling voice. She shook her head. "Only two young girls, but he left them this past se'enight..."

"Ye blamed idjit! Tell me all of it, the truth, now!" Bart squeezed her wrist so hard she almost fainted again, the blood leaving her face. She recovered quickly and nodded, the words tumbling out of her quivering lips as she hastened to tell her brother about Matthew's daughters.

He listened with a frown on his big, ugly face. "Seems to me, little sister," he began, speaking slowly through still clenched teeth, "that nothin', no real gain, will come to ye until yer gennelman husband and his lady daughters are dispatched from this blessed earth."

Dorothy paled and shivered as she realized the full extent of what Bart was saying. She was fond of Matthew. He was very kind to her, kinder than any gentleman had been to her in a long while. Indeed, he was the best thing that had happened to her in years. He was a doting old fool, yes, but he was *her* doting old fool.

The girls, his daughters...Dorothy hadn't been taken with them at Florette Dumont's, dismissing them as no more than typically spoiled daughters of the gentry, but she truly had nothing against them. Neither had done her harm. Bart, she realized, a chill creeping through her bones, was speaking murder.

Murder... And giving her no choice, no choice at all, if she, Dot, wanted to live.

❖

Eager to make up for the *débâcle* at the opera, and to ensure Sophia's absence at the Granthams' ball, Isaac sent a footman to her with a note. His message invited her to an intimate dinner that evening. Appallingly short notice, true, but, in the past, Sophia had never quibbled over such a lack of the niceties.

Secure in her answer, despite what had happened Saturday night, Isaac instructed Robbins to lay out his evening dress.

❖

Sophia Rowley was enraged!

Sapphire-blue eyes blazing, she considered tearing Isaac's dinner invitation in half and returning it. *Does he think I am his bought-and-paid-for demirep*, she fumed, *to be summoned by him with no prior notice, no consideration for any other plans I might have for the evening?*

She calmed herself, despite her great indignation, and decided to go to Duke Street and partake of Sir Isaac's fine wines and his French chef's excellent culinary creations. Then, she wanted to tell him to his arrogant, deceitful face, just exactly what she thought of his callous behavior toward her at the opera

"Joan," she called to her abigail, "do lay out my new pink silk dress with the black gauze overslip. I am dining at Duke Street tonight."

❖

Isaac greeted Sophia at the door, brushing a light kiss on her cheek. She looked lovely, as always. Saunders passed them cut-glass goblets of ruby red claret; the rich color of the wine shimmered against the pale pink silk of her evening dress.

"To you, Sophia," Isaac toasted her, quoting the Attic bard Homer, comparing her to Helen, the Greek enchantress whose great beauty had launched a thousand ships.

She smiled, returning the toast by quoting from—of all things for worldly, sophisticated Lady Sophia—the *Bible*, amused at his surprise as she whispered throatily, "*Drink no longer water, but use a little wine for thy stomach's sake*," slanting him an appraising glance over her goblet as she sipped the fine vintage.

He looked breathtakingly handsome in black, the white of his crisp linen stark against the dark trousers and tight-fitting coat. Her anger at him dissipated swiftly as she gazed at his cleanly chiseled features, which were set off by the old-fashioned simplicity of his hairstyle. No other man she knew could tie back that straight, thick hair with a plain black satin ribbon and look so marvelous. Truly one of a kind, she thought.

"I am so glad you came, Sophia," Isaac began, guiding her to the newly upholstered green and white silk Chippendale settee in the drawing room. She sat straight-backed, the folds of the loose black overslip falling to either side like gauzy wings. Dainty pink satin slippers peeped demurely from under the pink silk gown. The subtle almond scent of her signature Floris perfume, Frangipani, wafted sensually through the room.

She's very beautiful, Isaac thought, drinking in her perfect, creamy white complexion, shining blonde hair, and glorious sapphire eyes. Sophia's full, pouting red mouth promised untold erotic pleasures, promises, he reminded himself, she never failed to keep.

Her ripe, womanly form left little to the imagination, garbed as she was in that clinging, soft silk gown; her full breasts were barely restrained by the modest width of its flimsy bodice. No man could fail to be moved by her charms. Why, then, was he finding it increasingly more difficult to recall all the times she had stirred his senses clothed-nay, rather, barely clothed!-like this?

Why, he thought, and groaned inwardly, *am I tired of her already and wish this evening, only just begun, at an end?* This was a mistake. He realized he was making nothing but mistakes lately; if he wasn't careful, he would be a prime candidate for the Hospital of St. Mary's of Bethlehem. A Bedlamite-in-waiting.

Lady Sophia basked in what she interpreted as admiration from her lover, as his dark blue eyes drank her in. Her charms, she knew, were considerable; she had worked her sensual wiles on Isaac many times before. How silly she was to overreact, very silly indeed.

How could she have imagined her practiced charms would fail her? How could she have thought a mere chit of a country girl, a gauche bumpkin overdressed by a mediocre *modiste*, could capture the heart and soul of this cool, handsome gentleman?

She had panicked for no reason, she realized, and was relieved. She forgave him. All previous thoughts of arguing matters of absolutely no consequence vanished as she looked forward to a cosy dinner and its foregone conclusion when he escorted her back to her home.

She smiled seductively, raising her shoulders so the tiny sleeves fell ever so slightly down her plump upper arms, revealing more of her smooth, rounded, white bosom. Soon, with dear George's cooperation, she would be Lady Rebow.

She was sure of it.

❖

Sir Isaac came to escort Mrs. Davenport and his wards to Lord and Lady Grantham's ball. He explained Fraser would meet them there. He worried that Lady Sophia might also be present.

He remembered the most recent occasion he'd had the pleasure of Lady Rowley's company, and he winced involuntarily. A disaster of a dinner, following upon that *débâcle* at the opera... He had been less than attentive to his lady love during the many removes his chef presented. Finally, she had asked what the matter was. Actually, she had said, "*Isaac, you seem rather preoccupied tonight.*"

He had responded with the excuse of a muzzy head. A headache. She wasn't fooled. Sophia was well aware Isaac never complained of the headache. She had been livid! The large, dark amber cognac stain on his newly papered drawing room wall—cream-and-white flocked wallpaper purchased from Blew's warehouse—and the shards of fine Austrian crystal that had once been a brandy snifter, now imbedded in his new Axminster carpet, attested to that.

It was gratifying, however, to confirm that his quick reflexes in the face of imminent personal danger were still excellent. He had ducked just seconds before Sophia flung the glass at him. His ears, however, were still pink from the unexpected verbal abuse his ex-lover had heaped upon him. He was truly astonished at the variety and inventiveness of her oaths.

Lady Rowley! Who would have guessed...and he thought he had known the woman so well...

For all he knew, to spite him, Sophia might turn up at the Granthams' ball. Or, she may have finally returned to her ailing husband in Yorkshire. He hoped it was the latter.

"Are my wards ready?" He looked toward the stairs. "I fear it will be quite a crush tonight. The Granthams are popular hosts."

❖

She was here, glitteringly beautiful in cream satin and blonde lace. He could see her from across the room, her charms more than evident. Isaac's jaw tightened. If Sophia moved less than carefully, her voluptuous breasts would flow over the low, low cut of her costume. The leering gentlemen surrounding her seemed well cognizant of that possibility and were all but drooling in anticipation of the event.

Isaac fought back the urge to walk across Lord and Lady Grantham's crowded ballroom and order Sophia to cover herself. She was, however, no longer his mistress, and therefore no longer his concern. Both of them knew that. The members of *le haut ton* gathered here tonight, however, weren't aware yet of their severed relationship.

Mary could not help but notice Sophia, Isaac's friend from the opera, also. She noted, too, the twitch in Isaac's strong, square jaw, and the way he clenched his fists. She looked across to Lady Rowley again and saw that the lady and he made eye contact. Sophia appeared flustered; she brought her white-feathered fan up to her face and began to work it furiously. Then, quite deliberately, it seemed, she turned her back.

The cut direct! Aimed at Sir Isaac. Had that, indeed, just occurred? Mary looked about her. No one seemed to have witnessed what had happened...if, in truth, that had indeed happened. Her eyes flew to Isaac's face again, expecting to see his handsome features contorted in anger, but he was smiling. A grim, rather set smile, but a smile, nonetheless. He was holding out his hand to her.

"Come, my dear, let us have a turn on the ballroom floor." Her heart gave a glad little leap as Isaac led her into the *quadrille* now forming. The musicians struck up a familiar tune and she concentrated on the many steps and turns. *Isaac!* She was dancing with him, just as she had imagined in her dreams. She smiled with great happiness as she took his hand.

❖

Sophia turned as the orchestra began to play the evening's first dance. Isaac was partnering that young chit, his ward, in a stately *quadrille*. The girl was positively radiant. She glowed. As Sophia watched the graceful couple measuring out the intricate steps of the dance, she wondered if she had made the biggest mistake of her life when she had dismissed Isaac from it.

❖

Emma was also watching Mary and Isaac, her eyes troubled. That afternoon, she had interrupted a discussion concerning Lady Rowley's relationship to Isaac.

Sally had wondered, innocently, why the Baron was in Yorkshire whilst it seemed his wife had such an active social life in London. Emma, discreetly crossing her fingers behind her back, had remarked that Baron Rowley was elderly and ill.

Blue eyes widening in surprise, Sally had blurted, "Well, then, her place is surely with him! If my husband were sick and alone..."

Gently, Emma had countered, "Not alone, dear...I'm sure the Rowleys have an excellent physician and a multitude of servants to care for..."

Sally interrupted, shocked. "*Servants*, Emma? How can *servants* take the place of one's spouse? Why, if your Michael were ill, or my James, we would not leave..." She blushed deeply, leaving her sentence hanging.

Catching her '*my James*,' Mary had cast an odd look at her sister's flushed face. "That's the way of the *ton*, Sister. Doubtless, there are no strong feelings of affection between Lady Sophia and her husband, and so no one expects her to pretend to be his loving nurse."

"Mary!" Sally's eyes flashed. "That's unkind of you!"

Mary shrugged and resumed reading William Blake's *Songs Of Innocence* spread open upon the library desk. The pages of the slim volume were open to a charming watercolor in which she seemed engrossed.

Emma attempted to salvage the situation by commenting that perhaps the Baron wasn't so much sickly as elderly and preferred the relaxation of his country estate to the hustle and bustle of London. "For it is not up to us to judge others," she ended lamely.

Mary shut the book of poems with rather more vehemence than warranted. *"Hah!"* she snorted inelegantly.

Sally smoothed out the needlework on her lap and pulled a thread of colored silk through the fabric. "If the Baron expires, Emma, does it mean that perhaps Cousin Isaac might offer for Lady Sophia once her requisite mourning is over? I've heard they are good friends."

Before Emma could ask where Sally had heard this bit of news, Mary turned, her face ashen. In a low voice, she murmured, "Oh...oh, surely not..."

Oh, my! The child was besotted with her cousin!

The realization hit Emma with great force, and she neither responded to Sally's question nor asked her own question. Mary had run from the room, leaving them with mouths agape.

Now, Emma Davenport frowned, looking across the ballroom to where a frozen Sophia Rowley was watching the dancers performing the *quadrille*—watching, it seemed, two of the well-paired dancers in particular— and she wondered why the Baroness was present at the ball.

Nine

Charles Higginbotham and Lord Robin were delighted to greet Lady Rowley as they joined the Grantham crush. They sketched brief bows, expressing their pleasure as they paid her fulsome compliments.

Lady Sophia bestowed her most dazzling smile upon the young men, a smile that had snared three wealthy husbands. "Ah, Mr. Fraser's friends from the opera. How nice to see you again, gentlemen," she beamed.

They were much too young for her, of course, but perhaps there was a widowed father, uncle, older brother... *No, she had to stifle those thoughts!* She made a mistake, a severe mistake, but she could rectify it. Isaac wasn't entirely out of the picture. Not yet...

"I see Mr. Fraser across the room, there, do you not see him also?" Sophia pointed with her fan to the farther edge of the ballroom, where Emma Davenport stood with Sally and Fraser.

A slight furrow creased Bradshaw's smooth young brow. He turned to Lady Rowley. "Miss Martin," he said, referring to Mary, "is she not present tonight?"

Sophia's smile contracted slightly; she gestured vaguely with her fan. "I believe she's dancing with her guardian, Sir Isaac. He's her cousin, you know."

Bradshaw shook his head. "No, I didn't know...her cousin *and* guardian?"

Sophia bent her head toward the young man, whispering, "He keeps a tight rein on those girls. They are great heiresses, you see."

"Heiresses?" Charles made no pretense of not hearing Lady Rowley's whispered confidence. His ears fairly perked up.

"Yes," Sophia lied, embroidering the falsehood. "He's quite concerned they be kept safe from fortune hunters and libertines. If I know Sir Isaac"—here she tittered merrily—"and I believe I know him well, he shall personally handpick their suitors."

"I say!" Bradshaw's pale blue eyes positively gleamed. "That's interesting news." The girl was lovely. It had taken no great effort on his part to show interest in her, to flirt lightly and without altogether serious intent, but the news that the chit's family had deep pockets...

No wonder Fraser was mooning after the other sister! There was talk Jamie's father would cut him off entirely if he bought an army commission; if Fraser married well, that threat of disinheritance would mean nil. As for himself...the Bradshaws weren't so wealthy as most of the three or four hundred families comprising the *ton*; bringing an heiress into their family would do wonders for their diminished coffers and send his father and mother into the boughs.

Beautiful Mary Martin was instantly more attractive to him in light of this interesting information so freely supplied by kindly Lady Rowley. Bradshaw cast a dubious look at his friend, Higginbotham. He was well aware the man could keep nothing to himself. He, Bradshaw, would have to move quickly to press his suit before Mary Martin's substantial fortune became the latest *on dit* in the crowd of young, titled bachelors with markedly expensive habits and tastes.

"Well, Lady Rowley, I do beg your pardon, but the *quadrille* is drawing to a close, and I must get my name on Miss Martin's dance card before the demand for her company soars."

Sophia winced. The young man was correct. She had planted a tidbit concerning the Martin family fortune—of which she had no personal knowledge whatsoever—but the young woman's beauty alone would ensure Miss Martin more than her share of male attention tonight. Her ulterior purpose, however, had been only to keep that young woman from her guardian's side, to lessen their opportunity for another dance. For the truth was, she could not bear to see the two of them together.

They looked...and she bit her lip in dismay as she acknowledged the raw truth of it, as she saw them dancing, swaying towards each other, touching, gazing into each other's bemused and fascinated eyes...*they looked to the whole world as though they belonged together.*

❖

Mary was in high alt. *Never* had she imagined such sheer joy as the reality of dancing with Isaac. He was a very good dancer who moved gracefully. She was so used to his customary rigid military carriage and posture that she was quite surprised at his prowess on the dance floor.

She could dance with him forever.

❖

Isaac took Mary's hand and led her into the final steps of the *quadrille*. She responded with an agile twist of her body, her hand slipping easily into his. Tonight, she didn't seem to loathe his touch. Indeed, since that evening at the opera, their truce appeared to be working. They were behaving in a civilized manner toward each other, almost as if they were truly friends.

Was she finally accepting his guardianship and all it entailed? Or had she simply decided to make the best of an uncomfortable situation and wait him out until her father surfaced? Was it all an act for his benefit?

He almost hoped...no, though he had to admit she wasn't a child, but a beautiful and wholly desirable young woman, there was no possibility in the world that he and she could...

She was his first cousin, the daughter of his mother's brother. Matthew, her father, had abominable habits that no reasonable, thinking man would want to see carried on into future generations. Matthew was soft in the head, rather lazy, and his only sibling was a woman of the most disagreeable sort, Isaac's bad-tempered mother, Madam.

There were unfortunate strains in the Martin family. In-breeding among the upper classes, he had noted from his days at Cambridge amongst the scions of *le haut ton,* produced many such bad examples as Matthew Martin. If he had been a horse carrying such unfortunate traits, Isaac would've had his uncle gelded with no remorse. One could not geld human beings, however, and no amount of love and affection could overcome the negative effects of bad breeding.

Love? Affection? What was he thinking of? Isaac knew he had to stop thinking these thoughts, for such thoughts, such not-to-be-expressed desires, could lead only to madness. He was Mary's guardian, that was the beginning and end of it. Only that, and no more, no matter what else his confused mind and heart desired.

❖

"Mary, this was delightful," Isaac complimented his dancing partner as he guided her back to Emma. He squeezed her fingers gently for emphasis, then brought them to his lips.

Mary's face flushed from more than the heat generated by the strenuous dance and the closeness of bodies in the crowded ballroom. *His touch!* She longed for it...

"I wish we could waltz, Cousin Isaac," she blurted impulsively, regarding him with glowing eyes.

Isaac shook his head. "Young ladies, I believe, must have approval for the waltz." He looked to Emma. "Is that not so?"

Emma tapped her closed fan against her cheek. "The patronesses of Almack's are the arbiters of which young ladies waltz and which do not, is that not so?"

"I believe it is," Isaac replied.

"Is that only within the precincts of Almack's, Sir Isaac?" Emma wondered. "How unfortunate that your friend Lady Rowley is not present, for she would surely have the answer." She waited for Isaac to acknowledge that his *chère amie* was indeed there.

"Lady Rowley is here," Fraser interrupted, before Isaac could say yay or nay. "I saw her speaking to my friends."

Isaac didn't betray his knowledge of Sophia's presence at the ball. "Oh, is she?" He drawled his lie. "Perhaps she changed her mind at the last moment...Lord Rowley's no doubt doing well and isn't in need of her comfort."

Mary wondered why Isaac said he hadn't seen Lady Rowley. *She had given him the cut direct!* Mary darted a quick glance across the wide ballroom. Even from that great distance she couldn't miss the malevolence of Lady Rowley's icy glare. It physically jolted her. Sophia wasn't a woman with whom one trifled, she thought. Had she and Isaac quarreled?

Before she could reflect upon the situation, Lord Robin was asking for the next dance. Almost in the same breath, Mr. Higginbotham asked for the one following. She could only acquiesce, dimpling prettily at the attentive young men. Bradshaw led her out.

Bowing slightly, Isaac turned to Emma. "Mrs. Davenport? I promise not to trod upon your pretty slippers."

Emma tapped him playfully on the arm. "Little fear of that, Sir Isaac! I noted your skill on the dance floor." They stepped out, leaving Sally with Fraser.

Fraser smiled. "Shall we, Miss Martin? I'm not near so nimble as Isaac, but your slippers are safe with me, I vow."

"I have perfect trust in you, Mister Fraser," Sally murmured softly, placing her hand in his. The loving gaze she slanted up at him caused him to catch his breath and very nearly crush her dainty feet under his so much larger ones, but he recovered quickly and followed his friends.

Only Higginbotham was left partnerless, saddened that Miss May—daughter of a Cit whose family was excluded from invitation lists for *ton* functions—was absent. The thought that he had the next dance with Miss

Martin-the-heiress, however, consoled him considerably.

❖

Sophia was determined to face Isaac. With that end in mind, she positioned herself so she was directly in front of him when he and Emma completed the lively country dance.

She fumed to see him dancing with the governess as if unaware that she was there. He had looked straight at her—and through her—giving her the cut direct, just as she had done to him. She told herself it didn't bother her, even as her stomach churned with resentment and unhappiness.

"*Isaac!*" she trilled merrily, laying her hand on his arm and evading his cold stare.

"Sophia." His reply was curt.

"Mrs. Davenport! How nice to see you," she chortled.

Emma smiled and wondered what was happening. Whatever it was, it was clearly none of her business. She excused herself politely. "I must attend to the girls, Lady Rowley. Excuse me."

Sophia's smile was a shade too bright; she was thankful the governess was taking herself off so she could be alone with Isaac. She turned to him, moving the hand, still on his arm, familiarly up his broad chest.

"Isaac?" she pleaded, her voice a bit breathless. "Are you angry with me? The other night...oh, my very dear Isaac, I wasn't at all myself..."

Isaac smiled stiffly and removed Lady Rowley's hand from his coat. "On the contrary, my dear, I fear you were very much yourself." The memory of her unladylike actions and language still rankled, and he wanted her to know it.

Sophia's perfect red mouth trembled. "Isaac, don't, please. I deserve your anger, but not your scorn. Please, dearest, don't cast me aside for that country bumpkin you call your ward."

Isaac's face hardened into unforgiving planes. In a

soft, deceptively calm voice, he cautioned his former lady love, "Sophia, do take care. You tread on dangerous ground, my lady, I suggest you drop this matter and allow me to return to my party."

Sophia was beside herself. She swallowed a sob and clutched a handful of his black wool evening coat, crumpling the fine fabric. "My darling, please..." Losing all dignity, she pleaded, "At least, let us discuss this unfortunate misunderstanding."

The muted strains of a waltz floated towards them. Sophia looked at Isaac, her sapphire-blue eyes searching for signs of life in his dark, shuttered ones. "Isaac, waltz with me, my darling, please," she wheedled. "You know how much you enjoy waltzing with me. We must talk..."

Isaac sighed in exasperation. *This woman!* She was making a veritable cake, a spectacle, of them both. Curious eyes were beginning to turn their way. A waltz, then, and be done with it! Then he would take her outside, away from all prying eyes, and tell her, once for all, they were done. A brutal *congé*, and one too long coming. She was out of his life for good.

Now, all he had to do was convince her of that unalterable fact.

"Yes." He nodded as he looked down into her beautiful face, unmoved by that beauty and newly made aware of her capacity for indelicate, even vicious behavior. He wondered why he had allowed their relationship to drag on so long. Whatever had been between them died a natural death long ago. "Yes, Sophia, let us waltz." He swept her into his arms and into the dance.

❖

Mary, sitting out the waltz with Higginbotham and Bradshaw, had no illusions that Cousin Isaac was consulting Lady Rowley on the propriety of young ladies performing the waltz in public. Their faces had seemed full of passion as they conversed. Isaac had swept Sophia's tall, generously curved body into his strong arms with the familiarity of a lover of long standing as he bore her away and they glided effortlessly across the ballroom floor.

They looked like two gods, Mary thought. Beautiful, untouchable, belonging to no one but each other. She didn't know why they had glared so at each other. For it seemed painfully obvious to Mary, as she watched them dance the sensuous, romantic waltz, that Lady Rowley and Isaac would surely leave the ball together.

Mary wanted to cry out her anguish, but it would be a sad commentary indeed on her first London ball. Some things, she thought bitterly, were just not meant to be. She and Cousin Isaac were friends, and perhaps that was the best, the most, she could hope for. Someday, she might find the key to his heart, but not, it seemed, tonight. *Not with Sophia Rowley in attendance.*

Lord Robin smiled as Mary turned her back on the dancers and gave him her full and undivided attention.

❖

Mary had become an avid reader of the London newspapers. Ignorant of who was who in the *ton*, she nonetheless found the announcements and gossip fascinating. Two mornings after the ball, however, the items she chanced to read were hardly to her liking.

"Baron Rowley has died," she announced in a colorless voice to Emma and Sally as they sat together in the morning room.

"He has? Poor man." Sally jumped up to peer over Mary's shoulder. She read the notice through, then declared, "His wife was waltzing at the ball as he lay dying."

Emma set aside Miss Austen's latest novel to respond to Sally's quick, and perhaps unfair, judgement of Lady Rowley's behavior. "She may have been unaware he was at death's door, Sally. It takes time for news from the country to reach London."

Sally sniffed. "She had no business to be at any entertainment whatsoever, knowing her husband was so ill."

"Oh, now, Sally..."

Mary's cheeks were flushed as she thrust the newspaper she was reading under Emma's nose. "Mrs. Davenport! Look at this!"

Emma Davenport scanned the few lines of print, a shocked look on her normally composed features. "Oh my," she mouthed.

"Let me see." Sally wedged herself between Mary and Emma. She read aloud, "*It is rumored this day in London that Sir I----R----- reported ripped knuckles and a sore fist, whilst the notorious M--------- T--------, Lord S----, newly-returned to our shores, was seen to bleed profusely over his evening dress after an altercation behind the M------- mews of Lord and Lady G------. Could the cause of their violent dispute be the beauteous Black Widow, Lady S----- R-----, about to bury husband number three in Y--------?*"

"He told me he slipped and fell on the gravel after escorting Lady Sophia to her coach," Emma muttered.

"Jam...Mr. Fraser...said Cousin Isaac had a handkerchief wrapped about his hand and that was why he had to leave, to have his injury attended," Sally volunteered, the newspaper still clutched in her hands. "He said he had suffered a fall on the gravel walkway."

"I saw him leave the dance floor with Lady Rowley," Mary added. "You saw him after?"

The two women nodded, astonished and puzzled by what they'd read.

"And *who* on earth is *'Lord S---'?*" Mary wondered aloud.

❖

Their afternoon callers—among them Fraser, Bradshaw, Higginbotham, and a number of other young Corinthians who'd danced attention on the sisters Martin at the ball—enlightened Mary, Sally, and Emma on the identity of Lord S---, whom they believed to be the scandalous rake, Maximilian Trehearne, Lord Snow.

Henny May, calling with her mother, giggled at the

notoriety and drama. "Mary, how sheltered you and Sally were at Draycott Terrace, to be sure! No one you knew was in the papers then."

Henny was almost breathless with delight. Her bosom bow's guardian, that handsome and upright gentleman Sir Isaac, rumored to have engaged in violent fisticuffs with a notorious nobleman, a gazetted rake, over a beautiful lady! *How romantic!*

Henny was thrilled with the scurrilous gossip and with Mr. Higginbotham's renewed attentions. That young man had recently discovered that the Mays were wealthy, and was losing no time pressing his suit with pretty Henny. Higginbotham Senior, Viscount Armitage, had made it clear to young Charlie, a fifth son, that the family had no prejudice against wedding wealth engendered by commerce.

Mrs. May was in high alt. *A viscount's son paying court to her dear Henrietta!* Heady stuff, indeed. Meeting the Martin sisters had been a lucky day for the Mays. She helped Mrs. Davenport pour tea while she probed for intimate details on Fraser's courtship of Sally and Bradshaw's pursuit of Mary.

"Will we have news shortly, d'you think, Mrs. Davenport, concerning dear Sally and Mister Fraser, and dear Mary and Lord Robin?" she asked.

Emma, ever discreet—and not altogether sure she liked Mrs. May, whom she privately thought a toad-eater—simply smiled and shook her head. "Not for me to say. Mr. Fraser will have to speak to Sir Isaac...unless, of course, Mr. Martin reappears."

Mrs. May jumped at the mention of the absent Martin *paterfamilias* like a dog at a particularly tasty bone. "Dear Mister Martin! Wherever can he be? As I was saying to my dear Edward the other day..."

The afternoon's conversation quickly worked its way to the tantalizing item in the newspaper that seemed to implicate Sir Isaac, despite Fraser's vain attempts to steer the conversation into other directions.

"Have you seen our cousin, Mr. Fraser?" Mary asked Jamie.

"Yes, I have, Miss Martin," Fraser responded.

"Is he well?" Mary sipped her tea delicately, her eyes riveted on Isaac's close friend.

"Why should he not be, Miss Martin?" Fraser countered, passing her a dish of ginger biscuits and cream cakes.

"We've not seen him since the night of the ball in Mayfair, sir. Is he avoiding us?"

Fraser chewed thoughtfully on a biscuit. "Sir Isaac's a busy man, Miss Martin...he has many things to see to, parliamentary sessions to attend..."

"Has he gone to Yorkshire for Baron Rowley's funeral?"

That question hit Fraser unexpectedly. He had feared some inquiries concerning the newspaper gossip—which made it patently clear to anyone with half a mind who the participants were—and had resolved to be discreet. He had not, however, expected Mary to be so curious.

Isaac go to Yorkshire for old Rowley's funeral after he and Rowley's wife had carried on what most people characterized as an obvious liaison for years? *A most strange idea!* He had to remember, though, that the Martin sisters were innocents.

He shook his head. "No, I assure you, Miss Martin, Sir Isaac is still in town. He has no plans to journey to Yorkshire, despite his...ah...great friendship with Lord Rowley's widow."

"Is he, then, concerned we might ask indelicate questions concerning his hand injury, Mr. Fraser, after reading the newspaper account? Is that why he's not come round to visit?" Mary persisted.

Fraser blanched visibly, then recovered swiftly. "I'm sure he shall be visiting you soon, Miss Martin. His injury is simply a scrape. It had, however, bled onto his clothing...that was why he had to leave so abruptly," he lied, knowing full well the details of that "injury" as confided to him by a shamefaced Isaac the morning after the ball.

"I assure you all, Sir Isaac has no idea why that

scurrilous item was planted in the newspaper. Perhaps someone caught a glimpse of him slipping on the gravel after he saw Lady Rowley to her coach and decided to cause embarrassment to them by viciously altering the facts. Your guardian, I'm sure, doesn't know Max Trehearne personally. Indeed," he warmed to his subject, "neither of us had any idea Trehearne had returned to England."

"Why would someone malign Sir Isaac and Lady Sophia?" Sally asked, joining them where they sat apart from the larger group and leaving a giggly Henny May to entertain the young men paying calls at Queen Square.

Fraser gulped. He didn't relish lying to the lovely object of his tender affections. He shrugged and smiled, answering, "Gossip is indeed pernicious...there are troublemakers and rumormongers everywhere. Mayhap someone had a score to settle with Sir Isaac—or Lady Sophia—and is taking it out in this underhanded way."

"I say, Fraser." Bradshaw had now joined them, full of his own consequence and the belief that his pursuit of Miss Martin had no serious rivals. "So, shall you be seconding Sir Isaac Rebow one morning soon? Is it to be pistols or drawn swords at dawn?"

Sally paled. It wasn't lost on Fraser. The blood rushed to his head. "Robin," he warned his friend, "there are ladies present. Hardly a matter for funning."

"I apologize, ladies." Bradshaw smiled. "It is not, as my friend cautions me, a subject appropriate for delicate ears. Perhaps, as the afternoon unfortunately draws to a close, we should retire to Manton's and discuss this topic in a more fitting and congenial gentlemen's atmosphere. I'm sure Charlie and the others will join us." He winked at the sisters.

Fraser's nod was curt, his mouth a thin line. He rose to make his *adieux* and take his leave with the other young gentleman, their possible destination Manton's popular pistol range.

Sally turned a worried look on Mary. Her sister's face held a pensive expression, then she smiled. "They wouldn't be speaking thus, Sally, so lightly in front of us, if a duel were truly imminent."

"How can you be so sure, Mary?" Sally whispered as their guests took leave of them, only the Mays lagging behind for more personal good byes. "Jam...Mr. Fraser...seemed concerned."

"Cousin Isaac? *Dueling over a woman?*" Mary gurgled, laughing heartily. "Our so-very-proper guardian? Oh, Sally, Sally, you're funning me!" She shook her head, the tears streaming down her cheeks as Henny and her mother looked on, perplexed, and Emma frowned.

Ten

Isaac ran Mary down at Hatchard's Bookstore; the morose butler Mapps had given him her direction. Mrs. Davenport and Sally had an appointment with the modiste, but Mary chose to visit Hatchard's instead, to replenish her reading materials. Clara accompanied her.

Hatchard's was busy, full of its stock in trade, with its bow-fronted windows displaying new titles, its shelves and counters overflowing with books and journals. Agile young clerks scampered up high library ladders to retrieve items for customers.

Isaac frowned when he saw Clara idly walking the floor, some small volumes in her arms, exchanging flirtatious glances with a pink-cheeked clerk stationed at the sales counter. He would definitely have to speak to Mrs. Davenport concerning the abigail's loose behavior. Where was Mary? *Nowhere in sight!* He walked towards the back of the store, his eyes searching for a small, quick figure with hair dark as night.

She was in the Literature section, engrossed in a large, leather-bound volume that looked to weigh a ton. "Mary," he hailed her. She didn't seem to hear; he walked right up to her.

She was neatly and smartly dressed in a yellow pelisse slightly flounced at the hem. The ribbon in her chipstraw bonnet, tied in a crisp bow under her firm chin, matched the bright yellow of her outer garment.

Mary looked up as she heard footsteps, looked up, and, disoriented, fell into the dark-blue eyes of her guardian. She was suddenly a tiny, tiny thing, swallowed up in a vortex. Whoosh! What a strange feeling. She cleared her head. She had been delving into the more

114

somber of Shakespeare's love sonnets, *Sonnet XXVI*, which began *"Lord of my love,"* when Isaac had appeared. As if caught in a shameful act, she shut the heavy tome hurriedly and dragged her eyes from his.

"I am sorry," Isaac apologized, wondering at her agitation, at her flushed face. "I didn't mean to startle you." She looked very beautiful today, with that high color and those dark, smoldering eyes. Again he was aware of the subtle scent of rosewater surrounding her, almost like an aura.

Mary quickly regained her composure. "No, certainly not. You caught me unawares, that is all."

Isaac lowered his head to read the book's spine. *"The Works Of Shakespeare.* Do you intend to purchase this weighty volume?"

She shook her head. "No, I have the complete works at Alresford Hall. This is but a new edition, charmingly designed, pointed out to me by Mr. Hatchard, that I wanted to examine."

Isaac smiled. "An educated woman. You must be the family bluestocking, Mary."

Mary bristled at his teasing tone. "Emma believes all women should be educated as well as men. She intends to give her daughters educations equal to her sons." Mary shot Isaac a challenging look. "As I shall, also."

"Goodness, all this talk of offspring...have you become betrothed since the Granthams' ball without my knowing?" He still teased, but the knowledge that someday she would be wed to another man gnawed at his insides.

"You know everything, Cousin Isaac. You would surely know if I were betrothed before I did, I would not hesitate to wager," she countered, pushing the book to one side and pulling and tightening her York tan gloves over her hands.

Isaac frowned; she seemed out of sorts. With him? Fraser had warned that Mary was questioning him about Lady Rowley, and of course she had wondered about the newspaper gossip.

Unwilling to address that embarrassing event, he remarked, "Fraser tells me young Bradshaw's been spending a good deal of time in your company."

"As Lady Rowley spends a lot of time in yours, Cousin," she replied tartly, moving to a large stack of books on another table and perusing them intently.

Not any more, my love, he wanted to reply, biting his tongue, instead. *My love? Where did that come from?* Isaac cleared his throat. "Lady Rowley's left for York-shire. I believe it will be many months before she returns to London. She's in mourning, and shall be involved with the settlement of her late husband's estate."

Mary's heart gave an excited little leap; she smiled to herself. "Whatever shall you do, then? For compan-ionship?"

Isaac shrugged. "She was a close friend, but I've other friends, and, of course, my two wards to look after. The season isn't yet over. We've a goodly number of events and entertainments to attend in the next several weeks. You and I, Sally and Mrs. Davenport, shall be quite busy."

"You wish to see me married off so soon, then?" she asked, her eyes meeting his straight on.

That clear-eyed, direct gaze almost unnerved him, making him slightly dizzy. Recovering, he questioned, "What makes you believe I desire that?"

Mary shrugged. "Has that not been your intent, with this... guardianship?" She blew some particles of dust off a folio in his direction.

"Not at all," he responded, stepping back hastily from the floating motes of dust. He held back a sneeze. He spoke, his voice lowered, meant for her ears alone. "I felt it a shame you and Sally weren't putting your time in London to good advantage, shut up in Chelsea all those months with no company."

"We managed to keep busy, Sally and I, and when we met the Mays, we had others with whom to spend our time. True, the company wasn't at all sophisticated, the events we attended hardly up to the *ton's* high stan-dards, but we weren't deprived, Cousin Isaac."

"Your father had an obligation to bring you both out into society," Isaac answered firmly, "to meet your peers, your equals, to..."

"...marry us off," she finished his sentence for him.

"Not necessarily, my dear, but that was one possible outcome," he replied. *Lord, she was testy today!*

She turned away from him, back rigid, shoulders high. "What if we didn't wish to marry?"

He wanted to throw his hands up in exasperation. She was unsettling him again, just when he thought all was smoother between them. "A few moments ago, you were speaking of educating your children..."

"That was simply speaking hypothetically," she murmured, bending her head to riffle through the pages of an expensive, highly illustrated volume.

"That was what?" Isaac bent his head nearer to hear her better. They were almost nose-to-nose.

Startled at his closeness, smelling the lime-scented soap on his skin, she began to stammer. "I was speaking hypo...that is, I didn't necessarily mean what I said... I mean...not exactly..."

Isaac straightened up. "What on earth are you talking about, Mary?"

"I...I'm not sure...that is." She looked down at his large hands, covered in handsome dark leather gloves, and asked the question she'd been longing to ask for days. "To change the subject, Cousin, did you truly assau—I mean, did you have an altercation with a Lord Snow on the night of the ball?"

The little baggage! Isaac was completely taken aback. Well, Fraser had warned him that she was too curious by half. What happened between him and Snow was his business, and, oddly, the talk had quickly died down. Fraser said no one really believed any such incident had occurred; 'twas absurd to think of Sir Isaac Rebow, famous for his sense of propriety, in such tawdry circumstances.

What was left unsaid by his good friend was that no one could imagine a dull dog like Isaac would behave in such an overtly violent, passionate fashion. Also,

Sophia's removal from the scene owing to her husband's demise took away a good deal of spice from the tale. He had told Jamie the truth of what happened, and saw the near-disbelief on his friend's face.

If one of his closest friends couldn't imagine it... Isaac's fists twitched. The skin over his knuckles had healed, but the bones were slightly sore from the force of the blow to Snow's phiz. He wondered what condition his lordship's face was in after four days? The power of that well-aimed punch had cracked bone, he was certain.

And here was Mary, wanting to know the truth of it from him. Was there ever such a young woman? He had not encountered her like before, the curiosity, the stubbornness...*well*, he thought, *why not?*

"Yes," he responded honestly. "I had an...altercation...with Lord Snow. Are you satisfied?"

"No," she answered, just as honestly. "I want to know *why* it happened. Was it...Lady Rowley?"

Isaac drew a deep breath and looked at the true cause of his *contretemps* with the despicable Max Trehearne. *Sophia, indeed!* No, not Sophia at all. No, it was for...what did that cur Trehearne call her? Yes, for this *"delicious morsel"*—damn the man!—standing before him, all big eyes and flushed cheekbones.

Lord Snow had insulted her with his dirty mouth. Incredibly, though, his lordship had seen the bare truth of it, that Mary was indeed the cause of his break with Sophia. Those two factors had made him snap, had caused him to lash out at the unfortunate Trehearne, a man most decidedly in the wrong place at the wrong time.

"No, my dear little cousin, it had nothing to do with Lady Rowley. Come." He extended his arm towards her. "Let us find your abigail. I'll take you home."

❖

Mary wasn't sure what to make of it. Isaac Rebow, her oh-so-perfect cousin and guardian, engaging in fisticuffs with a notorious lord! So, the scurrilous newspaper account was true, in part at least. He did not deny it. As to the cause...if not Sophia, whom? Could she believe him, or was he—as the perfect, proper gentleman he was—simply shielding a woman friend?

She slanted a glance at him as they walked to Queen Square, her arm in his, Clara strolling sedately behind them. He was a soldier. She wasn't a complete ninny; she suspected he had killed men in battle. He was certainly more than capable of fighting with his fists, scuffling with another man, one-on-one, as out of character as it seemed at first.

Mary looked up at the sky. Blue, almost cloudless, a marvelous spring day. She frowned, contemplating the man at her side. He was a splendid physical specimen, fit and strong, and he possessed a temper. She had been on the receiving end of his temper on more than one occasion. She shuddered, remembering the times they had come to figurative blows.

Now...now they were friends...were they not? She remembered how exquisite it felt to be in his arms while they danced. She had tingled with delight, never wanted it to end. And then, to see him with Lady Rowley. Mary trembled with the memory, reliving the agony it had caused her.

"Cold, my dear?" Isaac murmured. They were walking with her arm in his, and now he clasped her fingers, questioning.

She kept her face averted. Her emotions were too quick to show on her face. She was sure he would guess she was thinking about him...and what she was thinking. "No...that is, perhaps just a bit. The wind seems to be shifting."

Isaac frowned. The day was still and windless. Not a newly furled leaf nor budding flower moved in the park as they skirted past. He hoped his ward wasn't taking a chill. She was a delicate little creature, fierce as she might appear to be at times. Hot tea! Ah, yes, that would warm her and avoid illness.

"Do you think we can prevail upon Emma to provide tea for us, Mary? I could do with a good, strong cup. She and Sally must surely be returned from the modiste by now."

"Most assuredly, Cousin Isaac," Mary agreed. Tea was a safer subject to ponder at this moment than her emotionally charged feelings about Isaac. As they turned the corner and approached the Davenports' house, she noted a large coach at the kerb.

"Who can it be?" she wondered. They weren't expecting guests. From time to time, after the ball, young gentlemen had been leaving their cards, but this visitor—? The carriage was unfamiliar...but...

Mary gasped as the portly, wispy-haired, middle-aged gentleman stepped down from the coach. His air of benign absentmindedness was all too familiar. "Papa!" she cried, disengaging herself from Isaac's arm and guardianship. Skirts lifted and a smile of joyous welcome wreathing her face, she ran toward her errant father.

Isaac stood stock-still on the walk, his face unreadable to the curious abigail who came abreast, watching the tableau of welcome and reconciliation being played out before his eyes. It seemed—out of the blue, blue, cloudless sky—that his reluctant guardianship was about to come to an end.

The day he longed for, was it not? Then why did he feel as if something unutterably precious had been stolen away, something he had no possibility on earth of ever again attaining? A cloud appeared out of nowhere and suddenly obscured the sun.

❖

The tears were many, the recriminations few. Sally and Emma had followed almost immediately on Mary's heels from their appointment at the *modiste's* and witnessed the tender reconciliation of father and elder daughter. Normally quiet Sally had shouted aloud and almost jumped off the walk and into her papa's outstretched arms, and now he held both his children tightly to him, his face wet with joyful tears.

Emma shook her head in amazement at the happy reunion. She looked at Isaac. There was an odd, set smile on the ex-guardian's visage. *Rather grim!* He should be gleeful, Emma thought, gleefully happy his unwanted duty was over, that his bachelor life was once again his, unencumbered by the awesome responsibility of guardianship for two young women he barely knew. He no longer had to play the chaperon, arrange entertainments, and dance attendance on his country cousins; for him, the season was ended.

Why, then, did he look so...yes, Emma thought, that was the only way to describe the bleak look in his eyes...why did he look so bereft?

Briskly, Emma swept into the house and, calling for Mrs. Pepperwit, ordered tea and cakes. Isaac was still on the sidewalk, silently observing the commotion and fuss taking place there. He had not moved an inch. Emma called to him softly.

"Sir Isaac, do come in, please. Let us have tea." She looked toward the Martins. "There is, I would venture, a good deal to talk about this afternoon. Clara!" She raised her voice slightly. "Do come in, girl, and stop your gawking."

❖

In honor of the occasion of Matthew's return, Mrs. Pepperwit had made tea in the fine new Neale jasperware teapot Isaac had presented to Emma as a gift. An ample store of white linen napkins were on hand for the copious tears still being shed by the sisters and their father.

Apologies abounded and forgiveness was freely given. Promises were fervently tendered for the future, and answers were finally forthcoming. Matthew had turned to Isaac and embraced him warmly, confirming that the newspaper notices had brought him to his senses at long last. He thanked his nephew and asked for his indulgence.

"I beg your forgiveness, my boy. I'm an old fool, and I know you must think the worst of me—for which I do not blame you one whit!—but I didn't mean to abandon my dear, dear girls." The girls, cuddled on either side of him, burrowed their heads into each of his sloping shoulders and wept afresh at his words.

Isaac wanted to wring his uncle's neck, but forbore to do so in front of Emma, the girls, and the servants, who were also weeping. It was a veritable weep-fest! Only he and Emma were not crying, and he felt quite the odd man out at this happy little reunion. It had happened much too quickly, too soon—had it really been only four weeks?—and he was unprepared. He didn't realize he would feel so reluctant to relinquish his responsibilities for Mary and Sally. Especially Mary. *Too soon...much too soon!*

Matthew was speaking, explaining his hurried departure from Draycott Terrace at midnight. Isaac could barely believe his ears as his uncle's tale unfolded.

The old fool had eloped!

"I fell in love, you see, and it happened so very quickly. Beaming, his puckish features lighting up his small, round face, Matthew turned to his daughters. "Girls, I want you to meet your new stepmama, my Dorothy, as soon as we can arrange it. I'm sure you two shall love her as much as I do. I'm the happiest of men!"

Arrange it? What was the daft old fool saying, Isaac wondered. He cleared his throat. "Uncle Matthew? You shall, of course, be taking the girls to your new home?"

Martin hemmed and hawed and ran a finger inside a cravat that suddenly appeared to be too tight. "You girls are so well settled here with Emma...and, ah, Dorothy, kind and good-hearted as she is, well, she does prefer us to be alone. Only for a little while, girls!" he assured his daughters, who ceased cuddling and were now looking at him with puzzled expressions.

"I'm hoping." He turned to Emma, a beseeching look on his countenance. "I was hoping Emma would kindly keep you here for a little while longer. Until Dorothy and I..." His face turned an alarming shade of pink. "Until Dorothy and I leave off our... harumph...our honeymoon."

Mary's lips quivered. "You mean you don't want us with you, Papa?"

Isaac's heart tore into pieces at Mary's sad face. She was hurt. Yes, he could strangle his unfeeling, uncaring uncle right now with no trepidation! He was breaking his girls' hearts. What was wrong with the careless old fool?

Matthew patted Mary's hand, meaning to comfort her. "Oh, only a little while, my love, until Dorothy and I get used to being married." He looked from his elder daughter to the younger, his voice full of deep emotion. "I know 'tis hard for you to understand, you're both so young, and never having a mama to discuss the nature of relationships between men and women..."

Emma broke into what was rapidly becoming too intimate a conversation. "More cakes, Squire? Sir Isaac?" She made a show of handing round the pastries brought up from the kitchen by Clara.

"Sally, Mary," she said hurriedly, covering up the awkwardness of Matthew's plea for more time alone with his bride, "it is no inconvenience for me to have the two of you—and Mapps and Mrs. P.—spend time with me whilst your Papa and new stepmama have more time to acquaint themselves with each other. Let us continue as before for a little while longer, shall we?" She smiled brightly at the assemblage.

Isaac sat back in his chair, his arms crossed against his broad chest, and regarded his boots. Those pieces of apparel had never before received such intense scrutiny from him. His valet would have been amazed.

Isaac was furious. His uncle, clearly, didn't want his daughters in his little love nest to interrupt his carryings-on with his new bride. The old man was caper-witted, indelicate to a fault. *Honeymoon,* indeed!

Bless Emma for her kind offer, he thought, but those poor girls! First, desertion with no explanation, and now, this pitiful show of selfish indulgence. What foolishness did their misguided papa have in store for them next?

The tea was bitter in his mouth.

❖

Fraser knocked on the door just as the remains of tea were being carted away by Mapps. He was inordinately pleased to see Matthew and took the opportunity to ask if he could call upon him soon. At that, Matthew looked from the one to the other of his daughters and caught Sally's shy, tremulous smile. He waggled his finger at her. "Aha! You minx," he teased.

Mary frowned. She guessed instantly Fraser's intentions. Catching Emma's eye, she commented *sotto voce* "He couldn't possibly! Sally's too young." Emma put a finger to her lips, cautioning silence. She invited the visitors in her drawing room to sup at Queen Square that night.

Matthew agreed with alacrity. "My Dorothy doesn't expect me to return so soon. That would be delightful, Emma, thank you." He turned to the other two men. "What think you, Isaac? Shall we retire to Brooks's, then, until dinnertime?"

Noting the look on his uncle's face, Isaac was aware that the expensive brandies and cigars available at the club would be on his docket. Some things, he thought wryly, will never change.

He was sure, also, that he would be privy to Jamie's offer for Sally's hand. The young man was chomping at the bit to get his bid in. *Well, then, perhaps I should let you, my dear Fraser, foot the blunt for this one,* he decided. Aloud, he said, "Excellent idea, Uncle Matthew."

Isaac stepped back to have a last word with Emma. "I'll stop at Duke Street and instruct one of my footmen to bring wine for dinner."

He wondered what Madam would have to say about her brother's remarriage. They still had no idea who *'my Dorothy'* was, nor where the newlyweds were abiding. Madam would, however, be pleased his cousins were off his hands and his purse shut for the nonce. No more expenses from that quarter; hence, more for Madam to spend. He turned to Mary, "Madam will be eager to hear this news. You will write to her?"

Mary nodded, her eyes downcast and her hand at her throat. She was upset, understandably so, that her father wasn't about to take her and Sally away. Isaac longed to comfort her, to assure her she'd always have a home with him, but it would be highly inappropriate. Mary had a home: Alresford Hall. She'd hie herself off to Essex before long. London held few attractions, and now it was painfully apparent that her father's new home had no room for her.

Isaac sighed. Dinner this evening mightn't be the happiest of occasions for either of them, albeit for differing reasons. He would have to make sure he consumed enough brandies at his club to dull the edge of his sensibilities. Only then could he face up to the reality that Mary's life was no longer in his hands. Her father had come back, and she would continue to do exactly what she wanted to do under his lax supervision, as she had in the past.

Further, he knew that whatever those things were she wanted to do, they would have nothing to do with him at all. The pain of that knowledge stabbed sharply, like a knife twisted between his ribs.

Eleven

He had been watching them for days.

He thought, yesterday, that he would have a chance at the dark-haired one. The women had split up, two of them going in the direction of Dot's dressmaker, the girl another way, to that bookseller the Fancy favored. Unfortunately, she took a servant with her, a hefty girl who looked like she had a healthy pair of lungs for screaming if anyone got too close to her mistress.

Bart Scofield swore. Doggedly, he had followed them to the bookstore and waited outside. The man came, then, the flash cove who was always going back and forth from Duke Street to Queen Square. He was a big one, he was. No sense tangling with him. Bart would keep an eye out for now, get the pattern of their comings and goings, get to know them like the backs of his hands.

He had time. The old cove, Dot's "husband", was going to change his will, put her in it. He was going to Essex to see his lawyer and get it straight. There was a lot of the ready there, but Bart wanted more. If his scheme worked out, the girls would be dead within a fortnight, and then all would go to his sister when he put a period to the old man.

Bart's big, rough hands itched. He wanted money, and would go to any lengths for it. Once Dot had her share of the Martin estate, it would be as good as in his pockets. His sister didn't dare do anything to anger him these days. Dot was on thin ice after her betrayal and cowardly disappearance. He wouldn't hesitate to dispatch her soul to its just reward alongside the souls of the Martin family.

Dot was a pretty enough little bitch, and had her uses, but Bart knew she was as stupid as they came. If anyone had gotten the brains in the Scofield family, it was him! That was the truth of it.

Now, he had to keep a close watch on the Martin sisters' movements, for, when he struck, he would have to strike swift and clean. A pity they were squandering so much good blunt on clothes they would never have a hope of sporting, if all went as planned. Too bad...*for them!*

❖

The last person Isaac expected to encounter at Tattersall's Repository, that classical temple devoted to the worship of prime horseflesh near Hyde Park Corner, was his Rebow-side cousin, Captain Tommy Adams.

Tommy and his lady wife, Grace, lived at Warley, an estate not far from Alresford Hall. They were neighbors and close since childhood. Tommy and Grace were connoisseurs of finely-bred horses and passionate followers of the fox hunt.

Grace was a rare woman, allowed to join in the local Chelmsford hunt alongside men. But then, Isaac acknowledged, Grace wasn't the most feminine of women. In fact, Isaac was mildly surprised Grace had not accompanied Tommy at Tatt's, though women as a rule weren't welcome. Grace was the exception who proved that rule.

He waved to Tommy, who was standing under the bare-beamed wooden roof with a group of like-minded horsemen. They were examining a skittish bit of prime blood being restrained by a sturdy groom. "What, ho, Tommy! All alone in town?"

Tommy Adams grinned at his rich, stylish cousin. Isaac was a good sort, if a bit of a stickler, high in the instep. Tommy said something *sotto voce* to the groom, who nodded and led the spirited chestnut stallion away. Joining Isaac alongside one of the Doric columns that enclosed the inner square of the Repository, he clapped him heartily on the back.

"Isaac! Been a demmed age, I vow! How are you? And Madam?" He was exuberant with pleasure at this chance encounter.

Isaac smiled wryly. "You probably see a good deal more of my dear mother than I, Cousin."

"Hardly!" Tommy guffawed, his long-nosed, sunburnt face creasing into a wide grin. "Never been fond of me or my lady, your mama. Must know that, Isaac! Not funning me, are you?"

Isaac shook his head. "Who is she fond of, Tommy? I've not found the person yet of whom she speaks that well...except perhaps for my Uncle Matthew's girls."

They were walking together slowly now on the packed brown earth of the enclosure. Tommy Adams nodded his head in agreement and added, "What's this I hear about your uncle? Officer in m'old regiment says he saw a notice in one of th' newspapers."

"Thank goodness, that matter's been settled! The old fool eloped—though we've yet to see his bride—and he left the girls to fend for themselves. At Madam's urging, I tried to take the situation in hand, and probably made things worse than they were."

Tommy disagreed. "Knowing you, Isaac, hardly think that's possible."

"Well, thank you, Tommy, but it was more than possible. Now Uncle Matthew's returned but refuses to take the girls. They're living with their former governess, so their housing situation has improved from the Chelsea rental, but..."

"Your uncle was always caper-witted, Isaac, begging your pardon. Could the girls not return to Alresford Hall? Had a good life there, seems to me. Remember th' older girl..."

"Mary," Isaac replied softly, *Mary, Mary, Mary*, savoring the taste of her name in his mouth.

"Yes, Mary. Good-looking girl, nice sort. Good dowry, too, I'm sure."

Isaac shrugged. "Good enough, if Uncle Matthew doesn't dip into it keeping his mysterious new bride in style."

Tommy stopped in front of the small, domed structure supported by Ionic columns in the middle of the enclosure; an idea hit him. "Have a mount with you, Isaac?"

"No, Tommy, I took a hackney." He thought back to the morning almost a month ago when Jamie had bounded up the stairs at Duke Street and invited him to Tatt's. A month? It seemed an eternity, so much had happened since then, so many changes.

Tommy was aware of how Isaac, the boy, had sought solace in Wivenhoe Park's stables. It seemed Isaac, the man, had similar need of solace from horses and men who appreciated them. "Well, then," he continued, "take my mount, and I'll ride th' chestnut I just purchased. Go to my place for a dish o'tea, or something stronger. Sure Grace would enjoy seeing you."

Isaac nodded agreement. The mindless chatter of the county horse-and-hunt set would be a welcome break from all his tribulations.

❖

Lean, long-legged Grace Philippa Adams was in her scarlet riding habit. The habit with the black-frogged embroidery, not the scarlet habit distinguished by gold military-style epaulets, nor the scarlet and green, fashioned from a Scottish clan tartan. Her wardrobe consisted primarily of riding habits, in point of fact.

Grace spent most of her time riding or mucking about the stables. Warley was known throughout Essex for its excellent stables; it wasn't known for much else. The gardens were ragged and unkempt; the bare-bones housekeeping left a great deal to be desired; furnishings were minimal; the food was barely edible, except when fresh game was available.

The Adamses didn't seem to mind their surroundings. They spent most of their time in the stables. Guests with the misfortune of not being horse lovers never returned for a second visit. Their small house in London,

near Hanover Square, was but a miniature version of
Warley, down to every detail, not the least of which was
the indifferent housekeeping. No, actually, it was worse,
as the Adamses spent hardly any time in town and never
entertained there.

Like her husband, Grace was tall, rangy, long-faced
and long-nosed. Isaac thought she looked rather amazingly like a horse, a sweet-tempered if not especially
pretty mare. He wondered occasionally if a nearsighted
groom at Warley had ever thrown bridle and bit over her
head and attempted to saddle her. It was a distinct possibility!

Grace was delighted to see Isaac, her cousin-by-
marriage. She threw her long, sinewy arms around him,
embracing him so hard he was almost breathless. Then
she threw back her mane of long brown hair and laughed
out loud at his surprised reaction to her effusiveness.
She took his arm and held on to it.

Isaac grinned; she was a good sort, if not exactly
fitting the image of a lady of quality. She bellowed below-stairs for tea and cakes, and, still holding on to
Isaac's arm, led him to her drawing room.

He knew from past experience the tea would be
weak and the cakes stale, and also that he would be the
sole one of the three of them to notice, or to care. As
Grace poured from a chipped stoneware teapot, slopping
the pale brew over onto the cracked saucers, Isaac politely refused the plate of dried-out cakes Tommy offered.

"Tell us about the Martin girls, Isaac," Grace asked,
settling back in her chair and crossing one scruffy
booted leg over the other. "We remember them well,
Tommy and I." She smiled a toothy grin at her husband
and Isaac again remarked her horsey countenance.

"They're well, Grace. I've been...that is, I was escorting them to *ton* affairs, which they seemed to enjoy.
Mary was reluctant at first, but she soon warmed to the
events. She made quite a stir at the opera and was be-
sieged by admirers at a ball given by Lord and Lady
Grantham."

"Pretty girl, Mary." Tommy nodded. "Enjoyed riding, not like t'other sister." He turned to his wife. "Believe she went riding with you numerous times."

Grace nodded. "Good little horsewoman. Sally didn't like horses. Stayed at the Hall and embroidered. Needlewoman, that one."

Isaac sipped the pale, weak tea and forbore making a face at its insipid taste. "I wouldn't be surprised to hear wedding bells pealing for Sally soon," he told them.

"Little Sally?" Tommy was surprised.

"Yes, scarce seventeen and the recipient of an offer of marriage from a young man of my acquaintance, James Fraser. Nice chap, good family, but seems determined to purchase an army commission." Fraser's news had been expected; no surprise there, for he had acted fast as soon as Matthew surfaced.

"Sally Martin following the drum? That fragile flower?" Grace seemed incredulous.

"Fraser might well have second thoughts on that commission," Isaac acknowledged. "A rough life for a sheltered young miss barely out of the schoolroom."

Against his better judgement, Isaac helped himself to a wedge of cake. One bite was all he needed to regret his decision. Hastily placing it on his plate, he continued, "So, I shall probably see you all at Alresford Hall, come the nuptials. Mark your calendars."

"Not blood relatives t'us, Isaac. Cousins to you, only, on the Martin side, Madam's side of the family."

"But surely you will be invited as close neighbors," Isaac replied.

"Oh, what grand fun! I do love a wedding." Grace smiled, drawing her upper lip over big front teeth and exposing a goodly amount of healthy pink gum. Isaac was fascinated; if she were a horse, such marvelous teeth and gums would make her a sound purchase indeed.

"Surprising, though, from what you say 'bout her success in London, that Mary didn't receive the first marriage offer," Tommy commented.

"Sally's sweet and docile. My friend evidently couldn't resist such an excellent temperament. She's quite pretty also." Isaac put down his teacup. "Mary, on the other hand, is an outspoken young woman who needs the guidance of a strong hand and a cool head. It would take a brave young man to offer for her. Though most say she's without doubt vastly more attractive than her sister."

Sally's a demure English rose, thought Isaac, *but Mary beggars description. A hothouse flower, a rare, precious bloom...*

"No." Tommy shook his shaggy head. "Don't mean that, Isaac. Meant, Mary being such a great heiress and all..."

What was Tommy nattering on about? Mary a great heiress? The sisters would have sizable marriage portions from his uncle Matthew, but hardly...there was some foolishness touted about since the night of the ball, that the Martins were extremely wealthy, but he had set that nonsense straight as soon as he heard of it. Whoever had spread such a falsehood? Isaac gave Tommy a puzzled look.

"D'you not know, Isaac, about Mary's fortune?" Grace asked gently, placing her large-knuckled hand on his sleeve.

"Fortune?" he repeated stupidly. "I cannot think what you mean." He looked from Grace to Tommy.

Tommy shot a glance at Grace. "He don't know, Gracie. Or—" he turned to scrutinize Isaac— "or he's had so little to do with that family of late that he's plainly forgot."

Isaac was well and truly bewildered. "What the devil are you two talking about?"

"Why, Alresford Hall, o' course, Isaac. Mary owns it outright. Came to her straight from her papa's family, no entail...and there's money, too."

"Tommy, are you mad? My Uncle Matthew is still very much alive."

Grace Adams looked from Isaac to her husband and then back again. "But, Isaac, dear, Matthew Martin ain't

Mary's father."

Isaac's puzzlement at Grace's statement wasn't at all helped by Tommy's whoop of laughter as he slapped his thigh in merriment. It was amusing, quite a joke, to get the better of Isaac, a man who usually had all the facts at the ready, who was not uninformed.

Isaac debated the weightiest issues of the nation in Parliament, he could discuss irrigation schemes for the Essex fens with ease, he was a military strategist of the first order who had distinguished himself in India, and a canny, astute businessman who couldn't seem to lose money.

Right now, however, in the middle of the Adamses' disordered drawing room, he was thoroughly dumbfounded.

"Then who? Who, by all that's sacred, is Mary's father?" he asked, bewildered.

"Elisabeth Martin's first husband, o' course, Viscount Barnard." Grace helped herself to a large piece of pastry, speaking with her mouth half-full and scattering crumbs on her lap and on the frayed oriental carpet.

She swallowed the cake and explained, "Lady Barnard was widowed when Matthew Martin married her. The babe, Mary, was young, scarce three months old. Barnard was killed in a coaching accident when Elisabeth was increasing. Mary never knew her real pa, Barnard. Stuck his spoon in the wall eight months before she was born. Always considered Matthew her pa."

Isaac looked from one to the other of his cousins. "Everyone knows this?" he queried them.

The Adamses nodded in unison.

"Then why—" he began.

"The Barnard family was never much interested in the girl." Grace responded gently, patting him on the forearm. "Her being female...well, the estate and title, excepting Alresford Hall, went to the closest male relative, some lordling in the west country, no, Tommy?"

Tommy shrugged. "Madam knows this story, Isaac. Surprised you don't recollect it. Mary knows Matthew isn't her real pa, so does Sally...'twas never a secret."

Isaac was taken aback. He had acted completely out of turn taking the responsibility for Mary. Her Barnard relatives should have had their say when Matthew Martin disappeared. Why hadn't Samuel Ennew...?

"Lawyer Ennew knew this?"

"Isaac," Grace said slowly, patiently, her hand still on his arm, "*everyone* knows this. Matthew adopted Mary, with the full consent of the Barnard family."

Isaac breathed a deep sigh of relief. He had not acted wrongly, after all. Ennew didn't misinform him. His uncle was Mary's legal guardian, and Ennew had stated that Isaac was named in Matthew's will should anything happen to him. It was a great relief, knowing he had acted properly.

Straight on the heels of that knowledge came a greater one: he and Mary weren't related by blood. Whatever were the defects of intellect or character exhibited by Matthew Martin, they had no bearing on the intellect or character of Mary Martin, née Mary Barnard. The Honourable Mary Barnard, daughter of a viscount.

She outranked him.

"How much of an heiress did you say Mary Martin was, Tommy?"

Tommy placed his hands behind his head, linking his long fingers together. "Seems to me, Cousin, you need t' have another talk with Lawyer Ennew in Colchester." His wife Grace nodded her head vigorously.

❖

Emma had to have a talk with Sally. As Squire Martin had reminded her, the girls were ignorant of marital matters, with no mother to inform them how things went between men and women. It was Emma's role to enlighten them. She spoke first to Sally.

Sally's initial reaction to Emma's delicate but truthful recital of the facts of married life was utter incredulity. She giggled girlishly, then covered her mouth with her hand. "Oh, surely *not*, Emma!" she protested.

Emma took Sally's hands in hers and spoke from the heart, reassuring her. "Sally, it is perfect bliss with the partner of your heart. There's awkwardness, to be sure, at first, maidenly shyness to overcome, and perhaps some painful moments...but you and Mr. Fraser love each other, and that's what matters. Give yourself over to the joy, my dear, and find your happiness with each other."

The clinical details she then proceeded to supply were followed avidly by young Sally, and she asked a number of intelligent questions. Emma was relieved.

❖

Sally could not wait to pass on her newfound knowledge of the marriage bed to her elder sister. Mary listened intently, then commented, "Sally, did you never watch the animals at home?"

"Mary!" Sally was scandalized. "Not at all the same..."

"It is," Mary replied sagely, raising her dark eyebrows in a knowing manner.

Her all-knowing air annoyed her sister, who countered, "It is not! According to Emma..." Sally's bold, confident narrative swept Mary in, enthralling her. She nodded, convinced at last by her younger sister's recitation.

"You're correct, Sally, there seem to be several marked differences. I look forward to the experience."

Sally shot Mary a sharp look. "I'm the one who's to be wed, miss. May I remind you of that?"

"Well, I've a good deal to imagine, then. Emma's words are truly food for thought." Mary patted her sister on the cheek and left Sally sitting on the bed wondering at Mary's self-satisfied look.

Mary walked down the stairs to the drawing room in a dreamy state of mind. She imagined herself in a flimsy nightrail in the embrace of her cousin and ex-guardian, the formidable Colonel Sir Isaac Rebow. Even better, she imagined herself as God had made her in Isaac's warm embrace. She pictured the splendor of his unclad, tall, muscular physique, like the drawings of Greek statuary she had studied in the art books at Alresford Hall's well-stocked library. A delicious shiver went through her body.

She looked forward to the experience, as she had told her sister; nay, she savored the fanciful thoughts now whirling through her mind. Mary had an excellent imagination, which was now serving her well. She skipped down the last four steps and smiled broadly to herself.

Twelve

'Tis an old saying that a dappled sky, like a painted woman, soon changes its face. As Mary, Sally, and Agnes Pepperwit prepared to journey to Knightsbridge for the crucial meeting with the new stepmama, high, thin sheets of cloud hung above Queen Square. The clouds looked like ripples on the marled bottom of a lake, or like the scales of a fish.

"A mackerel sky," Mrs. Pepperwit pronounced. "'Twill rain by and by, I suspect."

"It has been so lovely this entire week!" Sally exclaimed worriedly. "Do you think it is a sign?"

"A sign of what?" Mary's tone was exasperated as she drew on a pair of knitted black silk mittens. She was in a pensive, unhappy mood, not looking forward to this visit.

"I am not by any means looking forward to this dinner, Mary, if you must know," Sally admitted, echoing Mary's thoughts. "I have a foreboding which won't go away."

"Don't be such a peagoose, Sally!" Mary snapped. "You can be so missish! Do let's get this meeting over with, and get on with our lives." She swept past a startled Sally and called to Clara for an umbrella.

Mrs. Pepperwit heard her mutter under her breath, *"One may as well be prepared!"*

Mrs. Pepperwit raised her wispy white eyebrows at Sally and shook her round, plump shoulders. Sally shrugged, wondering at her sister's black looks and abrupt behavior. It was good that Emma wasn't there to overhear Mary's conversation; Emma would be most vexed at such rudeness.

❖

"My dear girls!" Matthew Martin clasped his daughters to his chest and embraced them heartily. His bride Dorothy stood at the drawing room door, a stiff smile on her face. She was dressed in a classic Florette Dumont creation, a forest-green silk frock, exquisitely sewn and demurely high-necked; over her shoulders was an artfully draped Cashmiri shawl with a long, knotted fringe.

Mary and Sally looked at Dorothy and then at each other. They immediately recognized the woman who had been in Mademoiselle Dumont's establishment. The woman whom Florette's two giggling seamstresses had said—almost swallowing the straight pins between their tittering lips as they took Mary and Sally's measurements—was a member of the muslin company. Seeing the sisters' total lack of comprehension, they had enlightened them further. The woman was a Cyprian, the apprentice dressmakers told them, a courtesan, a light-skirt, a high-flyer, a woman who sold her body to men for their intimate use.

And their new stepmama.

❖

That week, Mary described her father's new wife to Madam in a letter to Wivenhoe Park. *She is awkward to a degree, & more out of her Element than you can Conceive any body. My father is forc'd to exert himself most Amazingly, but they seem prodigious Fond & Happy. Indeed, They play together all day long, like a Couple of kittens.*

Their father seemed happy, indeed. He glowed in Dorothy's company, clearly besotted. The new Mrs. Martin didn't indicate, by look or word, that she had ever seen her new stepdaughters before this Knightsbridge meeting. She hardly spoke to them at all. She hung on to Matthew's sleeve and flirted with him in what could only be called a decidedly kittenish manner.

Afterward, Sally commented that Dorothy's constantly batted eyelashes had made her dizzy, and her monopolization of their father had made it impossible to converse with him. Her foreboding, moreover, had proven to be all too true.

Below-stairs, Mrs. Pepperwit had been regaled by the servants with tales of Mrs. Martin's vulgarity. The housekeeper sniffed that she was "not good *ton*" and wondered aloud why the lady never had visitors. The scullery maid volunteered that she had seen the mistress conversing with a strange man in the garden. The stranger, she reported, was dirty, extremely ill-favored in looks, and made her skin crawl in fear.

Mary and Sally, hearing Mrs. P.'s report in the coach as they rode home to Queen Square, swore her to secrecy then revealed what they had learned at the dressmaker's. It would not do for Emma—or Madam!—to learn what a cake their father had made of himself. They agreed they had to enlist Cousin Isaac's help in investigating Dorothy Martin's background.

"Tomorrow, Mrs. P., early, before Cousin Isaac steps out, we must see him," Mary decided.

Sally paled. "Mary, perhaps we should tell Emma, take her into our confidence. She could deal far better with Cousin Isaac, I think, in a delicate matter such as this."

"It isn't her business, Sally. It's a family matter." Mary took her sister's cold hand and squeezed it. "You mustn't even tell Mr. Fraser!"

"But I cannot say these things, speak of courtesans and the like, to Cousin Isaac!" Sally wailed.

Mary threw her hands up in the air. "Sally! You're being missish again!"

Agnes Pepperwit interceded. "Miss Molly, it appears to me you must be the one to speak to Sir Isaac. 'Tis plain, Sally's mortified to discuss such things, and I agree with you 'tis a family matter and no concern of Mrs. Davenport's." She patted Mary's shoulder. "I shall accompany you to Duke Street tomorrow, do not fear."

"Thank you, Mrs. P." Mary smiled weakly, darting

an exasperated look at her sister, soon to be married, but still, in her estimation, a child.

❖

For a countryman born and bred, Bart Scofield was as ignorant of the weather as any Londoner. A mackerel sky did not signify, not to him. As a consequence, he was soaked to the skin when he spied on the Martins that evening in Queen Square and cursed the stinging sheet of cold rain that pelted him unmercifully and dripped icy rivulets of water down his collar.

He was still keeping a watch on the sisters, still waiting for a signal from Dot that the old man had made the changes in his will. But no signal was forthcoming. He cursed Dot long and richly as the rain continued to fall, relentless in its steady rhythm, and sneezed violently.

❖

In Mary's room, late into the night, Sally's embarrassment at having to speak to Isaac about their disgraceful stepmama had given way to hysterical weeping.

"I cannot have her at my wedding, Mary," she sobbed. "Jamie's family...oh, what would they think when they saw her? I would die!"

"We shall make sure they won't meet her, Sally," Mary consoled her.

Sally looked up at her sister, hope flaring in her eyes. "Shall we arrange to have her abducted the week of the wedding?"

Mary seemed to consider the suggestion seriously for a moment. "It's a possibility, but I'll wager Cousin Isaac may have a better plan." She drew the counterpane over her sister's petite form. "Sleep now, dear, don't trouble yourself with this matter. I shall take care of it."

She rose quietly from the bed and went to the window. Opening it, she listened to the windblown rain, feeling some of the wetness on her cheeks, yearning once more for the uncomplicated tranquillity of her old

life in the country. Somewhere close by she heard someone sneeze.

Sighing, Mary began to shut the window, then left it
slightly ajar. She turned back to look at her sister and
smiled. *Poor little thing,* she thought. *All she wants is to
be married to her Jamie. And all I want is...*

To ask Cousin Isaac for his help, that was all, she
finished the thought and sat back in the rocking chair by
her bedside, tucking her bare feet under her. *He shall
help us,* she persuaded herself to believe, *oh, he must!*
She slept fitfully.

❖

Bart wiped his dripping nose on his rough woollen
sleeve. He cursed the weather, his sister, and all the
Martin clan. He was going to have to take the matter
into his own capable hands, he was.

Let the old cove diddle and daddle over changing
his will: Bart would pick off his tender little chicks one
by one in the meantime. And here, now, was one of
them. *Ah, lovely, lovely!*

❖

Mary slipped out of the house by her old escape
route, the servants' entrance off the kitchen. She would
try to see her cousin Isaac before he left for Parliament,
explain their predicament, and ask for his advice and
help. He was a man of the world and would know how
to deal with such things.

Cousin Isaac, she would tell him forthrightly, *it appears our beloved Papa has wed a Cyprian. Sally's devastated, fearing the effect Dorothy will have on her wedding festivities and on her future in-laws. What do you
think? Shall we contrive to have our stepmama abducted? And what shall we do about Papa?*

Mary sighed deeply. Life in London was much too
complicated. The country was never like this. To think
that she was used to complain about having to deal with

Madam! Dealing with Madam in Essex—with her end-less stream of instructions having to do with the refur-bishment of the Duke Street town house—was simplic-ity itself compared to this distressing new problem. Mary prayed Isaac would have the solution.

She was so deep in contemplation that she took no notice of the sinister-looking man huddled in an alley-way two houses down the street who began to move away from the buildings as she unlatched the wrought iron gate of the servants' entrance.

As Mary raised the latch, she suddenly stopped, re-membering something important she had neglected in her concern and worry. *Mrs. P.!* Releasing the latch hur-riedly and letting it fall into its socket with a loud clang, she ran down the stairs and into the house.

❖

What the—! Bart swore vehemently, drawing back into the safety and concealment of the alleyway. Where had that piece of fancy goods gone? He had planned to follow her and knock her down with force. She was a little bit of a thing; a hard fall against the solid pavement of the sidewalk would render her unconscious, kill her for sure.

She had come out again! He stepped out eagerly, then groaned as he saw she wasn't alone. That fat old woman from last night was with her, holding on to her arm.

Damnation! Bart let loose a long volley of graphic curses that would've done any one of his criminal class proud, as Mary once again eluded his evil grasp.

❖

More than a dozen anxious pairs of eyes lined up before their master's cold, dark blue stare in the ser-vants' dining hall at Duke Street. Colonel Sir Isaac Re-bow had summoned his staff with no prior notice on *'a matter of some urgency.'* Now, he walked slowly up and down the rigid line comprised of maidservants, scullions, footmen, butler, housekeeper, and cook, looking neither to the right nor to the left, but straight ahead. In a deceptively calm voice, he began to address his household staff.

"I've an important question to ask all of you, and I hope you'll consider your responses carefully. *Very carefully*. Do think before you speak. Now, then..." He came to a halt and moved back a step, noting the collective discomfiture of his wary servants, fixing his eye on each of them in turn.

"I would like to know the circumstances of your hiring, good people. Who was it who hired you, Saunders? Betty? John? I shall leave Robbins out, as he came with me from Wivenhoe Park, but all the rest of you...how came you into my employ here at Duke Street? I was much too busy to interview and hire staff personally before my move here. Who conducted this chore for me?"

Saunders, the tall, distinguished-looking butler, his spine straight as an iron rod, stepped forward as if volunteering to speak for the assembled group. No one took a breath as he began.

"Why, Lady Rebow, Sir Isaac. She hired us from the Servants' Registry in the Strand." The butler's deep voice was firm and confident.

Isaac snorted in disbelief. "Nonsense, Saunders! Madam never stirs from Wivenhoe Park. An emissary came in her stead to choose from among the applicants at the Registry. I simply want to know who that person was, and I do not intend to waste my time waiting for an answer to be forthcoming."

He glowered at the lot of them. It had the intended effect. Eyes were lowered; feet shuffled nervously; puffs of held-in breath were expelled. Saunders cleared his throat. "Umm, yes. Yes, sir, it was..."

"*Saunders? Betty?* Why is no one answering my knocks?" Mary Martin's distinctive, throaty voice floated huskily below-stairs, cutting short Saunders's attempt to answer Isaac's question.

Relieved at the reprieve, the staff, as one, relaxed, falling out much like an army regiment at their ease. Isaac's head jerked up in surprise. He was prepared to hear Mary Martin named as the individual who had hired his staff without his knowledge, but not to have her appear in person on his doorstep at the very instant of the revelation.

"Cousin Mary," he welcomed her. "Mrs. Pepperwit," he acknowledged the Martin family retainer. "What a delightful surprise. But what brings you to Duke Street so early?"

"A matter of some urgency, Cousin Isaac," Mary began. Someone snickered, and Isaac darted a quelling look toward the assembled serving staff.

"You're dismissed...for now," he advised them. "We shall take the...ah...other urgent matter up at another time. Be prepared." Isaac cast a meaningful glance at Saunders, whose broad brow was lightly bathed in sweat.

❖

Mary settled herself on an upholstered leather sofa in Isaac's dark wood panelled library, hands folded primly in her lap, trim ankles crossed. Mrs. Pepperwit, grumbling that her breakfast at Queen Square had been interrupted by Mary's urgent summons to accompany her to Duke Street, had gone below-stairs to have tea with the servants.

What a sweet picture of docile femininity she makes this morning, Isaac mused. *I wonder what she wants? I'm no longer her guardian, after all. Has she had a problem with her papa?* How ironic that she had interrupted the interrogation of his servants. It had taken him far too long to come to the conclusion that Mary was responsible for the staffing of his household.

He had underestimated her badly. No wonder she chafed under his guardianship; the girl was fully capable of taking care of herself, and managing others competently as well. *More fool, he, for not knowing that from*

the first. It might have saved both of them some unpleasant moments. As it stood, he had applied too heavy
a hand and ruined any chance he might have had...

"Shall I ring for tea?" he offered.

"No, no thank you, Cousin Isaac." She shook her
head.

Isaac sat down in a leather-covered armchair opposite her. She looked delectable this morning, he thought,
fresh and innocent in a green-sprigged muslin frock and
dainty white kid slippers. A vision. A lovely, unattain-
able vision...

"Cousin Isaac?" Her voice brought him back from
his musings.

"Yes, Mary?" he answered. "What's this matter so
urgent that Mrs. Pepperwit must needs be spirited away
from her breakfast?"

Mary smiled at his query, dimpling, then sobered
quickly. She looked down at her hands, still folded demurely in her lap. Her voice, when she spoke, was low
and even, yet imbued with that husky sensuality of
which she appeared to be so innocently unaware.

A courtesan, Isaac thought, not for the first time,
would kill for a voice like that. He held his breath.

"This is...this is a matter of some great delicacy,"
she began, her eyes still lowered.

"Go on," he urged her gently.

Mary looked across at him, her large eyes dark and
troubled. "We need your advice, Sally and I. She is concerned about her wedding, you see." She paused to
gather her courage.

"Never say she's changed her mind about young
Fraser!" Isaac blurted. "Ah, but I knew it was a com-
mitment entered into too swiftly, this engagement. Too
bad, but if she needs time to think, urge her to do so. If
she decides to break it off, it will be no great disgrace. I
can speak to Jamie..."

"Oh, no, no." Mary shook her dark curls emphati-
cally. "Sally would never dream of calling off her wedding to Mr. Fraser. They're very much in love. No, no, it
is not that."

Perplexed, Isaac sat back in his chair. He steepled his long fingers against his chin and propped his elbows on the chair rests. "Well, then, whatever is it?"

"Our stepmama, Cousin Isaac. Dorothy M-M-Martin," she stuttered, "Sally and I have met her, and...and...you see...we are quite distraught."

"Why are you so distraught, my dear?" Isaac asked. The girl did indeed look distressed; her lovely brow was furrowed.

"We believe her to be a Cyprian, Cousin Isaac," Mary blurted. A quick flush painted her cheeks.

"You...what?" Isaac couldn't believe his ears. He stared at his so-called cousin in disbelief. Would she never cease to astound him? A Cyprian? What did the chit know of Cyprians? And who had enlightened her? Was this all part and parcel of Emma Davenport's radical ideas on the education of women?

By God, he'd have it out with that insufferable bluestocking! He willed himself to speak slowly, to breathe calmly. "Mary...you should not be discussing such matters with me."

Mary made an impatient, dismissive movement with her hands. "Yes, yes, Cousin Isaac, I know. Men think that gently-bred women like myself and Sally shouldn't know of such...things, much less discuss them. But we do know about them and there you have it, Cousin Isaac. Our stepmother *is* a Cyprian, and Sally is mortified that Dorothy will ruin her wedding to Mr. Fraser, that Mr. Fraser's parents will make him cry off when they see it is such an unsuitable alliance.

"You're our only hope, Cousin. To whom else can we possibly turn?" Her large eyes sought his out. She leaned forward, intent on his reply.

He ran his hand abstractedly through his hair and dislodged the riband holding it back. He didn't notice that it fell softly, sinuously, onto the carpet. "Mary, you cannot..."

She stood up and went to him. Her eyes bored into his. "Oh, please, Isaac, you're a man of the world, and we need you. I need you. I..."

He was aware, dimly aware, that she had dropped the "cousin" entirely and was calling him intimately by his first name. She was warm flesh and blood, though not of his blood, and scant inches stood between them. He was attracted to her since their first meeting and had not been able to dismiss her from his mind, despite long harangues with himself whilst he was awake. Neither could he banish her from the fantasies that obsessed him during sleep. All he had to do now was reach out, as she repeated over and over in that sultry, bedroom voice that she needed him...

Isaac backed away. He felt the jut of the windowsill cutting into his hip and ignored the dull thud of pain as he made contact with the hard wood. He placed both hands palms backward on the windowsill and forced himself to hear what she was saying and to dismiss the lewd fantasies that were threatening his tenuous grip on sanity and his rigid sense of propriety.

"Mary...I would rather not have this conversation, but it is best you tell me all you know–or believe you know–immediately." He gritted his teeth.

She nodded, relating their first encounter with Dorothy at the mantua-maker's, Dorothy's behavior in Knightsbridge, and the servants' gossip there. "So you see, Cousin Isaac, we're quite concerned and have no one else to turn to. Will you not help us? Please?"

He looked into her dark eyes, wide with worry. As distasteful as this conversation was, he owed it to her and her sister to do what he could to clarify the situation. There was a Bow Street Runner, Jonas Latham by name, whom he had almost contacted in the matter of his absent uncle. He would make an appointment to see him as soon as possible. Latham could investigate Dorothy's past for him.

"All right, my dear, set your mind, and Sally's, at ease. I shall see to this immediately." He spoke reassuringly and she nodded in relief.

"Thank you...I'm so sorry if I've upset you again, but it seems to be the cross you have to bear, Cousin, in dealing with me." She smiled impishly at him.

Isaac drew a sharp breath and ran the fingers of his right hand through his long hair, wondering briefly what had become of the riband that usually held it back. Mary's enchanting, heart-shaped face was very close to his, as she had stepped forward while making her impassioned plea for his help. Her eyes were large and dark, her lower lip full and enticing.

He could smell the rosewater fragrance she favored emanating from her person and registered the shine on her glistening black hair. Her sweetly curved woman's body swayed slightly toward him, and he couldn't help but note how the thin muslin fabric both caressed and outlined the full roundness of her lovely bosom.

He was lost. There was no running away. She had literally backed him up against a wall—or, in this case— the library window. Fully realizing that he was probably making the worst mistake of his formerly orderly life, he pulled her unresisting body to his. He held her close and felt the loud, erratic rhythm of her heart as her soft breasts pressed against the hard musculature of his chest.

He lowered his head, his loosened hair falling against his face and over his cravat, and kissed her deeply and thoroughly upon the mouth. His senses rioted with the powerful impact of her clean, sweet scent and the feel of her gentle, yielding form as her soft lips parted under his. He could feel the trembling in her arms as he ran his tongue lightly along her lower lip and gently invaded the warmth of her welcoming mouth.

Mary didn't hesitate but she took his hot, seeking tongue into the soft recesses of her mouth. She moaned inarticulately and allowed him full ingress as he probed and caressed in a kiss more intimate and exciting than she had ever imagined in all her girlish daydreams. Boldly, she imitated his movements with her own eagerly searching tongue.

As if from far away, she heard him gasp, then groan. He was fondling her neck and shoulders, inching his way down to her breasts. His fingers stroked their soft smoothness, exciting their tender tips. She felt them pebble into hardness and whimpered, arching her back.

She rubbed against him, wanting more, so much, much more.

He heard her purr like a satisfied kitten as she moved her hips against his groin. He grew stiff in response to the pressure of her soft, sweet flesh; the few layers of clothing between them were scant barrier to the heat that now rose from their close embrace. His right hand moved lower, pulling at her frock; he caressed her limbs with long, gentle strokes. She didn't stop him; nay, she was cooperating fully in her seduction.

He realized he was having his way with her, with the girl-woman who haunted his dreams, in his very own library, with the door shut. In a few moments he would have her on her back on the oriental carpet. Her sweet young thighs would part, and he would...

Dear Lord! Was he out of his mind? He pushed her away, his shaking hands attempting to restore some semblance of order to her dress. Her dreamy, unfocused eyes stared up at him in bewilderment.

"Isaac?" she murmured, confused.

He looked down at her soft, swollen mouth. It appeared bruised from the ardor and force of his love-making. Her lips were parted, moist, waiting for him to continue to make love to her, to kiss her to distraction, to bed her...

"Oh, my dear," he apologized, his voice low. "My dear, I'm so, so sorry...forgive me..."

She frowned, puzzled. "Forgive you? Why?" She nuzzled his cheek with her head, wanting him, willing him, to take her in his arms once more.

He took her hands in his and kissed the tips of her fingers. "I've behaved abominably, Mary. I am an unspeakable cad...I'm so sorry."

Incredulous, she looked at him. Her face felt hot, so did her whole body. He was gripping her hands so tightly that they hurt. She heard him repeat his apology, but it still made no sense. She moved away from him angrily, humiliated and hurt.

"Isaac! Stop it!" she cried. "Don't, please don't!" She took her hands from his grasp and balled them into fists. She pounded them on his chest with barely contained fury.

"Mary..."

"No! Stop it! Listen to me, you great fool!" There were tears in her eyes now, and her lower lip was trembling. "Why are you apologizing? What is wrong?"

He drew back in surprise at her reaction. He had taken unjustifiable liberties with her innocent young person. She didn't seem to comprehend that his behavior was unforgivable, beyond the pale; rather, she seemed angry that he had interrupted their lovemaking. What was wrong with the girl? She should be exhibiting righteous anger at his licentious behavior, not this!

"Mary, please, calm yourself." He took her wildly flailing fists between his large, strong hands. "You shall do yourself an injury if you don't calm down." And injure him as well, he added silently.

She was weeping now, crying openly. He didn't know what to do, or say, except...he knew he wanted her, wanted her quite desperately. He was a victim of his debauched lust, a rake and a cad, no better than the universally despised Maximilian Trehearne. There was no way out. No, there was a way out, only one. *Only one thing to do.* A thing wholly approved by the society of which they were a part. As a proper gentleman, he knew what it was, for he had tempted her into lust, compromised her terribly.

"I shall call upon your father this afternoon, never fear. I've behaved badly and I recognize that. I shall offer for you, Mary, do not be so upset. I don't know what came over me...but I shall set things right."

"Offer for me?" She had stopped crying now and was looking him full in the face. *"Set things right?"* she whispered. Isaac's hair was wild, his cravat crumpled, his clothing mussed. He had a look of acute mortification upon his face. She had never seen him in such an imperfect, non-Isaac-like state. It was strangely attractive. But, what was wrong with him?

"Isaac...I...I don't understand." She tried to speak, to make sense of what was happening. Her insides were churning, all her senses askew. Why was he behaving so strangely after kissing her so wonderfully and touching her in such an exciting way? What had she done to repel him? Was it—the thought crashed through her brain— was it because she was not Sophia Rowley, but a poor substitute?

Isaac's face was solemn, at odds with the wild disorder of his hair and costume. "Mary, I've compromised you. We've been alone together in a closed room, and I have taken improper, unconscionable liberties with your person. The proper thing, the only thing, for a gentleman to do is to make an offer for your hand."

"You always do what is correct and proper, whatever the circumstances, do you not, Cousin?" she asked, her voice soft and cool, her eyes level with his. Outwardly, she appeared calm; inwardly, she seethed.

Isaac's head jerked back in surprise at her statement. No, he wanted to say, no, I'm going to do this because I want to, because I want you, but not like this, not now. Instead, however, and to his everlasting shame, he answered, lying through his teeth, "Yes. Yes, Mary, I do."

Mary's face paled. He cared not a whit for her. What he cared for, what concerned him, were appearances only. They were both disheveled, their grooming and dress clear evidence of what they had been doing in this private room. Anyone who chanced to walk in would see it clearly. He was caught in a situation he had, without doubt, carefully avoided for years.

Then a thought came to her, sudden and unbidden. By so doing, by making her his offer, he destroyed forever any chance of marrying his *chère amie*, Lady Rowley. Thanks to this misbegotten encounter with her, those lovers would now never wed. How could he ever forgive her that? He would hate her for forcing him into this situation. Hate her every day of their lives together...

Shaken, she moved away from him. She smoothed her short crop of curls, pulled her dress and chemise to order, straightened her stockings, and covered her half-exposed bosom. She knelt down abruptly and came up with the narrow riband that had held his hair back. It had fallen to the floor.

"Here," she said, holding the riband out to him, her tone of voice brisk. "Do repair the damage to your hair. You must set it to rights. You are overfond of setting all things to rights, are you not?" The foolish tears were dry; instead, she felt hollow, empty, inside.

He could only stare at her in disbelief, unmoving. She looked down at the slender length of material and shrugged, then walked behind him and all but pushed him into the chair. "Sit down," she said. "Allow me."

Her fingers trembled slightly as she ran them through his thick straight hair and smoothed it back from his face. She tied a neat bow, as adroitly as any his fastidious valet had ever knotted. Cocking her head to one side, she nodded, satisfied with the results of her work.

"There." She ran her hands down the sides of her frock, rubbing off the slightly waxy residue of his hair pomade "That is that."

She smiled stiffly and bent her head in order to adjust his ruined cravat. Her nimble hands unmade the numerous creases passion had engendered, but here Robbins would have wept at what he would have considered desecration of his good work.

Isaac took her hand. *"Stop it,"* he ordered, irritated at her fussing.

Anger flared warningly in her eyes, then subsided. "Please let go of me, Cousin. I would like to leave now."

"No," he answered. "Not until you understand exactly what it is I must do."

"Do whatever you want, Sir Isaac," she snapped. "It is hardly a concern of mine, I assure you."

"Mary." His voice was weary. "Please, you don't understand the enormity of this situation. Don't make matters even worse than they are now."

"Worse?" Her voice rose in anger. "I don't know what's wrong with you, Isaac Rebow! You kissed me, I kissed you in return, then you..." She blushed, remembering the heated caresses that had followed. "No one has to know what happened here between us," she argued.

"You need not offer for me, Cousin." She fixed him with a steely glare. "I would not accept you, at any rate."

"Mary." His voice cut like a sabre blade. "You do not know what you are talking about. I've compromised you. We are as good as betrothed right now. There is no way you may refuse me, not after I speak to your father and tell him what has occurred."

"We kissed each other, Isaac! You placed your tongue in my mouth, and I placed my—"

He clamped his hand over her lips, shocked to his very proper core, and quelled her brazen words. "Stop that," he warned. He shook her slightly and was about to remove his hand when he felt her sharp little teeth bite into the fleshy part of his palm.

"Bloody hell! You little vixen!" Not thinking, simply reacting to the sharpness of the unexpected pain, he brought the palm of his other hand down hard against her round rump. She jumped, squeaking in surprise.

"How dare you!" she accused him, rubbing her hand against her offended *derrière*.

"How dare *you*, miss!" he replied, breathing fire, shaking his injured hand as if waving away the hurt.

"I loathe you, Isaac Rebow!" she cried. "I loathe and despise you, you...you...*odious man!* I would never marry you! I would die a spinster, first, and lead apes in hell!"

"If you refuse my offer, you may well lead apes in hell, miss, for no one else will have you!" He brought his hand up to his mouth and sucked the sting out of his bruised palm; she hadn't broken the skin, but she came perilously close. He remembered their first meeting, when he had the urge to take her over his knee for her saucy ways and impertinent speech. *The hoyden!* He should've followed his first instinct then and brought her to heel.

Mary didn't like the threatening gleam in his eye. He wasn't a man to cross, not ever. She put both hands to her tingling bottom and backed away. *"Do not dare,"* she warned him.

"Only a madman would offer for you, miss." He moved slowly and menacingly towards her, until she was flat up against the door.

She shut her eyes tight at his words, then opened them fully, gazing up at him. Her lips trembled, and she replied with her husky, tantalizing voice, "Only a madman such as you."

"Yes." He sighed, all anger flown, all tension abated. "That is the truth of it: only a madman such as I." He placed his hands on either side of her flushed face and bent his head. His forehead brushed hers briefly. The touch of warm flesh on warm flesh sent her pulse racing.

For a long, mad, minute she thought he would kiss her again. *Oh, yes, yes,* she pleaded silently. Her mouth trembled in anticipation, then whatever remained of her wracked and confused senses got the better of her. She reached behind her and quickly unlatched the door before he realized what was happening.

She made her escape, and the door shut sharply in his face.

He slammed his hand against the wood. Unfortunately, it was the same hand she had bitten. He cried out in pain and regret. *Why had he not simply told her he loved her?*

For there was no denying it any longer. Despite his best efforts to deny the truth, he loved her. He loved her quite desperately and beyond understanding.

And she had made it quite clear that she loathed him. The pendulum of their relationship, always contrary to the laws of nature and science, swung relentlessly backward, never forward. He sighed and looked down at the ruined mass of linen at his neck. Now he would have to go to his chambers and summon his valet to make repairs.

It wouldn't do to appear before his father-in-law-to-be with a less-than-perfect cravat. Robbins would never forgive him.

Thirteen

The awful irony of asking his uncle for his daughter's hand on the very day he engaged a Bow Street Runner to investigate that same uncle's new wife wasn't lost on Isaac. The further irony was that both interviews had gone remarkably well.

Latham had acted with alacrity, promising results before week's end, and Uncle Matthew was delighted with Isaac's suit. Their lands marched together! They were kin! Isaac was like a son to him! In Matthew's eyes, it could not be better.

Isaac omitted relating the fiery scene he and Mary had enacted in his library and his compromise of her virtue. Mary was perfectly correct: no one had to know what occurred there. Despite what he said in the heat of passion, he could not stoop so low as to insinuate they had been about to make love, and, by so doing, force the match.

Love. How had it happened? How had he fallen in love with that unreasonable chit? He had done what he purposely avoided all of his bachelorhood, become enamoured of a difficult woman. He was, truly, a madman, and, as Mary herself said, a very great fool.

He stared at the books stacked on his orderly bookshelves and wondered what new and terrible coil he had gotten himself into. He had vowed for so long to keep his distance from difficult, unreasonable, headstrong females. Had he not learned a grim lesson from his parents' unhappy marriage?

Isaac grimaced. He had traveled to Colchester after his interview with Matthew to see Lawyer Ennew again, this time to discuss marriage contracts. Whatever hap-

155

pened between the two of them, Isaac was determined
Mary wouldn't lose Alresford Hall nor her dowry from
the Barnards, her real father's family. If the marriage
failed, if she wanted to live apart from him, she would
have ample means to live alone and well. She would not
suffer at his hands.

Ennew was also delighted at the news of Isaac's offer for Mary. His eyes had twinkled merrily. "Couldn't
make a better match. And right under your nose all these
years, my boy," the older man had crowed, as he tied red
ribbon around the black-and-white ledgers containing
the details of Mary's dowry.

"One of the greatest heiresses in the county. Nay, in
at least five counties! Lovely and accomplished, to boot.
You're a lucky man," the lawyer had added gleefully.

Isaac wryly acknowledged Ennew's comments.
"I've been blind to a remarkable degree, sir. My eyes,
believe me, have been opened at last." *At what price?*
He wondered if Mary would, indeed, accept him. Matthew had promised he would bring her around after
Isaac admitted she wasn't interested in his offer. He had
kept to himself her comment that she'd rather lead apes
in hell than marry him.

From Colchester he went to Wivenhoe Park to tell
Madam, in person, that he had asked for Mary's hand.
He was perversely curious to witness her reaction.

Madam was at tea in the blue and white drawing
room when Isaac arrived. She ignored his presence, and
his possible need for refreshment, as she instructed her
young companion, Miss Japp, newly come from the
Servants' Registry in The Strand, to pour her another
cup of Darjeeling tea from her favorite imported Chi-
nese willow pattern teapot.

Ignoring his mother's pointed rudeness, Isaac in-
sinuated himself directly between her and Miss Japp.
There was murder in his eyes. "Dismiss this young
woman, Madam. I would speak to you alone. *Now!*"

She nodded curtly to Miss Japp, who left the room
hurriedly. Madam narrowed her small blue eyes and
looked daggers at her only son. "What is it?" she asked

testily as Isaac seated himself across from her in a Sheraton wing chair.

"You, Madam, have a good deal to explain," he began, leaning forward, hands clasped loosely between his knees.

"What are you talking about?" Mary Rebow didn't intend to allow her son's barely contained annoyance to affect her. She thrust back at him with the mixture of rudeness and contempt that always served her encounters with Isaac.

"I'm talking about our last discussion, on the subject of the sisters Martin, Madam," he persisted, ignoring her usual bad manners.

"Ah," she drawled. "*That* discussion. When you refused to listen to my good suggestions? Was *that* the one? Do kindly refresh my memory." Her face seemed set in stone as she faced him down across the tea table.

"Yes, Madam, *that* very discussion. You somehow neglected to mention Mary Martin is not our blood kin." He noted with pleasure how the lines on his mother's face seemed to deepen.

"So?" she countered. "What of it? It's no secret! Everyone in the county knows Mary's the daughter of Viscount Barnard."

"Everyone?" Isaac tapped his heel in a hard, threatening staccato on the polished hardwood floor and looked unblinkingly at his mother. "Everyone, it seems, but I."

Madam shrugged. "You knew. You simply forgot. At any rate, your uncle adopted her. Why such a to-do about this now?" She took a deep draught of her tea and pursed her lips.

"Did you, knowing how strongly I feel about marriages between cousins, fear I might be tempted to ask for her hand if I knew she isn't my blood kin?" Isaac parried.

Madam's lips parted thinly in a cruel smile. "Call the gel what you will! Blood kin, not blood kin! What does it signify? *You* shall never wed, we both know that."

Isaac rose from his chair, smoothing the wrinkles from his gray pantaloons and adjusting his navy blue waistcoat. "We shall see, Madam." He bowed very slightly, a mockery of filial respect, a tight smile about his lips.

Madam leaned forward. "Disabuse yourself of the notion that the chit would accept any offer of yours," she hissed.

"Why would she not, may I ask?" Isaac replied.

"*You* ain't the marrying kind, and the chit's no fool. You know only Cyprians and lightskirts, just as your father before you. You offer for her, and I shall tell her all about you, Isaac Rebow, and the blighted seed from which you sprang." Her venom spurted into her son's face; she relished that he paled at the viciousness of her words.

"No, the chit ain't going to accept *you*, my dear, not after I get through with her." She smiled smugly, self-satisfied.

"You are wrong, Madam. Mary has accepted me," he lied, lying further, "and I have already signed the marriage contracts at Lawyer Ennew's."

He shot her a scornful look. "I do suggest you contemplate a move to the Dower House. It would be wise to prepare. I give you fair warning, Madam."

Madam's double chins shook in fear and in anger. *"You lie!"* she bellowed, as she watched him leave the room. "You lie," she whispered to herself, less confidently, as he left.

Isaac strode angrily from the Park and mounted the high-strung steed a waiting groom held for him. He dug his heels into the horse's heaving flanks and raced away, Madam's icy contempt echoing in his ears.

❖

Jonas Latham was a tall, rough-looking fellow, but a proud member of the Runners fraternity. He was plain-spoken and wise enough to hold his counsel, preferring not to speak unless it was absolutely necessary. He had listened with rapt professional fascination to Isaac's tale of conniving Cyprians during their initial interview.

Latham had promised to get on to the case immediately; he had many excellent contacts among the Covent Garden abbesses, and reliable informants in the low gin shops and gambling hells in that crime-ridden precinct. Isaac had advanced him a goodly purse to coax them to talk about Dorothy Scofield Martin, whose previous surname he'd gotten easily from his uncle.

Now, as Isaac awaited Latham's news, his hands supporting his head as he sat at the desk in his library, his feet in Hoby's finest Hessian boots propped on a needlepoint-embroidered footstool, he wondered how long it would take his uncle to talk sense into his stubborn daughter's head.

Isaac's life, as he'd known it, had come to a complete stop. Nothing mattered now except his suit for Mary's hand. The unruly chit had re-ordered his priorities and made a shambles of his life, and, surprisingly, he discovered he wouldn't have it any other way. She had to say yes; she simply had to.

❖

Latham's news was as bad as Isaac feared. He sat, almost numb, disgusted by the cheap publication the Runner had brought him. Some years old, creased, dog-eared, dirty, a listing of several pages similar to the notorious annual once issued by the infamous pimp Jack Harris, which supplied names, descriptions, addresses, and prices for the compliant ladies of Covent Garden.

"Here, Sir Isaac." Latham pointed to a paragraph at the top of page five, "I believe this is the person you are looking for. Dot Scofield, she called herself then."

Isaac read the listing dispassionately: *Dot Scofield, Russell Street, Covent Garden. Buxom, a true Blonde, pretty and very agreeable as to her Person. She is like a Kite, sometimes high, flying o'er the treetops and sometimes sinking low into the gutter. A fat purse pleases her above all things. Never approach her with less than Ten*

*Guineas in your hand, and half-a-crown for her servant,
for her connexions are mostly with Gentlemen of Rank
and Fortune. Other times, discarded by her Patrons,
she's to be found in the safe keeping of the renowned
Abbess, Mother Nell.*

He thrust the rag from him in revulsion, bile rising
to his throat. *How could his uncle?* He turned to Latham,
"You're sure? This is the Dorothy Scofield who married
my uncle?"

Latham nodded, adding laconically, "There's more
to tell, sir."

Isaac grimaced. But, he might as well have it all.
"Say it, then. Spare nothing."

"The lady's already married."

Isaac nearly jumped out of his chair. *"What!"*

"She was married to a farmer, Ezekiel Smith.
Smith's still alive, the marriage never legally dissolved.
Your uncle is not therefore legally wed to the wench.
Further, she's guilty of bigamy."

"Excellent news!" The Cyprian had gulled the old
man expertly. Isaac would delight in exposing her. Bigamy was a serious crime; Matthew would be grateful.
Or would he be? Isaac put that disturbing thought aside.
"Is there any more?"

Latham nodded. "Yes, sir. She's a dangerous piece
of goods, this Dot. Your uncle's in serious danger. His
daughters are also in danger."

Isaac felt the blood chill in his veins. "What are you
saying, man?" His mouth was dry.

The Bow Street Runner's tone was grim. "She and
her brother were engaged in a confidence game on the
streets. That's how she chanced to meet your uncle. He
was a cove they intended to cull, but Dot cheated her
brother and married Martin instead."

He paused to take a sip of the fine French brandy
Isaac had poured for him. "Her brother, Bart Scofield, is
a felon but lately escaped from Newgate Prison, a murderer who missed his date with the hangman. He has
caught up with Dot. My informants tell me he's boasted
openly, whilst in his cups, that he'll kill her husband and

his family for the money the husband's promised Dot in his will.

"And..." Latham paused again. "I'm told these murders will take place soon."

Isaac swore a fierce and coarse oath. He gripped the edge of his mahogany desk so tightly that his well-manicured fingernails were left with ragged edges as they scored deeply into the thick, topmost layer of veneer.

❖

Mary Martin wanted to die.

Was there ever such a wretched person as she? What could Isaac think of her after their disastrous interview in his library? First, she played the wanton, all but throwing herself into his arms, then she attempted to injure him when he thrust her away in disgust. As if those actions were not bad enough, there came the worst part, his reluctant offer to marry her.

Isaac was a man of high principle. Society, the rules of the *ton*, dictated that he make that offer. It was obvious to her that he did not want to do so. He was extremely agitated; she had never seen him thus. Isaac was *always* in control.

Yet... Her fingertips moved tentatively over her bruised mouth. She could still feel those passionate kisses on her lips. So heated, so wild. Mary trembled. What was it between them? The constant push-pull of emotions, the harsh words, the tender caresses. Too confusing! She couldn't think about it without coming totally undone.

To whom could she talk? Emma? Oh, she would die of embarrassment! Sally? Her sister would never understand. Sally and Fraser were two perfectly matched peas in a pod. Theirs was a smooth, uncomplicated relationship, no great highs, no deep lows. This, whatever it was, between her and her former guardian, was painful and hurting, blissful and joyous, at the same time. She feared for her sanity, for, surely, it would make her mad.

She returned to Queen Square in a dark mood, and the mood didn't lift. It permeated her being and surrounded her with a palpable cloud of unhappiness. She knew Emma was deeply concerned, and now Papa sent a message that he was coming to see her. She knew it concerned Isaac's offer. What was she to do? She wanted him, had wanted him for a long time, not any more as a child longs for a fairy-tale prince, but as a woman grown wants a man, as husband and lover. She knew the difference now. Bittersweet knowledge!

Did he want her? That, indeed, was the question. Had she forced him into a situation he could not, as a gentleman of high moral standards, ignore? He was in love with Lady Rowley, was he not? Surely they were longtime lovers. Now that lady was free, free to marry him.

He had already beaten one gentleman to a bloody pulp over Sophia's honor, and Mary had come between them, now that the lady was finally free to wed. Did Isaac hate her for it? *How could he not?*

But his kisses... They had told her a different story, had they not? For all her ignorance, her inexperience, she knew he had not been so reluctant to embrace her, to kiss her. Was it only because he couldn't resist his manly lusts? Was that it? She had played the wanton, knowing his lady was away, forcing him into ungentlemanly behavior he would otherwise...

Oh! It was all too confusing! She would truly go insane.

❖

Mary received her father with trepidation. Isaac had wasted no time. She smiled bitterly to herself. Was she simply another military campaign to Colonel Sir Isaac Rebow, one he had to win at all costs? Or was she just another political issue for Whig politician Sir Isaac to debate in the House of Commons? What had he told Papa? How persuasive had he been?

Now here was her papa, pleased beyond belief, wishing her happy on her engagement to Isaac. "He's like a son to me, Mary, and you are the best of daughters. You have my blessings, my dear, on this union. Mayhap we could plan a double wedding, Sally and Mr. Fraser, you and..."

"No!" She leapt from the sofa, pulling her hand from her father's. "I mean, that is..." She gave him a beseeching look. "Papa, I'm not sure..."

Matthew frowned. "Not like you, Mary, to go missish. What's wrong, my dear?" he asked kindly, patting the sofa, asking her to sit down.

Mary flushed. She, *missish!* How unfair, how could Papa... But she was acting like a milk-and-water miss, indecisive, stammering; he saw the truth of it. She took a deep breath. "I shall not marry Cousin Isaac."

"Whyever not, Mary? I assumed, that is, I thought you always looked upon him with favor. Has he done anything to displease you?" Martin's face was troubled.

He has not told him, she realized, surprised. Isaac hadn't told her father about the compromising library incident! Why? He said Matthew would have no choice but to see his offer accepted when he knew...but he had not told, or else Papa would be adamant she accept.

That had to mean he did not want her so much after all.

Well, so be it. Regret cast a gray pall over the afternoon. She lied, "Papa, I am not so sure I want to wed."

Matthew guffawed. "Nonsense, my girl! D'you wish to be put on the shelf for the rest of your life? What is there for a woman save marriage and children?" His tone softened. "I want to dandle grandchildren on my knees 'ere I depart this earth."

She bit her lips; heat stung her cheeks. Matthew rose halfway from the sofa and gently pulled her down beside him. "What is it that really concerns you?"

Mary couldn't look at him. She spoke through stiff lips. "If I do marry, Papa, I must be sure there is love."

Matthew smiled. "I took that for granted, my dear. Isaac's inordinately fond of you."

"Fondness isn't love, Papa," she replied faintly.

Matthew patted his daughter's hand. "That must

come first, Mary. In our set, regrettably, it don't always happen, neither the fondness, nor the love."

He shook his head, causing the wispy, flyaway hair to float around his face. *He looks like an aged cherub*, Mary thought. She felt guilty that she had asked Isaac to investigate her new stepmama's background. She had no desire to cause her father pain and half wished she had not set those events into motion.

"You wed for love," she murmured softly.

A faraway look gave a mysterious cast to Matthew's pale blue eyes. "Your mama was my great love, child. No other woman could hope to..." He sniffed away a tear, unable for a moment to continue.

He patted her hand briskly. "I'm happy enough now with what God has sent my way." He beamed with pleasure.

Dorothy, Mary thought, could not, by any stretch of the imagination, have been sent by the good Lord. Poor Papa! Still lonesome for Mama, and making a terrible mistake in trying to assuage his loneliness by marrying Dorothy. Her heart went out to him.

"Papa, I don't believe I can be persuaded in this. If you tell me I must..." she began, looking at him earnestly.

"Nay, daughter, never would I tell you, or Sally, you *must* wed anyone!" he stated firmly. "But I feel you are making a mistake, my very dear child, to refuse. Isaac's a serious man, perhaps too serious for a girl of your tender years, but you can turn him up sweet, eh?"

Desperately, Mary countered, "Papa, I fear his affections lie elsewhere. I cannot..."

Matthew looked puzzled, then his countenance warmed pink. "Ah, I see," he responded. "You are, perhaps, thinking of, *another lady*?"

She nodded, miserable. *Lady Rowley.* Isaac's true love. What chance had she with that sophisticated beauty as a rival?

"Do not think me unaware or remiss in my duties toward you, daughter," Matthew reassured her. "Between us, and do not repeat this to anyone, I saw fit to bring up the matter of that lady."

Now it was Mary's turn to blush pink. "You did?"

Her father nodded. "Isaac, my dear, has been a bachelor for a long time. Men...to be frank," he continued, his frankness causing heat to flush his features once more. "Men have certain needs that must...er...suffice it to say, my dear, that the issue of that lady is quite resolved. A dead issue, in point of fact. Isaac, I assure you, shall be a true and faithful spouse."

"He does not care for her?" Mary was surprised at her father's frankness, elated with his news.

"It is over and done with, Mary. Leave it at that, my dear," he replied, evading her direct question. "Now, give me your promise you will think on Isaac's offer."

Mary turned her head slightly. "Think on it?"

Matthew spread his hands palms out. "Most certainly. 'Tis not a decision to make lightly. I wish you and Sally happy, with good husbands of your own free choice. Sally has chosen well, my dear, and I wish the same for you."

So he wasn't going to force her to accept Isaac immediately, then. He wanted her to take her time and consider it. Mary thought her father not nearly as dimwitted as most people believed. He was wheedling her into a promise to consider Isaac's proposal of marriage rather than having to go back to his nephew with her outright refusal. He knew her well, her papa.

"A good place to think, away from the distractions of town, would be Alresford Hall. Leave London for the nonce, my child, consider your future in the peace and quiet of the country. What say you?"

He knew her even better than she realized. *Alresford Hall! Oh, how she longed for it!* Yes, at the Hall she would consider all her options. He wasn't going to pressure her, and a separation from Isaac would be telling. Could she live without him? By herself, at Alresford Hall, she could come up with an answer. There was much to decide, but Matthew was leaving the decision to her.

"Oh, Papa!" she cried, throwing her arms around

him. "I love you! You're the best of fathers!"

"I love you, child of my heart," Matthew reassured the daughter of his much-beloved first wife, the child of his heart if not of his loins. She did need time, and space, he thought, to ponder, but he was also sure that decision would make him, and his nephew Isaac, the happiest of men.

❖

Time, Emma thought, *to have it out with Mary.* The girl had been blue-devilled for days, sometimes surly, other times seeming on the verge of tears. She retreated into her music, strumming her Spanish guittar for hours on end, or beating away discordantly on Sally's harpsichord. Her fluctuating humors were unhealthy and beginning to grate on the ears of all at Queen Square. They needed to talk.

"Mary?" Emma knocked on her charge's bedroom door. "May I enter?"

There was no answer, just muffled sounds. Matthew had been by earlier. After his departure, Mary had raced to her room and absented herself from the household for several hours. Was she sobbing her eyes out?

Worried, Emma tried again. "Mary?"

No answer. Emma was becoming alarmed, and not a little angry. She tried the door. Locked! *"Miss!* Open the door this instant."

There was a thump, as if a large object had fallen, then silence. The governess was sorely tried. She pulled out the last weapon in her arsenal. "Mary," she called, exasperation in her voice, "if you don't unlock your door this instant, I...I shall ask Mapps to break it down."

In spite of herself, Emma began to laugh quietly. If that was not the feeblest of feeble threats. Mapps! It would take a great deal more energy than that poor soul possessed to attempt to break into Mary's room. The thought was ludicrous! The old servant could barely shuffle from one room to another. Emma held her sides, trying not to burst apart with laughter.

From inside the locked room, she heard the patter of bare feet on the wood floor, then the latch slid open. Mary's face peered out. *"Mapps?"* she queried, dumbfounded.

The governess pressed her lips into a straight line and shrugged, holding back her laughter. "Well, it was worth a try." She stepped into Mary's room and noted the *portmanteaux* on the floor. That was the sound, then, baggage thrown to the floor. Mary's eyes were dry. No weeping jag.

"Where are you going?" Emma asked, puzzled.

"Alresford Hall, Emma. Did Papa not speak to you?"

Emma shook her head in surprise. "No, my dear, he didn't. How did this come about?"

Mary sighed, sitting cross-legged on her disordered bed. "I'm going to Alresford Hall to think things over."

It was Emma's turn to be dumbfounded. She found her voice. "What things?"

Mary screwed up her face. "Cousin Isaac's proposal of marriage, for one, Emma."

"My dear! Was this why you came back from Duke Street in such a terrible humour the other day? Why did you not tell me?" Emma's hands flew to her heart in dismay.

Mary couldn't look into Emma's eyes. "I am sorry, truly, but I could not."

Emma jumped to the worst of all conclusions, given the circumstances. "What did that man do to you? That monster! How did he dare!"

"No, no, Emma, no. He was all that was proper." Mary was still not able to look at Emma. "After he kissed me, that is..."

"Kissed you!" Emma squawked, a most unladylike noise. "Where was Mrs. Pepperwit whilst all this...this *kissing* was going on?"

"Breakfasting below-stairs," Mary began, then added hastily, "but, Emma, I kissed him, also. It was not entirely his fault."

Emma stared incredulously at Mary's remarkably

serene face as she attempted to explain. "No, Emma, you don't understand, I *wanted* him to kiss me."

So, the tension between Mary and Isaac was naught but strong mutual attraction. Emma had wanted so many times to ask Sir Isaac what was behind their odd behavior, but it was none of her business. She was neither kin nor guardian. It was a bumblebroth, and she washed her hands of it.

She hugged Mary close. "I wish you happy, then, my dear, and I shall hope for the best."

"Emma, your wishes may be premature. I am not certain I shall accept."

Emma frowned. "My dear, he placed you in a compromising situation..."

"Please," Mary begged. "Papa doesn't know! Nothing so terrible occurred," she lied. "Isaac and I are, after all, adults."

Adults! The one certified adult hadn't behaved as such, and this young woman was far from adulthood, but Emma kept her counsel.

"Yes." She smiled wryly. "I have the utmost confidence in both of you." Behind her back, the governess crossed two sets of fingers.

Fourteen

The land surged with late spring blossoms, swelling with Nature's bounty. Jade-green grass pastures swayed in the gentle breezes blowing off the sea, foaming with flowering yellow cowslips, golden marigolds, the torch-like crimson heads of red clover. Reed warblers and whitethroats darted out of nests in bramble and barberry bushes deep in hedgerows; the loud 'hooeeet-tac' of the redstart sounded from nesting crevices in low stone walls; plump red-breasted robins pulled plump recalcitrant worms from the earth; the harsh, rattling call of Mistle thrushes soared from high atop black poplars.

Along the canals threading through the Essex fens grew blue corn-cockle, tall bullrush, fragrant meadowsweet, common mallow, English hibiscus, spiky musk mallow. Wild herbs perfumed the fresh country air as the golden sunshine released volatile oils in the afternoon's warmth. Feathery fronds of fern spilled over wet waterside rocks like so many green lacey fountains.

Bees swarmed in large clumped masses, following impatient newborn queens to even greener pastures, more intriguing woodlands and stone crevices. The flowering promise of the fields foretold the copious gathering of nectar by those diligent insects, and Mary was reminded of her own bees and hives, becoming more anxious than ever to set foot again at Alresford Hall.

She was eager to listen once more to what her beloved grandmother called the laughter of the bees. Grandmother said those cunning and wise creatures well understood how short was summer, and how it must be fully savored and enjoyed.

The cares and problems of dark, dirty London slipped farther away with each milepost. They'd soon stop for refreshments at the Rose and Crown, on the River Colne, a Colchester inn dating from the era of good Queen Bess. Travelling in her father's old-fashioned, badly-sprung coach was tiring, and she needed to stretch her cramped limbs. From Colchester, the road wound easily past Wivenhoe and thence to Alresford. She would be home soon.

John Coachman pulled up in the innyard of the Rose and Crown, bringing the tired horses to a halt. A post-boy scrambled to open the coach door. Mary hopped out, extending her hands to Agnes Pepperwit and Mapps.

Mapps grumbled. His rheumatic old bones had suffered mightily in the uncomfortable coach, and he saw little reason not to vent his spleen. Mrs. P. endeavored to jolly him up with the promise of a tankard of good English ale and a jellied pork pie in the inn's coffeehouse, and they tottered in together. Mary assured them she would follow shortly, but she needed to walk about before sitting down again.

A familiar whoop and holler drew her attention to a tall, rangy gentleman alighting from a magnificent, snorting chestnut stallion. Isaac's cousin, their Warley neighbor, Captain Tommy Adams. Smiling and holding out his big hand, he advanced on Mary.

"Miss Mary Martin! Back home, eh?" he boomed.

Mary acknowledged Tommy's greeting. How good it was to see his long-nosed, familiar face. She took a deep breath of crisp country air. "Yes, Captain Adams, I'm here for a while. I've so missed the Hall. How's your good wife Grace?"

"Well, well. Lovely to have you come by sometimes, Mary. Have a spirited mare, a sweet goer, y'might like. Your mare's getting on in years, should imagine, no?"

"Why, that's most kind of you. Yes, I think 'tis time she retired to pasture. I'll come see you in a day or so, thank you." She gave him a broad smile and waved goodbye, surprised and pleased at his offer to sell her one of his prized cattle.

One of her greatest pleasures was riding through the woods and fields. She had ridden in Hyde Park but was constrained by the sidesaddle females were expected to use and by the restrictions on galloping through the park. The thought of once again riding astride, running like the wind in her old leather breeches, exhilarated her. She couldn't wait to regain the freedom she had temporarily lost in London.

How had she managed those constraints? She shuddered inwardly, while conceding it hadn't been so bad in the beginning. At first, it was thrilling to be in such a large metropolis, part of the hustle and bustle of large crowds. She liked the sights and entertainment: musical events, the pleasure gardens of Ranelagh and Vauxhall, the Chelsea Physic Garden, the menagerie at the Tower, the equine acrobatics at Astley's Ampitheatre.

But the lack of open spaces in which to roam freely, the dirty air, and the unspeakable smells had finally gotten to her. She had not lied when she told Isaac she was a country girl at heart.

Isaac... If she decided to accept his offer, would she be expected to live at Duke Street? Worse, would she have to move to Wivenhoe Park? That hit her with a jolt. She wasn't partial to the Park's stone-cold neo-Palladian grandeur. Alresford Hall was a half-timbered black-and-white painted Tudor mansion, modest and simple in comparison with the ordered classical rigidity of Wivenhoe Park, but it was home.

Then there was Madam. How could she bear the brunt of Madam's company and scrutiny twenty-four hours a day? The thought was daunting. She and Sally had always shared the burden of Madam's foibles and constant demands. Now, Sally was to wed and follow the drum with Fraser. *How she'd miss Sally!* They were so close, bosom bows as well as sisters.

Sally had greeted the news of Isaac's offer with great delight. Next to Fraser, she thought the sun rose and set on Cousin Isaac. She couldn't understand why Mary needed time to think about accepting his suit. She had exclaimed that Mary was indeed the luckiest of women. *Hah!*

❖

After partaking of refreshments, Mary and her servants climbed back into the lumbering coach for the last leg of their journey. They rode along the River Colne, past the large and busy shipyard at Wivenhoe, and the neat 17th-century cottages hugging the riverbank, then turned inland.

They left behind the Colne estuary, with its muddy channels filled with a rich variety of water and sea fowl: dabchicks, tufted ducks, mallards, coots, Brent geese, cormorants, ringed plovers, redshanks, curlews, great grey and purple herons. Mary's sensitive nostrils caught the welcome and tangy salt smell of the nearby sea as they made the sharp right-hand turn at Alresford Creek. Only a few miles now...

She was home.

❖

Fraser was ebullient. "Isaac, old fellow! So, we're to be brothers-in-law! I wish you happy, my dear friend, most happy!" He noted how well Isaac looked, for once splendidly turned out in a coat that couldn't possibly have come from that obscure military tailor on Conduit Street. No, that exquisitely fitted garment of bottle-green wool draped handsomely over Isaac's impressive physique could only have come from one tailor, the estimable Weston. *Robbins must be in the boughs,* he thought.

Isaac smiled ruefully at Fraser, unaware that his splendid new Bath superfine coat was causing such a reaction. "I wish I could accept your good wishes, Jamie, but they're premature. Miss Martin hasn't yet accepted my offer."

Fraser's good-natured face fell. Dumbstruck, he sat down heavily on the nearest chair in Isaac's drawing room. "I say, Isaac, I'm sorry. I didn't...that is, Sally told me..." he mumbled.

Isaac clapped a hand on Fraser's shoulder and assured him he had not spoken out of turn. "No, never say you're sorry, Jamie. The young woman is...well...she has not made up her mind to accept me. She has gone to Alresford Hall to contemplate my suit."

"I say, Isaac." Fraser twirled his curly-brimmed beaver hat in his hands. "You seem altogether quite sanguine about this state of affairs."

Isaac shrugged, his obviously unpadded shoulders lifting the fine fabric of his coat; he poured brandy for his friend. "What is there to do? I cannot, nor am I about to, force the lady into acceptance. That—" he grimaced—"would be odious. "

"Can you...are you free to discuss the matter, Isaac?" Fraser ventured diplomatically as he took the brandy snifter.

Isaac collapsed wearily onto the elegant Chippendale sofa, an addition to his recently refurbished drawing room, and sighed. "Miss Martin," he began, carefully choosing his words, "isn't so sure she wishes to wed anyone."

Fraser looked perplexed. "What, then? Does she want to remain a spinster?"

Isaac smiled. "She is an heiress in her own right, Jamie, and can do whatever she desires. She's an independent woman, not dependent on any man for status, wealth, or happiness."

"So, it's true?" Jamie murmured.

Isaac's ears perked up. "What's true?"

"Oh," Jamie leaned forward, elbows on knees, snifter loosely held in both hands. He rotated the glass slowly. "It was rumored at the Granthams' ball that Mary was a great heiress."

He grinned, looking very much a roguish boy, as he further explained. "My old chum Bradshaw became immediately and completely enamored of her on that notable occasion. As did several other young men in our set."

Isaac snorted derisively, remembering that impertinent young whelp's attentions. "Bradshaw, yes, I've heard his noble family could use an infusion of gold into their diminished coffers. Too bad for our young lordling that Mary insists she wants no part of marriage."

"He believes your offer has taken her off the Marriage Mart, Isaac." Fraser grinned. "You're a major catch, a man who's successfully avoided the parson's mousetrap a good many years. And family, to boot."

Isaac shook his head. "Pshaw, Jamie! My offer was simply the first made. If she turns it down—" He winced, knowing that occurrence all too possible, "Well, then, young Bradshaw and the others will have their opportunities to approach Matthew. My chances are not necessarily better than those of anyone else."

"You shall have to woo her, Isaac," Jamie advised. "Woo her seriously and sincerely and without letup. Seems to me she's confused. Her life these last months, with the disappearance of her father, and your guardianship, and now the new stepmama...you must admit, it's been a life more than unusually full for a simple country girl."

He looked closely at his friend, his blue eyes narrowed. "That is, if you *really* want her, if this offer of yours isn't merely a farce."

Want her? Isaac thought. *Want her? She's become life itself to me, Jamie,* he wanted to say. His natural reserve and intense dislike of expressing publicly his most intimate concerns held him back, however, even from his closest friend.

"A farce? What nonsense! Of course I...want her, Jamie," he said stiffly. "I've offered for her, as you point out, after all these years of sidestepping eager mamas with eligible young daughters in tow."

"Do you love her, Isaac?" Jamie asked in a quiet voice, his eyes never leaving his friend's face. "More to the point, have you *told* her so?"

❖

Honey is too good for mere bears, Thomas Fuller

had written in his *Gnomolgia,* and Mary agreed. She loved the smooth, sweet, soothing taste of honey and had never feared the busy, buzzing yellow-and-black-slatted insects that worked Essex's fields, woods, and fens.

Silas Grey, the Hall's bee master, had taught her well from childhood. He took her to see bees working in the fields; he showed her the bees that populated Alresford Hall's hives and the fatter, hairier bumblebees that lived in the earth; he pointed out the strange mason bee, a solitary bee that makes its cells in mortar or sandy riverbanks.

Farmer Grey told her the story of the honey-making process, described the roles of the queen, the workers, and the drones, and was patient with the young child's questions. He permitted her—clothed in protective garments, gloved, veiled, straw-hatted—to help him smoke the hives with rush straw and the powder of dessicated puffballs.

She collected honeycombs and set them into linen bags that would be hung to allow the honey to drip from the combs into pots. The combs, later melted, would provide the beeswax for candles and furniture polish prized by the Hall's housekeeping staff.

In winter and early spring, she helped the bee master set out shallow dishes of water and wooden troughs filled with boiled honey-rosemary water or ale-soaked bread crumbs. These would keep the bees well watered and help them stave off starvation.

Mary learned how bee skeps, those coiled and plaited hives of rye straw collected from the harvest, or rush and reeds taken from marshy fens, were constructed. Each skep had only one opening, because the wee creatures detested drafts. Silas took care to keep his hives protected from rain, vermin, and marauding animals, placing them against southern-facing walls, and onto suspended wooden platforms.

The beehives at Alresford Hall were in the orchards and in the flower gardens behind the kitchens. In the spring, Silas built empty hives for the bees beginning to swarm, so they had homes to inhabit. The bee colonies were a hardy lot, consisting primarily of native and hybridized British bees.

Mary quickly got into the routine of country life. She helped with the bees, collected the herbs comfrey and horehound for medicinal concoctions, lovage and rosemary for culinary use, selected flowers to cut for house decoration, harvested tasty early lettuces and radish from the kitchen gardens, rode the mare Tommy had sold her, and fished quietly in the Colne.

She was gradually regaining the peace she had yearned for all those last troubling weeks in London, and the endless round of activity pushed aside the decisions she had come to the country to make. She thought of Isaac, but only at night when her restless mind was otherwise unoccupied. When she thought of him, she was helpless, still not knowing what to do.

She kept putting off the inevitable, making her days even more purposefully busy, so she would be too tired at night to ponder the future. *She hated her indecision!*

One afternoon, two weeks into her country retreat, she was playing gardener, using a razor-sharp knife to cut heavy branches of late-blooming purple lilac intended to fill the twin Ming vases in the front hall. She took a deep breath of the lilacs' fragrance, a sensual, heady perfume that suffused her entire being. It made her slightly dizzy.

She heard the heavy tread of footsteps behind her and assumed it was the under-gardener. Without turning to look, Mary instructed him to take the garden trug filled with lilac blooms into the stillroom.

"Your servant, ma'am, but I am not so sure where this still room is," a rich baritone voice answered.

Her heart stopped. *Isaac..Isaac! Here!*

She caught her breath, but she couldn't move. Her feet were rooted to the spot. Isaac reached for the trug and set it gently on a rustic wooden bench.

"I do hope you're not planning to do anything dangerous with that tool," he teased, indicating the sharp-honed kitchen knife she had been using to cut the tough branches.

Mary turned, then, and faced him. He was hatless, dressed in riding clothes, and carried a riding crop in one hand. Time played a trick on her, and she saw the young Isaac as she knew him when she was a child. He wore the buckskin breeches she remembered, a crisp white linen shirt open at the neck, and high, black leather riding boots. His unbuttoned, loose-fitting coat was buff-colored. The intense feelings she had for him then collided with the feelings she had for him now, and she felt a rush of such strong emotion, she could barely stand it.

"How are you, Mary?" he inquired softly, his midnight-blue eyes scanning her intently.

How could she tell him how she was? She barely had words for what she felt. She forced herself to recover quickly. Very carefully, she placed the menacing-looking knife atop the lilac blooms in the basket. Willing her lips not to tremble, she faced Isaac with a welcoming smile.

She was garbed in an unfashionable, country-style dress cut to follow her natural waistline and looked as though she'd just stepped out of an old family portrait. The dress was a pretty green and white patterned cotton with elbow-length sleeves ending in a froth of plain lace. The round neckline was modest; a half-apron of white linen with a scallop-edged border completed the costume's look. She was the very epitome of an unspoiled country miss.

Isaac thought he had never seen anyone, anything, so beautiful in his life.

She glowed with good health and loveliness, her dark eyes sparkling, her cheeks rosy. His eyes lingered on her mouth, full, moist-lipped, inviting... He remembered their last encounter, and how softly and eagerly that dear, sweet mouth had yielded to his. His lips felt dry; he licked them quickly, nervously.

Finally, she returned his greeting. "I'm fine, Cousin Isaac, and how are you?" The day was slightly humid. The morning sun slanted through the tall bushes, highlighting the auburn sheen in his dark hair. Her hands itched to reach out and up and run her fingers through those thick, soft strands, to loosen his long hair from its restraining riband.

She loved his hair, the sensual way it contradicted the severe propriety of his usual everyday costume. She imagined him a swashbuckling pirate, gold ring in one ear, leaping from a ship's mainmast and catching her by the waist, his long hair sweeping across his shoulder and brushing her face. She could feel the texture of those soft, individual hairs against the warm flesh of her cheek. She felt hot, as if the day's humidity had suddenly overcome her.

He noticed the quick flush that came and went and reddened her neck and chest, and wondered what was going through her mind. *Why did he make her so nervous and out of sorts?* He clenched the riding crop tightly and willed himself to ignore her reaction.

But the silence between them had already grown too long and too heavy, weighted with things unsaid. He spoke hurriedly. "I— Madam and I, were hoping you would join us for dinner? Madam says she's not seen much of you since you returned from London."

Mary bit her lower lip. She was purposely avoiding her aunt. Her days were serene, and she had no wish to disrupt them with Madam's demands. Dinner with her and Isaac would be a strain. "Tonight?" she repeated.

He smiled down at her. "Tonight, or tomorrow night, if you prefer. I apologize for the short notice, but it is the country, after all. We have always been less formal here, have we not?"

Mary swallowed. She suspected this dinner invitation was simply a ploy: he had come to the Hall for her answer. She could continue to stall, but to what purpose? Tonight, tomorrow night, now, 'twas all the same. She owed it to him, to Papa, to give an answer.

As if he read her mind, he reassured her. "I've not come to press you for an answer to my offer, Mary. Pray set your mind at ease. This call's on a different matter entirely." He looked about the garden, only a stone's throw from the bustling kitchen quarters. "Is there a more private place than this where we can sit and talk?"

She felt foolish. Her agitation was showing. *The curse of her expressive face!* She could hide nothing from him. She led him to a bench in the formal Tudor garden, the oldest of the Hall's landscaped gardens.

The Tudor garden was a serene and pleasant spot, a square, walled enclosure sited by the landscape architect to be overlooked from the small side terrace that abutted the Morning Room. Four knot gardens, that intertwining Elizabethan conceit made up of herbs, small trees, and flowers, were set in each corner of the square.

A marble fountain bubbled gently in the center; it was surmounted by a woodland sprite, an eternally mischievous smile sculpted on its fey face. Silas had set several straw skeps into the low, enclosing walls, two on each side, and the low, buzzing murmur of bees could be heard under the sounds of the falling water.

Isaac looked about the placid garden setting and commented, "Alresford Hall has so much more charm than Wivenhoe Park. The Park's severe and cold, reeking of classical proportion to a fault. No wonder, Mary, you hate to leave your home."

Yet another reason for saying no to your offer, Mary thought. Masking her inner feelings, she indicated the simple white wood bench. "Pray be seated, Cousin."

Isaac sat, absentmindedly flicking the leather crop against his tight-fitting breeches. Mary found herself drawn to the unconsciously rhythmic movement, fascinated by how closely the buckskin clung to her cousin's muscular thighs. She quickly pulled her eyes away, embarrassed he might catch her bold stare. Her eyes then lit on his bare head, and how his hair shone in the bright sun...

She was flustered; she couldn't stop looking at his face, his hands, his long, athletic legs. She was starved for the sight of him, that was the truth of it. But Isaac seemed not to notice her blatant stares; he focused his gaze above her dark head, as if momentarily transfixed by the behavior of a colony of swallows as they swooped for insects in the kitchen gardens and flew up again on a passing current of air. He cleared his throat slightly, his eyes still on the noisily-chirping birds.

"Mary, I've come to relate to you the outcome of the investigations into your stepmother Dorothy's background, as you requested."

Mary snapped to attention. Heedless of her recent decision to hide her emotions, she clutched at Isaac's sleeve. "Oh! You must tell me, Isaac! Was...is...what we feared, true?"

Isaac was amused by the childlike eagerness of her voice, at the unselfconscious way she clung to his sleeve. Mindful, however, that it was hardly an amusing matter, he stifled his smile and took her hand in his, gently turning it over, palm up. "Not a pretty story, Mary," he warned her.

"Oh dear...is it very bad?"

He nodded, keeping her hand cradled in his. She was so eager to hear him, he noted, she didn't pull away. He stroked his thumbs against the smoothness of her soft palm and savored the sensual touch.

"I engaged a Bow Street Runner, Jonas Latham. He was able to get to the heart of the matter. In short, Mary, without going into the unsavory details, your stepmama, or, I should say, your ex-stepmama, was exactly as you and Sally suspected."

"Ex-stepmama? Has Papa had the marriage annulled?" Mary's eyes searched Isaac's face; her customarily husky voice was high and excited.

Isaac gazed at her thoughtfully and turned her hand over in his. "There was no marriage, Mary. Dorothy already has a husband. She deserted him years ago, but they are still legally man and wife. Your father was never legally wed to her. In point of fact, Dorothy is a bigamist."

"Oh," Mary whispered, as the full implication of her father and Dorothy's relationship hit her. "Oh! Poor Papa!"

"Yes, just so," Isaac commented wryly. "Latham and I met with your father and told him the full story. I didn't," Isaac assured her, "tell him anything of your part, or Sally's, in this sad scenario. I...er...I pretended that Dorothy seemed familiar to me...that I had...um... run into her. That is, that I had seen her...in a particular...ah...situation...some years ago."

Mary nodded, not noticing his stuttering embarrassment. Her heart was beating rapidly. Isaac had done this, as he said he would. He kept his word; he had done it. And it was true, all of it. A terrible thing, and all true. *Papa! She could weep for him.*

"I must tell you, however, Mary, that I would have let this whole affair be, let your father be happy with his new bride, unsuitable though she was, if not for two things."

"What things?"

Isaac shifted his weight on the fragile bench, crossing his legs. "One, that Dorothy already had a husband, and two, that she and her vile brother, a criminal of the lowest sort, were planning mischief against your family."

Mary shot from her seat. *"What!"*

"Sit down, love, sit down," Isaac pleaded, unaware of the endearment that had escaped his lips. "Latham and I have taken every precaution to guard all of you. Don't fear." He grinned, "What do you think of your new groom, Jeremy Walker?"

Confused by this abrupt change of subject, Mary nonetheless answered, "Jeremy? He came from Warley, along with the mare Tommy Adams sold me. Tommy said Jeremy was an excellent groom and would help me train Blossom. We did need another stablehand, so I hired him."

Isaac continued to grin. Dimly, Mary noted she had never seen him smile so broadly. A dazzling smile it was, too, one that changed his entire appearance, made him seem younger, less stern, made him even handsomer...

He said, "I brought my cousin Tommy into our plans, Mary. I hope you don't mind what I had to tell him, but it seemed best at the time. I bought Blossom from Tattersall's and asked Tommy to pretend it was from Warley, and that Jeremy was one of their stable lads. Jeremy is actually a fledgling Bow Street Runner, a *protégé* of Latham's."

A tiny gasp of admiration escaped Mary's lips. "You're truly an amazingly resourceful gentleman, Sir Isaac Rebow. Did you learn your strategies from the Indian Wars or from the Byzantine machinations of your Whig politics?"

He laughed, a rich, throaty baritone that quite took Mary's breath away. She had never heard him laugh before! Like the grin, it was dazzling. He was a different man, more appealing, more human. Why did he not laugh more? He had grown far too old, far too serious, all too soon. She harkened back to her childhood and realized he was old even then, an old man in temperament when in reality a mere youth.

Oh, Isaac, she pondered, *what made you grow so old so soon?*

Isaac continued his sad tale of the disintegration of her father's marriage. Matthew had closed the Knightsbridge house and moved to Queen Square. Emma was apprised of the situation and was only too willing to help.

Never would he forget the look on the old man's face when he and Latham had revealed the truth about Dorothy. Matthew was devastated, heartbroken. Watching his expression, Isaac swore he had aged ten years in ten minutes, before his very eyes.

Mary pressed him to supply more details. Isaac sighed and continued. "We confronted Dorothy and showed her the proof we had of her sordid background. She attempted, of course, to lie, but to no avail. She had to admit her guilt, and her knowing, if—as she protested—unwilling complicity in her brother's criminal actions."

Mary wiped away a tear, a tear for Papa and perhaps also for poor Dorothy, and remembered how playful the two had been that day in Knightsbridge. Like two affectionate kittens. She wanted to believe Dorothy had some feeling for Papa. There was no denying that Papa did care for her.

Again as if reading her thoughts, Isaac spoke. "Your father was a very lonely man, Mary. He had been lonely for a good long time. He loved your mother very much and had never gotten over her untimely death."

Mary nodded, unable to speak, choked up with sadness for her father, for Dorothy, for the death of love. No, that wasn't true. *Love didn't die!* Papa kept his love for Mama in his heart, and it was still there; it would be there long after he forgot all about Dorothy.

"Mary?" Isaac was looking at her expectantly. She had allowed her mind to drift, and Isaac wanted to finish his story.

"Now," he continued, taking hold of her hand once again, "we had to apprehend Scofield, Dorothy's vile brother, before he could harm any of you. However, he had the wind up from his criminal cohorts, the ones who accepted Latham's bribes for information."

Isaac shook his head, a wry half-smile on his visage. "Honor among thieves... To sum up, Bart has disappeared from sight. No one knows where he is."

"Surely," Mary argued, "he cannot mean to do us damage now, not when you've uncovered his schemes? Why would he..." Her voice trailed off.

"I wish I could agree with you, my dear." Isaac's voice was somber. "But Bart contacted Dorothy and warned her he would have his revenge on us for thwarting his plans. Dorothy was terrified, out of her mind with fear, and told us."

Isaac squeezed Mary's hands, which had gotten cold, and noted her face was blanched of color. "Don't worry, Mary, we shall apprehend him. In the meantime, you're all under watch, just in case Bart makes an appearance."

Isaac searched Mary's face closely. "You know I would not let anyone harm you, do you not?"

She met his gaze and could not mistake the tenderness and concern she saw there. "Yes," she whispered, meeting his eyes. "Yes, I know that." Isaac would take care of her. He took care of her and Sally when Papa abandoned them and although initially reluctant, had been a protective, if over-protective, guardian. His good word was his bond, she had no doubt of that whatsoever.

He rose from the bench, picking up his riding crop, "That is the full tale of Dot and her villainous brother. Quite a pair, but I have strong hopes we've seen the last of them. Well, Mary, shall you be dining with me and Madam tonight?"

"I don't know, Isaac. You've given me much to think about, to absorb..." She was a trifle breathless, aware he still held her hand in a firm grip. She saw a disappointed look flit across his face.

An inspired thought struck. "Why not dine here, with me? There are still a number of questions I would put to you."

Isaac grinned and pointed out his casual attire. "What? Dine at table with you, dressed like this?"

She laughed, a high, pretty sound. "It's the country, after all, Cousin. We can dispense with formalities here. I can send a footman to the Park to say you'll be dining here, and I'll gladly dine with the two of you tomorrow night."

"That sounds excellent, Mary, so long as you're sure you don't mind." Again, he indicated his clothing with a sweep of his riding crop.

"Set your mind at rest, please! As you can see"— she pointed to her own attire—"this is not the latest fashion by any means, and, to keep you company, I shall not change. Now, while I consult with the cook, will you not take your ease in the Library with a glass of Madeira?"

Isaac's face had softened with her invitation. "You look lovely, my dear, and it's most pleasing to see a woman's waist where Nature intended it!" he teased.

Mary blushed at his bold reference to her body but accepted his compliment with a smile. It had been an amazing afternoon, she thought. She and Isaac had conversed in a civilized, adult, respectful manner, neither sparring verbally nor falling indecorously into each other's arms.

It boded well for the future, a future they might share together, did it not?

Fifteen

Isaac relaxed in the spacious Library. He sipped a glass of excellent Madeira and looked out at the exquisite Elizabethan knot garden, where he had just had the most extraordinary conversation with Mary.

That conversation, the sorry tale of a courtesan who manipulated a simple minded country squire into bigamy, was not what was extraordinary. That he and his ex-ward had managed to converse in harmony without quarrelling was the extraordinary thing, a major step forward in their checkered relationship. They were mutually courteous and respectful, had conversed as adults, and it ended with Mary inviting him to dinner.

Extraordinary!

He sipped the excellent wine slowly and considered the situation. Perhaps now was the perfect time to ask for her considered decision. It was several days past the time she had agreed to give him an answer. Despite his pledge earlier in the afternoon not to press her, they were in such good accord, that perhaps now she would accept his suit. Surely, their ease with each other boded well, did it not?

This was a good Madeira, he thought, as good as any he had in his own cellar. Curious, he pressed the curled label flat so as to read it better. Why, that...! It was from his cellar at Wivenhoe Park! Matthew had done it again. The man was incorrigible. He grinned and toasted him in absentia, "Here's to you, you old reprobate!" He drained the glass in one swallow.

Isaac was supremely sorry for his uncle. He had expressed his honest feelings to Mary concerning the advice he would have given Matthew to minimize the embarrassment of inadvertently taking an ex-Cyprian into his family. It could have been done, he had told her, but Dot would have had to be hidden, kept in the background. No association with the family would be allowed.

However, Dot was not simply a Cyprian, but also a bigamist, and the sister of a murderous felon who was threatening the lives of the Martins. Isaac was sorry his uncle was robbed of a chance at happiness in his twilight years, but there was no other recourse. Dot had to go.

Matthew knew she had to go, and that knowledge had broken his spirit. Dorothy's protests that she was given no choice by her brother save to do what he ordered, had fallen on deaf ears.

Matthew was forced to accept the whole, sad truth of it: Dot would have allowed her villainous brother to murder them all for Matthew's money and the guarantee of her own life. The poor man, Isaac mused, had sincerely believed Dot loved him.

Love. Isaac sighed. A dangerous and fearsome emotion. He knew that; it was the reason he'd avoided it conscientiously for years. Now he wondered if, like poor Uncle Matthew, it would destroy him, too.

❖

Bart bid his time. He was patient. He had acted instinctively the day he missed his chance with the old cull's chick, when he followed the girl and her fat servant to the flash cove's house on Duke Street. He overheard the first part of their conversation, about Dot's notorious past, from a listening post outside the library window. He knew, then, they were in for it.

The game was up. Bitter knowledge. He wanted to hear more, but left in haste when a big, hulking groom came out of the stable mews and almost spotted him hunkering below the window.

Dot! That stupid bitch! He knew she would tell all and put the finger on him. Her survival first, that was how she thought. He was right, too. A few days later, when the flash cove and the Runner Latham—he spat at the name—had told all to the old man, he had heard it all. Dorothy threw herself at her so-called husband's feet, begging forgiveness. He saw it all, Bart had, right under their noses, outside the window again, the whole time.

Well, the bitch paid for it, and the others would, too. He'd caught up with his sister and slit that pretty, lying white throat ear to ear when she had run to the Gloucester Coffee House in Piccadilly, to purchase a ticket for the Dover stage. Her numbskull of a husband had given her a fat purse and sent her on her way, even wishing her well.

Bart snorted. Wished her well, indeed! She'd fallen right into his hands. She didn't have a chance to call for help. Her wide, panic-stricken eyes saw their last of this sweet green earth when they saw him, waiting for her in the alleyway behind the ticket window.

The Royal Mail guard would find her in the morning, and he would be far away, with Martin's fat purse in his pocket. *Traitoress!* She paid the price for double-crossing him. So would they all pay the price...he couldn't wait to settle the score.

He stole a horse out of the Royal Mail's stables and made his way north and east for Essex.

❖

The fish course was remarkable, two fat brown trout served in a smooth, tasty, tarragon-flavored wine sauce. Mary had caught the fish with her own hands that morning in the Colne. Isaac complimented her extravagantly, both on her fishing skills—she had caught the trout with a fly-casting rod—and on her cook's elegant presentation.

Mary dimpled prettily. Cleverly, she reminded him of the old English saying, "Fish must swim thrice—once in water, a second time in sauce, and the third time in wine...in one's stomach."

He was charmed by her sweet, vivacious demeanor

and once again reminded of her competence and skills.
It was past time to tell her that he had finally discovered
that hers had been the guiding hand in the setting up of
his Duke Street household.

Over plates of good English pastries, maids of
honor, apple tanseys, Shrewsbury cakes and ratafia-
puffs, he apologized for underestimating her. "You
should have told me, Mary, the very first time I came to
Draycott Terrace. I was mortified to learn how much
time and energy you expended interviewing for my
household staff, hiring tradesman, neglecting your own
household in the process. Madam allowed me to believe..."

She stayed his speech with a look. "Over and done
with, Cousin. I am glad I could help." she shrugged her
shoulders. "Madam does things for her own reasons. She
did not want me to tell you, nor to contact you."

"Yet," said Isaac, frowning, "she was extremely upset when your papa disappeared and commanded me to
see all was made right."

"She wanted you to pack us off to Alresford Hall, so
we would be at her beck and call at Wivenhoe Park. I
am sure she did not want you to give us a season. She
expressed unhappiness in her letters that you were so
determined to be a concerned, active guardian."

Isaac fiddled with his dessertspoon. She had the
right of it; Madam hadn't wanted him to interfere. He
had bungled her plans for the girls, bungled them well.
Madam wanted them in Essex, under her thumb, but
now Sally was to be married off, and Mary...yes, Mary...
'Twas time.

"Shall we retire to the Library for more of
my...er...your excellent Madeira?" Isaac suggesteed.

Mary nodded and signaled to the footman to clear
the table. She rose. "Or port, if you prefer. Papa has an
excellent aged port..."

Isaac groaned inwardly, picturing that wine. *Indeed!*
he thought, *I can just imagine that excellent twenty-two-
year-old port. Yes, a fine vintage. I'm sure I know it well.*

❖

Mary had refused to consider his apology for not acknowledging her work in the refurbishing and staffing of the Duke Street townhouse, but she was secretly pleased he finally knew the major part she had played in setting up his household.

Isaac had enjoyed dinner, complimenting her lavishly on all the simple courses, far less extravagantly prepared than his French chef's creations at Duke Street, but she knew she set a far better table than the Park. Madam had a cheeseparing soul, and it was reflected at her table.

Mary was quite overcome by the flattery, and said so. He was drinking port out of a beautifully cut crystal goblet; she was drinking tea. "I am not used to such compliments, Cousin, and particularly not from you. You shall turn my poor head, I fear!" she teased.

Isaac took her comments to heart. He was ashamed of how badly he had treated her. Was it any wonder, given their history, not the least of which was the regrettable occasion when he had tempted her into lustful behavior, that she would not want to consider his offer of marriage?

"I am endeavoring to make up for my disgraceful behavior toward you, Mary. It's not meant to be mere flattery. I'm truly sincere. I have treated you badly."

Mary pitched her glorious voice low. "Isaac, please don't, I beg you...the past is forgotten." She smiled brightly. "We're friends now, remember?"

Desire gripped him, out of the blue, destroying the promises he had made to go slowly with her. He heard himself say, "I'm remembering something quite different, my dear. The last time we were together, in a library much like this one..."

She panicked at the sensually-charged images his words evoked, images that haunted her dreams and woke her at midnight. Picking up her teacup and saucer, she went to the long, arched Tudor windows overlooking the gardens. The late spring sun was setting in a blaze of golden yellow. A bucolic scene, totally at odds with the rising tide of strong emotion in her bosom.

"I apologize, Mary. I seem to have a gift for unsettling you," he said, belatedly coming to his senses.

"As I have a gift for unsettling you," she whispered, half to herself. She knew it could not last, this truce between them. If they weren't quarreling, they were teetering on the brink of inappropriate behavior. Now, she feared he was going to stand behind her, and she would feel his warm breath on her exposed neck. She would quiver and moan and...

The teacup and saucer fell to the carpet in a soft splash, spraying her white kid slippers and the hem of her dress. *"Oh!"* She was embarrassed at her clumsiness.

"Allow me," he said, rushing to pick up the china, which, miraculously, hadn't shattered. "Are you all right, my dear?" he asked, concerned at her sudden pallor.

"Oh, how clumsy! If I break any more of Mama's best china, Sally shall never forgive me," she explained, placing the intact teacup and saucer on a low table.

"You've broken other pieces?" he asked. "Well, fragile porcelain breaks easily."

She laughed. "Especially when one flings it in a fit of pique at one's mantelpiece."

He looked at her, amused. "You flung your Mama's best china at the mantelpiece? Here?" He indicated the magnificent carved dark-oak Tudor mantelpiece that dominated the room.

She shook her head. "No, at Draycott Terrace, when you first came to visit. I was so angry at you!"

His lips twitched. He remembered, also, recalling how he thought she needed a good spanking from a strong hand...his. "I was rather...pompous and overbearing that day," he acknowledged.

"Overbearing! Pompous!" She faced him, arms akimbo, the high color back in her cheeks. Her dark eyes flashed. "You were *odious,* Sir Isaac Rebow! What I wanted to do was throw the entire set of china at you,

never mind merely one teacup and saucer at the mantlepiece. A poor substitute, sir!"

He threw his head back and guffawed. His laughter rang out merrily; it was infectious. She couldn't help herself, but she joined in, holding her sides to keep them from splitting.

"It was all I could do," he roared, tears streaming out of his eyes, "to keep myself from taking you over my knee!"

"Oh!" Her face was contorted with hilarity. "Had you tried," she informed him, "you would have had a grand battle on your hands, I promise you!"

He sat down on the leather sofa, weak with the effects of their joviality and laughter. "Come, Mary, sit."

She looked at him dubiously, seeming to measure the size of his large hands, their strength, and his possible intent. "I think...not." She dimpled. "Not after what you've just admitted."

He was astonished. "You cannot think...surely!" and then he laughed again at her sly implication. "My dear, nothing could be further from my mind."

He looked at her archly and raised his dark eyebrows, teasing her with his next words. "I gave up the idea of beating sense into you long ago."

"So, you realized how futile it was?" she countered.

He responded with a straight face. "Absolutely."

They regarded each other with an odd mixture of fear and longing as the air between them shimmered with tension. It was strangely quiet in the large, well-appointed room. They realized they had both stopped laughing. She moved tentatively toward him.

"Come, love," he whispered to her, his eyes hooded. Come..." He held out his hand.

"Ah, Isaac," she replied, her voice soft, "can it be so very easy, then?"

"I sincerely doubt that, Mary." His voice was low and husky now. "I believe nothing between us can ever be easy, my dear. But, perhaps, if we both try..." He held both arms out to her, as if in supplication. She swayed slightly toward him, then stepped back.

"Isaac!" Her voice rose in panic, high and frightened, as she realized where this would lead. "Don't ask me, not now, please, not now, I beg you." She backed away from him.

He rose from the sofa and forced a polite smile on his face. He fumed inside, aware how badly he had rushed his fences. His old riding master would've been furious with him. No surprise, then, that he had fallen on his face. Best he left now, before he made an even bigger fool of himself.

He remembered his mother's cruel, taunting words. They reverberated with force inside his pounding head. She said Mary would never accept him, and it was true. True! Time enough he took that to heart. He could not make her love him; Madam told the truth. *The whole ugly truth.*

He picked up his riding crop from the side table and clenched it hard in his tensed hand. "Good night, then, Mary, I shall see you tomorrow night?"

"Ye-yes, Isaac. I shall be there," she stammered. She couldn't seem to look at him. The early ease between them had dissipated entirely. Black tension hung in the air like crepe on a door dressed for mourning.

"Well, then..." He sketched a bow and took his leave. He turned briefly. "The Adamses will be there, Tommy and Grace. I didn't think you would mind."

"N-no, not at all. I enjoy their company. It will be good to see them." Her face was pale, and he wanted to kick himself for making her so uncomfortable after such a pleasant dinner and their earlier light repartee.

If he had any pride remaining, any pride at all, he would release her from consideration of his proposal and hie himself off to London. Surely, given enough time...he would forget her. Or, he would not.

❖

The Runner Latham was concerned. He heard from a valued informant that Bart had gone to Essex, swearing to avenge himself on Sir Isaac and Mary Martin. The man seemed completely mad; matters were becoming serious. Latham had to protect young Walker, his *protégé*, as well as his clients. Jeremy was inexperienced, and Bart was a murderer.

A Royal Mail guard had found Dot's lifeless body at the Gloucester Coffee House just before sunset. Her throat was savagely torn from ear to ear, her purse was gone, valuables and jewelry stripped from her person. The crime scene was drenched in her dark red blood. It bore the vicious signature of a vengeful Bart Scofield.

Latham had no choice. Leaving another Runner to guard Matthew and Sally at Queen Square, he rode hell for leather to Essex, a brace of pistols in his saddlebags. He had to reach Wivenhoe Park and warn his employer, Sir Isaac.

Pray God he would get there in time!

❖

Mary spent a sleepless night. She wished she could relive the evening, an evening that had begun with such promise, only to end in disaster. Isaac had wanted to take her in his arms, to hold her close, to...yes, to kiss her. And she had panicked, not wanting him to know how much she desired exactly those things.

Those kisses, those caresses, the opening of the floodgates of lust, would wring a *'yes'* from her lips; she would accept his proposal. Marriage would satisfy the proprieties Sir Isaac Rebow lived by, which he insisted on above all things. He had compromised her virtue, led her into lustful behavior, therefore he had to offer for her, though she knew he did not really love her.

It was Lady Rowley he loved with all his heart, and she, Mary, knew she was the cause of his losing her, for now—*consummate irony!*—the lady was finally free to wed, the impediment of her husband gone.

She remembered the way Isaac and Sophia looked at each other as they danced to the sensual music of the waltz... The image would forever haunt her. They belonged together. It was obvious to anyone who saw them, was it not?

But she loved him desperately and could barely keep from throwing herself in his arms. Her desire was unbearably humiliating. He must never know how much she loved him, when it was so clear to her that his heart belonged to another. She had to accept that.

Could she?

Mary pounded her pillow in frustration and despair as sleep eluded her and churning storm clouds rumbled outside, tossing and turning in the night sky, mimicking her movements as she tossed and turned in her bed.

❖

The bee master was up early, planning to catch a swarm. He had observed that these particular bees were itching to leave their old, crowded hive; busy scouts were already out searching for a new home. The weather, however, had been slightly humid, with the promise of rain. It had thundered mightily all last night, but no rain fell. Silas knew bees would not swarm in unsettled or rainy weather.

The unsettled weather gave him time to catch up on hive construction. To give him additional time to properly prepare the new hive, he had an under-gardener beat a pan vigorously, simulating the sound of thunder after the actual thunder had ceased, fooling the insects into believing the storm threat hadn't abated.

He worked quickly, scenting the fresh hive with herbs he knew bees loved, rosemary, bee and lemon balms; he prepared a swarm screen to lift the bees when he was ready to take them from the old hive. He also sprinkled the old hive with water, using an apparatus he rigged from a perforated garden hose to simulate rainy weather until the appropriate moment to take the swarm. Later, Miss Mary would help him; she liked to participate in anything having to do with the bees.

❖

The humidity had risen sharply, and the morning had turned rainy in earnest, a light, misty rain the next step up from heavy dew. Enough to keep the bees inside their beehives, but not enough to keep Mary from donning her breeches and shirt and riding Blossom to the river. Fishing was excellent when it rained. She hoped to catch more fine, fat, trout for Isaac's table; he had enjoyed them last night.

She pulled on a scuffed pair of leather riding boots, good enough for the country but hardly passing Hyde Park muster, and placed a rather disreputable looking farm laborer's hat upon her cropped curls.

She swallowed a cup of hot, strong tea in the kitchen and made herself a breakfast packet of bread, cheese, and apple, wrapping the whole in a large white napkin. Ignoring Mrs. Pepperwit's protest that she "sit down for a right proper breakfast," she hurried to the stables and saddled Blossom.

The mare didn't mind the soft, misty rain either. What energetic Blossom minded was lack of exercise. The two creatures moved as one over the pastureland, through the woods, and down to the riverbank. Rain curled the wispy tendrils of fine, dark hair that ringed Mary's brow, and the fast gallop brought a rosy redness to her cheeks and a glow to her great dark eyes.

Mary had a favorite fishing hole, a deep pool she could reach easily by way of a number of wide, flat rocks, steppingstones in the middle of the river. She would fill her creel with fat, silver-flanked trout in no time.

For Isaac.

Sixteen

Latham rode all night. When he reached the Wivenhoe Park gatehouse, the gatekeeper looked at him askance, then ran to the house to confirm the Runner's appointment with Sir Isaac. Isaac took one look at the exhausted Bow Street Runner and insisted that he rest. Though he protested, Isaac instructed a servant to find Latham a bedroom. There would be time enough to confer with Jeremy and ensure that young man had a cocked pistol at the ready should Scofield dare to show his ugly phiz at Alresford Hall.

For Latham confirmed Isaac's worst fears: Bart was in Essex to wreak vengeance on the Martins. The news that he had murdered Dot in London was chilling, but not entirely unexpected.

❖

Now Isaac sighed, rubbing his close-shaven chin thoughtfully as he peered through the tall, floor-to-ceiling windows in his library. Bart could be out there even now, behind a tree, watching, brooding, plotting...

Or he could be at Alresford Hall...

Isaac shuddered. Jeremy was conscientious, but it was not the easiest of assignments to keep track of Mary. She was her own mistress, adhering to no fixed schedule, going her own way at the Hall.

At least, Jeremy's cover as a groom had been better than most ploys. He knew that, when Miss Martin went to the stables to have Blossom saddled, she was leaving the house grounds. Those times, he could shadow her quietly. Now that Mary knew Jeremy was functioning as her bodyguard, however, it was harder to keep track of her. He had to be clever, indeed!

Isaac smiled at the thought that came to him when he was speaking to the young Runner, that it might be wise to keep Jeremy in his employ after he and Mary wed. The threat of a murderous felon notwithstanding, he saw the value of having another pair of eyes save his keeping watch on his impulsive young bride. His bride... Why did he persist in this torture? Why did he imagine she could ever be his?

If he had half the intelligence with which he was credited, there would be no marriage talk tonight. She had bucked violently when he tried to tempt her the evening before, knowing too well what was on his mind. He was foolish; it was a waiting game. The lady had to be wooed slowly, as Fraser advised, not tempted back into his lustful embrace.

He walked to his solid, English oak desk and unlocked the middle drawer, pulling out his old army pistols. Isaac kept them and another pair cleaned and in prime working order. An excellent shot, he practiced at Manton's range in London whenever he could and took game with the Park's keepers when in residence. His aim was lethal, whether with stationary or moving targets, but it had been a long time since his object was killing a man.

A coach drew up, heralding the arrival of dinner guests. It would be an early dinner, befitting his taste for country hours. Drinks in the drawing room, a leisurely meal in the grand dining hall, music in the drawing room afterward, then an early departure for his guests. Latham, having rested and supped, would accompany Mary back to Alresford Hall, his pistols at the ready.

Isaac rubbed his temples in a fruitless attempt to work out the anxieties that were overtaking him. The night loomed long.

❖

The Adamses were announced by Swinton, Ma-

dame's heel-clicking, very proper butler; Isaac greeted
them with genuine pleasure. It was a long time since
they were guests at Wivenhoe Park. Indeed, it was a
very long time since there had been any guests at all at
his country residence. Madame wasn't fond of her
neighbors, and the sentiment was mutual.

"Grace! Tommy! How good to see you. May I offer
you sherry? Claret?" Isaac shook Tommy's hand and
kissed the tips of Grace's fingers. He gave Grace another
glance. She was in looks tonight, splendid looks; she
positively glowed. Grace Adams was almost pretty.
And, wonder of wonders, she wasn't attired in one of
her many riding costumes.

A flattering blue muslin gown draped Grace's tall,
Amazon-like figure, emphasizing her high, full bust and
long, straight legs. Her body, Isaac realized, could have
served as a model for classical Greek statuary. What a
lovely form! Why had he not noticed it before? Those
riding habits had effectively hidden her womanly shape.
Well, well, he thought, *what a surprise.*

"Sherry's fine with me, Isaac." He looked at his
wife. "Think Grace could do with some lemonade, if
y'have it."

"Of course! Swinton, please see to a glass of lemonade for Mrs. Adams." Isaac went to the liquor cabinet to
pour Tommy's sherry. He wondered briefly why Grace
was eschewing hard liquor. Good old Grace could put it
away as easily as any man he could name. Perhaps she
was indisposed? He hoped not. To make certain of a
quality meal, he had sent to London for his chef, Monsieur René. Isaac well knew the Park's ordinary fare left
a good deal to be desired.

Heavy wheels crunched on the gravel outside. Another carriage. *Mary...*

Isaac's heart skipped a beat, then made up for the
omission by beating in double time. *I am behaving like a
lovesick schoolboy,* he thought, all the while knowing he
had never once been lovesick, schoolboy or no.

"Mary! 'Tis been an age!" Grace positively whin-
nied as Mary made her entrance, enveloping her slight

form in her strong arms, lifting her off the floor.

"How good to see you, also, Grace...and Tommy." Mary smiled, dimpling, as she slowly extricated herself from Grace's exuberant greeting. "Isaac." She extended her hand tentatively, her eyes warming as she regarded his dinner costume.

Isaac hadn't wanted to overdress for country dining, but his black trousers and coat, contrasting with a crisp white linen shirt, grey silk vest, and simply arranged neckcloth, suited him to perfection. He rivaled the Beau in his understated elegance.

Mary was dressed in one of Mlle. Dumont's most elegant creations, a bright apricot high-waisted, low-necked, sprigged muslin that flattered her glorious dark coloring and gave more than a hint of her curvy figure.

Remembering the feel of her under his hands, Isaac's eyes warmed with pleasure. As he looked at her, he saw that she, too, remembered. A light flush had arced along her high cheekbones. *Delicious.* Achingly delicious... If Tommy and Grace were not present... He brought himself under control and brushed his lips lightly but intimately over her knuckles. Her flush darkened perceptibly.

Tommy, not noticing the suppressed excitement crackling in the air, broke in, evidently feeling he must make an apology concerning the mare, Blossom. "Did not want to deceive you, Mary, with Blossom and Jeremy, but Isaac thought it best."

Mary laughed. "You two rascals wouldn't make successful conspirators, I think. You're scarcely able to keep a secret for very long! But I thank you, both, for Blossom. She's a dear."

"Speaking of secrets," Isaac began, pouring a glass of sherry for Mary and another for himself.

Mary's ears perked up. "You've news of..."

Isaac nodded. "Yes. Tommy doesn't know the latest, either. The Runner Latham arrived early this morning and related the news of Scofield's whereabouts." He paused and took one of Mary's hands. He noted how cold it was, and chafed it with his.

"That the felon who wanted to do your uncle in, Isaac?" Tommy asked, frowning.

"The very same, Tommy," Isaac replied. "Suffice it to say, for now, we must all be very careful. Latham suspects Scofield may be lurking in this vicinity."

Mary paled. Tommy stifled an oath. Grace looked concerned.

Isaac attempted to sound reassuring. "Latham and his *protégé* are on alert. We shall also inform all of the servants." He omitted mention of Bart's cold-blooded murder of his sister.

"Does Madam know anything about this, any of it?" Tommy asked.

Isaac smiled thinly. "The less Madam knows, the better. At any rate, Latham's resting from his hard ride. He shall be ready to accompany Mary back to the Hall tonight with Jeremy."

"What about you?" Brow furrowed, Mary questioned Isaac. "Who will guard you?"

He was touched beyond measure at her concern. "I shall be fine, my dear. I have superb survival instincts, honed to a turn in India...*and* Wivenhoe Park." He laughed, drained his sherry glass and poured another.

Grace spoke. "Isaac? Mary could stay with us at Warley until this villain's apprehended."

"Kind of you, dear Grace." Mary squeezed the older woman's hand, "but Jeremy accompanies me at all times. With both Runners on the case, I have no fears."

Isaac patted her shoulder. "Nor should you, my dear. They are excellent fellows. No one will slip by them. As for me, with the protection of my firearms here at the Park, and, of course, the presence of Madam—" he pointed toward the Constable portrait hanging over the white marble Adam mantelpiece, "*Who* would have the audacity to storm Wivenhoe Park when she is holding court?"

He was chuckling when Madam entered the room, snorting, "*Holding court*, indeed! What foolishness are you chattering on about now?" She was garbed in a full, old-fashioned cream satin gown that laced up the front and exposed more bosom than was seemly. Emanating from her square, stocky person was a heavy, flowery scent that quickly permeated the room.

Her face was painted a ghastly white and her cheeks were rouged carmine. Greying white hair stuck out in poufs all over her head, threaded through with strands of pearls. Large ruby drops hung heavily from her ears.

"Seems to me, dear son, rather than my holding court, 'tis you who should be holding your tongue." Heels clicked behind her and she turned to see Swinton arriving to announce that dinner was served.

"I must thank you for taking time from your busy schedule to join us." He crooked an elbow towards her. "Do allow me to give you my arm." He extended his other arm towards Mary. "Cousin Mary, please take my other arm. I vow, I don't know when I have had two such lovely women on either side of me. I am well and truly blessed this evening."

Madam wasn't about to let what she interpreted as blatant sarcasm pass unnoticed. She was also irked at his reference to her tardiness and sloth. News of his various lady-loves had reached her from time to time—dropped by ill-intentioned acquaintances—and so she seized the opportunity to chide him, however inappropriate the occasion.

"I doubt 'twas so long ago, *dear son*, that you had more than one woman on your arm...mayhap you've had more than one in your bed, as well," she snapped at him, flourishing her large feathered fan in his startled face.

She leaned across Isaac's broad chest, her powdered hair dusting his dark jacket and leaving a white streak in its wake. "A fine guardian, you, for Mary and young Sally! *A rake for a guardian!* Never have I heard the like! I wonder how that old fool Ennew allowed it."

Tommy, bristling, leaped to his cousin's defense. "Never a rake, not Isaac! Rebow men don't run with that sort, never have!"

Madam looked at her late husband's nephew with disdain. "Why, Tommy, I didn't notice you and your wife were here." She cast Grace a contemptuous glance.

"How could you *bear* to leave your stables, even for one night?"

She jabbed Isaac in the chest with her fan. Bits of feather fluttered onto his powder-dusted coat and stuck there. "Like father, like son! Ladybirds and light-skirts...that's a *Rebow* man for you." She marched off, escorting herself to the dining hall.

Isaac slowly and deliberately took a large white linen handkerchief from his pocket and flicked it at the white smear on his chest. His face was mottled red with humiliation and anger, but his voice was strangely controlled. "There, that's better. Now, shall we go in to dinner? Mary?" He folded the square of cloth and extended his arm.

He seated Mary at his right hand; his mother seated herself at his left. Tommy seated his wife beside Madam, and he took the place next to Mary. Both Adamses appeared mortified, noticeably embarrassed by Madam's vicious remarks. Mary lowered her eyes to the table, her discomfort apparent.

Isaac sat down at the head of the table and carefully unfolded his napkin. His mother was in rare form. He knew it would only get worse. *Much worse!* His guests were probably wishing Madam, and, no doubt, him, at Jericho, while wondering why they had been so foolish as to accept his invitation. He had to control himself, as he always did, to ignore Madam's pointed barbs and vicious attacks, for all their sakes.

It would not be easy. He knew from long, sad experience it never was.

❖

Mary was shocked to the core at Madam's atrocious behavior. The realization hit that she had never, ever, seen Isaac and his mother interacting. Madam's loathing for her son was unremitting; she did not let up on him throughout the interminably long dinner.

Isaac, who soon regained his characteristic unruffled composure, continued to ignore all of her vicious sallies, her belittling of his appearance, his ambitions, and his idiosyncracies. His conversational *ripostes* were airy, witty, and sanguine. He did not allow Madam to get under his skin, while deflecting any barbs she attempted to throw at their guests. *He was,* Mary thought, *magnificent.*

How does he do it? she wondered. Madam seemed oblivious to their presence, hers and the Adamses, paying scant attention to her guests while constantly finding fault with her son. *Has it always been this way?* Mary wondered. *Is this why he so dislikes living at the Park? Is it why he joined the army?*

Mary and Sally had always found Madame burdensome and demanding, but this, *this* was excruciating. *She was a demon.* Poor Isaac! She wanted to tell her aunt to stop, to let Isaac be. Worse, she had the urge to hurl the largest platter on the sideboard at her, to stifle her appalling comments. Mary was ashamed of her base thoughts, while the poor Adamses were speechless.

Desperately, Mary cast about for something to say, to interrupt the cruel monologue dominating the conversation, to lighten the tension. Nothing came to mind until the fish course was removed.

"I am sorry Monsieur René chose not to prepare the trout I sent down from Alresford Hall, Isaac. Perhaps he didn't care for the wine sauce receipt? But Colchester oysters are a lovely delicacy, and they are presented so beautifully..."

She got no further. Madam turned a baleful eye on her niece. "*Trout?* What trout? Kindly explain yourself, my dear."

"The trout I caught this morning in the Colne and had Wilson bring to you," Mary began.

"Oh, those! I instructed the servants to cook them for their supper. Without the wine sauce, o' course! *Foolish* to waste good wine on the likes of servants." She harumphed.

Mary attempted to hide her disappointment. "Well, do save the receipt, then, for the next time Monsieur René considers serving trout. He may find it interesting."

Madam dug into her scalloped oysters with gusto. She answered with her mouth full. "Cannot. Tore it up. Cook—Mrs. Bates—said it was of no account. Agreed with her."

Isaac was incredulous. *"You tore up Mary's receipt? You gave the fish she caught for me, for us, to the servants for their dinner, Madam?"*

Mary broke in quickly, glossing over Madam's rude rebuff of her gift. "'Tis of little import, Isaac. I go fishing all the time. I shall send you more the next time I go."

Isaac appeared thoughtful. "Perhaps I shall accompany you, Mary. It has been a long time since I fished the Colne. The last time...I don't remember, Tommy, was it with you and your father?"

"Did a lot together when we were young 'uns, Isaac. Fishin', ridin', huntin'," Tommy mused nostalgically.

"Good times, Tommy, good times." Isaac smiled, remembering those salad days.

"And little Mary!" Tommy chortled. "'Member how she tried t'tag along, Isaac? Dogged our footsteps regular-like, she did! Used to hide in the stable hayloft when we curried the horses... Caught her once, eyes big, listening to our boys' talk."

Mary blushed. "I remember hiding, Tommy, but I do not remember you ever caught me. Indeed, I'm sure you barely noticed I was alive, although I admit I endeavored to follow you both. Alas, I was too small, my legs too short. I couldn't keep up." She smiled. "You were so tall, so big and marvelous...quite overwhelming creatures for a little brat like me."

"You were never a little brat, Mary," Isaac assured her tenderly, his eyes filled with warm regard.

Mary flushed, basking in his ill-disguised admiration. Madam, eyes narrowed, looked closely at them and snorted.

"*Little brats*...that's one thing I'm grateful for, Isaac. Couldn't abide *little brats* running about the Park. Bad enough when you were small! Good thing no one will have you. Would quite ruin my peace and quiet to have *your* brats underfoot."

Snapping her fingers at Swinton, she signalled for the course to be removed, oblivious to the cutting cruelty of her last vicious remarks.

There was stunned silence at the table. The carefully aimed dart had hit home. Mary saw the telltale muscle twitch in Isaac's strong jaw. Madam had finally gotten past his strong defenses.

Grace tried to defuse the tension as she marveled at the great haunch of venison a servant was bringing in. Garnished with wild mushrooms, surrounded by a chestnut puree, dotted with tiny early root vegetables and seasoned with a red wine sauce of lightly crushed peppercorns and juniper berries, it was a splendid presentation.

"Monsieur René's outdone himself, Isaac! This haunch must be from the Park's deer herd, no?"

Isaac forced himself to ignore Madam's last barb and answered his cousin's wife politely. "Yes, the gamekeepers took it a few days ago. It's been hanging in the larder to develop flavor." He added, "I shall have them shoot a buck for you and Tommy. With that, and Mary's trout, we can feast together one night soon."

Mary smiled. The tension had dissipated. Madam was a vicious old woman who seemed to enjoy hurting others, but Isaac wasn't going to allow her to completely destroy his dinner party. He had gained a good deal of her respect this evening, and she was finally beginning to understand the forces that shaped his youth.

She had a clearer picture of what it was like for him to grow up in this big, frozen showplace of a house— never a real home—with an absent father and a cold, critical mother who seemed to have no love at all for her only son. Mary wanted, suddenly, to take and comfort that lonely little boy, to cuddle and love him, for it appeared no one had ever done so. She began to understand Isaac; she had misjudged him terribly.

Swinton brought in port for the gentlemen as the ladies rose to take tea in the drawing room. The food had been superb, up to Isaac's highest standards, but the tension had been so thick only the sharpest of knives could have cut through it. Mary vowed never again to repeat the ugly experience.

❖

"Don't know how you take it, Isaac," Tommy Adams spoke, breaking into Isaac's brooding silence.

Isaac forced a wry smile. "She is the same as she has always been, Tommy. She drove my poor father away with her evil tongue and tries to do the same with me." *But her days here are numbered,* Isaac promised himself. *Whether I wed or not, she goes to the Dower House. Soon.*

"Don't you give up on the notion of wedlock, cousin," Tommy said. "My babe will need someone of his age t'play with at the Park, just as we two did." There was a shy, proud smile on the tall man's tanned face.

Isaac stared. "What the devil! Tommy...don't tell me that Grace...she is breeding?"

Tommy nodded somewhat sheepishly, then blushed full crimson as Isaac leaped out of his chair and threw his arms around him in a crushing bear hug.

He hooted joyfully. "Tommy, you old dog! I wish you happy, man! You and your lady wife."

The Adamses had been married many years with no issue. Everyone, Isaac included, simply assumed Grace Adams was barren. It was not unusual. People had said knowingly, "What can one expect? All that riding and hunting!" Well, Grace had come through, despite her addiction to rough riding. She would not be the youngest of mothers, but she would be a mother.

"Oh, bloody hell, Tommy! Madam's remark..." Madam's tactless comment about not abiding little brats at the Park was truly ill-timed. "You must understand she speaks only for herself. You and your offspring are forever welcome here, so long as I'm in charge."

"Know that, Isaac, no need to say it. Grace was a bit

taken aback, but, then, she's a bit more sensitive these days than she used to be."

Isaac recalled the request for lemonade, and the lovely glow surrounding an uncharacteristically serene Grace. "Increasing becomes your lady, Tommy. I've never seen her looking so well, truly."

"Happy, that's what she is. Here I thought, long's she has her horses, everything will be all right, she won't miss having a babe...hid it from me very well, she did. But she does want this. Wants it more than anything."

"I am so very glad for you, Tommy. You shall make fine parents."

"And you, Isaac? Shall you remain a bachelor forever, to spite your mama?"

Isaac grinned ruefully. "I'd spite her *if* I wed, Tommy, and that's the truth of it."

"Don't spite *yourself,* Isaac," Tommy warned.

❖

In the drawing room, the ladies sipped tea and conversed lightly. Grace was curious to hear of Sally's upcoming wedding, detail by detail, and Mary was endeavoring to impart as much of the plans as she was privy to, though not having seen Sally for some time, however, she wasn't quite up to the task.

She assured Grace that Jamie Fraser was the handsomest and kindest of men, and the young couple adored one another. Mary sincerely wished her sister well, but, at the same time, was ashamed to admit her jealousy of Sally's great happiness.

Madam, bored with talk of weddings, looked on indifferently. She interrupted to comment acidly, *"Pooh!* All this chatter of love! It gives one the megrims! I shall have to call Japp for my headache powders!"

Spying the never used pianoforte, she had a better idea. She asked her niece to play for her. Mary protested, "I do not play as well as Sally, Madam. I fear you would be greatly disappointed."

"Nonsense," Madam sniffed, brooking no feeble excuses. "I have heard you play, my gel. Modesty ill becomes you now. Come, before I tire. 'Tis nearly my bedtime."

Coerced, Mary sat down before the instrument and began hesitantly to pick out tunes as she leafed through the music on the stand. There was nothing there she knew well.

"I hope you like this, Aunt," she said, humming the first few bars of one of hers and Sally's favorite folk ballads, one she knew well enough to play and sing from memory, the haunting Scots border air, "Barbara Ellen."

Isaac and Tommy joined the women just as Mary was coming to the end of the lovely folk song. Her rich contralto voice was plaintive and compelling as she sang of love unwisely scorned and sadly lost.

> *"Come, mother, come, make up my bed/Make*
> *it both long and narrow/My true love died*
> *for me yesterday/I'll die for him tomorrow..."*

Isaac paused. He had admired Sally Martin's pure, clear soprano; high and sweet, it was a young girl's voice. This, however, this deep, rich sound, was the passion-filled voice of a woman. Mary's voice thrilled his entire being. If he had only known...

Before he could praise her beautiful voice and her lovely song, Madam saw fit to remark frankly, "Pretty voice, my gel, but that song! Morbid choice for a young chit, love and loss! You gels"—she waved her pudgy arms and hands, including Grace as well as the absent bride-to-be Sally in her indictment—"thinking love's all! There's a good deal more to life than that mere trifle, I warrant you!"

"How would you know, Madam?" Isaac asked quietly from the drawing room threshold.

Madam's eyes flashed a cold pale blue fire. "Don't you pretend you do, my son," she spat. "Doffing your breeches in a married woman's boudoir don't signify love, and 'tis all *you* know of the subject!"

Mary reeled at the coarse rejoinder. Grace, noting her sudden pallor, rushed to her side, a worried look in her kind eyes. Tommy was once again struck speechless.

Isaac closed his eyes and put a hand to his forehead. He seemed immeasurably weary. Through clenched teeth, he spoke to his mother, "Madam, I believe it is time you wished our guests *adieu.*" To himself, he thought, it is past time she was moved to the Dower House. He would do it himself, if he had to.

Madam's bravado seemed to depart. Finally, she had gone too far, and there was no going back. Isaac's quiet request left her no doubt that her days as *doyenne* of Wivenhoe Park had come to an end. She gathered up the shreds of her tattered dignity and exited, looking neither to the left nor right, her high-bridged nose in the air, purposely and rudely ignoring her guests.

Inwardly, she quaked at her son's new, quiet dignity, and worried that he would come after her and insist she make her polite *adieux* to Mary and the Adamses. She scurried quickly down the hall, her footsteps clattering loudly on the marble tiles.

Isaac did not follow her, however, inordinately content to see the last of Madam. The final sad and awful battle between them had been waged, and she had quite clearly lost. Isaac sighed, and the sharp release of his withheld breath removed the last modicum of tension from the drawing room. He was somewhat pale and shaken, but relieved.

Grace went to Isaac and kissed his cheek softly. "We shall make our good nights, Cousin, and we hope to see you, and Mary, soon."

Tommy nodded in agreement and shook Isaac's hand. They kissed Mary good-bye and departed, having been assured that both the Runners would accompany her to Alresford Hall.

Mary, alone now with Isaac in the quiet room, reached a hand out to him. "Isaac," she said softly.

Seventeen

Isaac took Mary's hand, turning it palm upward and rubbing gently with his thumb. The slight roughness against the smoothness of her skin was blatantly sensual; it sent a shiver through her arm.

"I apologize," he said, "for this dreadful shambles of an evening."

She didn't pull her hand away, savoring his touch's tingling aftermath. She shook her head slowly. "Not so much of a shambles...I enjoyed the Adamses' company...and yours."

He smiled wryly and drew her down next to him on the sofa. "My dear, you are compassionate to a fault. The sad truth is that this evening has been a disaster. Madam and I should have kept our evident mutual dislike, and never-ending quarrels, to ourselves. It was rude and inappropriate behavior and I do most humbly apologize."

Mary's eyes reflected the pain she felt for him. "Poor Isaac," she murmured sympathetically. She laid the back of her hand against his cheek.

He took it and turned it over, placing a soft kiss on the smooth palm. "Mary," his voice was husky, "we have to talk."

"Do we?" she whispered, reluctance evident in her tone.

He nodded. Holding on to her hand, he explained, "I realize that I cannot continue to hope you might accept my offer of marriage..."

Mary's eyes widened. "Isaac, don't...not now," she pleaded.

He ignored her. "My parents were unhappily joined

in the bonds of matrimony. They despised each other. I don't know why. Perhaps Madam was always vindictive and mean-spirited, perhaps my father was unkind in ways I could not understand when I was a small boy. Some people, perhaps, should never marry, as the married state is somehow contrary to their natures."

"Isaac," she interrupted.

"Nay, Mary, hear me out, I beg you." He gave her a beseeching look, quelling her objections. "I have no right to take your life away. I always thought I would never marry, and perhaps I was right. And it makes no sense for me to force you into a union that would make us *both* unhappy."

If she could not love him, he should not attempt to force her to do so. That would be odious in the extreme. She had the right to refuse him.

"I shall speak to my uncle and tell him we do not suit. He can be persuaded to accept our mutual decision." There, he had said it. He gave back her freedom.

He could not read her face. She should be glad, should she not, of his decision? But...if he did not know better, he would say she was enraged. He frowned, puzzled.

"How dare you, Isaac Rebow!" she spat, freeing her hand from his and rising abruptly from the sofa. Her color was high; she was trembling.

"Mary? Have I offended you? Was this not what you wanted?" He fumbled over his words.

"Do not presume, *Sir Isaac"*—she drew out his title slowly and deliberately—"that you know what I want. We had an agreement, and I thought you were a gentleman."

Confusion showed in his face. He ran a hand through his hair, loosening the riband holding it tight. He gazed at her in complete bewilderment. "Mary," he tried again.

She put up a hand to stay his speech. "You agreed I would have two weeks to make my decision, Cousin. I hold you to it. According to my calculations, the two weeks end tomorrow." She fixed him with a steely glare.

"I shall be glad to give you my decision then," she finished, "but not a moment before."

Mary was trembling inwardly after her bold speech. What nonsense! The two weeks expired two days ago; she had counted every hour, every minute of those two weeks, not wanting to end the waiting, yet all too aware of it. She had put off this discussion, like the coward she was, but his words were not what she expected to hear. *He, release her!* No, he would not! He could not!

She loved him. How could she let him go? She would be damned forever in hell for forcing him to honor his offer, for obliging him to give up Lady Rowley, the love of his life, but she couldn't let him go. She would die if she let him go. *She was dying a little now...*

"Tomorrow, Isaac," she stated firmly, "at Alresford Hall. Please, instruct Swinton to order my carriage."

Isaac was dumbfounded. He assumed she would be overjoyed to hear of his decision to release her. Why was she carrying on so? Was it that she wanted to be the one to end it, to refuse his suit before he could withdraw? Had he insulted her by reneging?

He would never understand women, and that was the truth of it. Neither Mary, Madam, nor his late, unlamented love, Sophia. He had mastered many subjects, but females were truly beyond his ken.

"As you wish, my dear. I shall, then, visit you on the morrow. I shall see that your carriage is ready and Jeremy and Latham are set to accompany you." He left the room quickly, so quickly he didn't notice his hair riband had unfurled and fallen to the floor.

Mary watched his departing back, a look of deep longing on her expressive face. She fell to her knees to retrieve the slim band of dark fabric. She clutched it tightly to her bosom as she rose and followed Isaac out the door.

❖

Latham and Jeremy rode on horseback on either

side of Mary's ill-sprung carriage. The old vehicle jangled all the nerves in her spine, but she barely felt the rude jarring. Her mind was spinning wildly with deep, hurtful thoughts.

He didn't want her.

She would humiliate herself forever on the morrow by accepting him. She was shameless, she thought, as she sank back wearily on the worn velvet squabs. She could not release him, no matter what the cost to self-esteem. She wanted him, and she would have him, whatever the price.

Was there ever such a fool for love?

She clenched Isaac's hair riband and felt the textured grosgrain biting into her sensitive flesh. She brought it to her nose and caught a faint but seductive whiff of his lime-scented hair pomade. She inhaled its scent deeply.

❖

Bart remembered enough about life in the country to understand he must dress the part. He traded his London clothing for the breeches, shirt, and leather jerkin of a farm laborer he had met on the Colchester road after he'd allowed his stolen horse to gallop away. He trimmed his long, greasy hair and shaved off his moustache and beard, exposing the ugly, zigzagging scar he had always hidden.

The scar was the constant reminder of a brutal knife fight on the Isle of Dogs, in the heart of the London docks. His old chums in the Seven Dials stews wouldn't have recognized him. Surely, he wouldn't fit the description of a heavily-bearded man those supposed friends had given to the Runner.

Imitating the country folk, Bart shuffled, moving slowly. He kept his eyes down, further playing the part. He was enjoying this acting, but he would enjoy what came next even more. He felt for the dagger hidden between his leather vest and rough linsey-woolsey shirt. He had honed its sharp edge so it would slice like a razor. The knife with which he'd dispatched Dot hadn't been half as sharp.

Dot! He still fumed when he thought of her betrayal. *She paid, the bitch!* As would the others. As would his so-called London friends.

He formulated a plan. He would call at Alresford Hall, at the steward's office, and ask for work. He had heard from others on the road and in Wivenhoe village that itinerant farm laborers were treated kindly there. Jobs were always to be found, from thatching tenant cottage roofs to planting potatoes, and the food was good and plentiful. The Hall had an excellent reputation.

Bart would insinuate himself into the daily routine, get to know the people and the lay of the land, and strike swiftly. Kill the girl first, the dark-haired one who started all the trouble, then move on to Wivenhoe Park to stalk the lord of that manor, the flash cove, the one who set the Runner on him.

His instincts said they weren't expecting him; he was absolutely certain he had the element of surprise on his side. He had brains, Bart did, and he figured all this out by himself. Yes, he had gotten all the brains in the Scofield family; he knew that for an indisputable fact. Dot was the stupid one, and look what happened to her!

Lost in the whirl of his scheming stratagems, he didn't see the large bee buzzing close to his head, a lone emissary sent out to scout a new home. He heard it, however, and flinched, ducking his head. He raised his hand to swat the insect hard; it fell and he stepped on it, grinding it mercilessly into the dusty earth. Bees! He hated bees. He hated everything about the country, but especially bees.

As a child, Bart had attempted to steal honey from a beehive, and he had experienced swift and painful retribution. Bart had almost died from the hundreds of stings inflicted on his body by the angry army defending its hive. Even now, there were few things the grown man feared as much as he feared bees. Those humble insects, in full force, were objects of fright to him even as the lowly mouse is reputed to be a fearsome object to the mighty elephant.

❖

It stopped raining. Scout bees located and approved of the new hive Silas had installed under the sweetly blooming lilac trees adjacent to the kitchen gardens. Only a matter now of trapping the placid, honey-filled creatures on a screen. There, they would cling in a great bunch like so many fat, winged, yellow-and-black-striped grapes, and be easily deposited at the new hive.

There was no danger of being stung by the honey-bees during this process. Each bee, knowing it must move on, prepares for the move by packing its honey bag, the pouch that bulges at its rear end with the sweet stuff of its hard labor. That filled pouch interferes with the workings of the bee's stinger, rendering it useless. The bee is helpless to protect itself, even if it senses danger, for its stinger won't function.

Even so, Farmer Grey took no chances. He knew from experience that bees were sensitive, easily startled creatures. He and Mary took the precaution of wearing heavy gloves and thick-veiled hats. They forebore smokers, however. Timing, now, was all. The transfer between hives must be accomplished quickly, before bees went too far astray.

Mary was delighted to see the bees lost no time streaming out of the old hive. She and Silas held the big screen, holding it steady as the insects dropped upon it in a huge, blurry motion of round, honey-swollen bodies and whirring wings.

Grasping the edges of the screen, they maneuvered it gently but firmly toward the lilac bushes, moving gracefully in what seemed like the steps of a languid, solemn country dance.

Suddenly, a scruffy man appeared from behind the heavily-laden lilac blossoms. Mary gave a start, noting—even through her thick veil—his desperate-looking eyes and the ugly, jagged white scar that crossed his lean face. She saw a sharp, shining object descending towards her breast like a silvery pendulum in swing. As one, she and the equally alert Silas tipped the dark mound of buzzing, moving bees onto the intruder's surprised face.

The man screamed, a high, keening wail of fright that shattered the idyllic peace of the country morning. He dropped the dagger and flailed at the noisy, swarming insects with agitated, uncoordinated motions of his limbs. He was sweating profusely.

The collective brainpower in the Scofield clan didn't amount to much. Growing up in the country hadn't educated Bart in country ways and lore. He had no idea swarming bees are incapable of stinging.

He had only the excruciating memory of the pain of that unfortunate childhood mishap. The suffering had gone on for weeks. He had hovered swollen and bumpy betwixt life and death, feverishly turning in his narrow cot, tender, oozing, and red as an over-ripe raspberry.

He fell backward, catching his ankle awkwardly on the leg of a wooden bench. Trying desperately to keep the feared, hated bees out of his eyes and face, he couldn't immediately right himself. Thus, he continued to fall...onto the seat of the rustic bench, on a garden trug full of wilted, cut lilac branches—lilacs that were never collected and taken to the still room—on a discarded kitchen knife sticking out at an odd angle amongst those dry, dead blooms, over a sharp blade that pierced his heart and lungs and spurted shockingly red arterial blood all over Mary, Silas, the bees, and the lilac bushes.

Bart's anguished scream brought the kitchen staff running from the house. Mrs. Pepperwit's wails rang though the gardens and ricocheted to the stables, where Latham and Jeremy, unaware of the great danger to Mary, were currying their horses.

"Blood! There's blood everywhere! Oh, help, help, help! Someone please come help Miss Molly!" the housekeeper screamed.

❖

Isaac heard the shouts and screams as he rounded the curve of the lane taking him to Alresford Hall and Mary's long-awaited response to his marriage offer. He spurred his great steed Nizam into a fierce gallop and raced behind the house, past the formal Tudor knot garden, in the direction of the loud noises, the kitchen gardens where he had approached Mary scarcely two days before.

There were bees buzzing angrily everywhere, bees hovering heavily about the heads of fearful servants attempting to swat them away, bees underfoot in dusky masses. Many had attached themselves solidly onto the white aprons of kitchen maids and the footmen's dark livery. Silas could be heard above the throng, shouting, "Leave them be! Leave them be! Do not smite them! They will not sting, they are afeard!"

Few paid attention as they hopped about, evading one group of bees only to be set upon by others. The maids were hysterical; the male servants swore long and lustily. There was blood everywhere.

Bright crimson streams and stains of blood gave an aura of dreadful carnage to the wild scene. Isaac cringed, remembering battlefields, the slaughter of men and horses, the coppery, pungent smells of blood and fear. He was on the edge of panic as he reined Nizam in sharply, looking for Mary. Where was she?

Mary...Oh, God, please, he prayed, not Mary! Please, not Mary!

Isaac saw the two Runners calling for order among the swarming bees and hysterical servants. It was horribly clear to Isaac that whatever happened, had already happened. All was done, save for this mad shouting and the blood spilled upon the ground and splattered onto the trees. It was over. *Oh, lord, 'twas over...*

He was too late.

❖

Mary lay still and unmoving in Farmer Grey's arms, her dress streaked red. A confused bee wobbled on the folds of her skirt, weaving back and forth indecisively as if drunk. Mary had fainted. Silas removed her straw hat and was fanning her vigorously as she regained consciousness.

Between the sweeps of the broad-brimmed hat she had seen Isaac dismount from his horse and run toward her. How strangely white was his face! Bloodless in the midst of so much blood. She smiled at him, knowing at that moment no one would ever menace her or her family again, and that Isaac had come for his answer, *come running!* And she had it ready for him.

Then she fainted again.

❖

She was in his arms now, and he was murmuring her name over and over. There was a wan smile on his handsome face and concern in his deep-blue eyes. Never had she seen him look so wonderful. He was alive. She was alive. "Isaac," she breathed.

"How are you, my dear, brave girl?" he whispered, his soft lips at her temple.

From the corners of her eyes, Mary could see Mrs. Pepperwit, tears streaming down her plump face, twisting a corner of her apron. Silas and the under-gardener were busily engaged in getting the bees into their new hive. Servants stood around in small groupings, talking excitedly, alert to the drama being played out before them as the Runners wrapped Bart's lifeless body in an old blanket and dragged him out of sight.

She looked up at Isaac. "I never faint," she averred.

"I'm sure you do not," he agreed, his eyes never leaving her face.

"It was an exception," she went on, "for...for it isn't every day someone attempts to set upon me with murderous intent."

"I...I am sure they do not."

She saw his lips were trembling now with what

seemed suspiciously like barely-suppressed mirth. *Was he going to laugh?* Mary fixed him with a stern look. "I fail to understand why this is a cause for such hilarity."

"It is not, Miss Martin," he stated firmly, wiping at his eyes with two fingers.

What, why was he weeping now?

"Isaac!" She sat up, thoroughly confused by his mixed reactions, still dazed by what had happened to the intruder who came at her with a knife. She and Silas...oh, they hadn't meant him to come to harm! That forgotten blade on the bench...she shuddered as she remembered the man's slow-motion fall to his death.

"I'm sorry, my dear...it is simply that I didn't expect such a spectacular drama to accompany your decision to accept or reject my suit. It quite...unmans me." Isaac smiled at her, his eyes still suspiciously moist, his smile, meant to be reassuring, suspiciously wobbly.

A quick flush brought the pinkness back to her cheeks. As if anything could 'unman' this most masculine of men! *Hah!* she thought. *Look at him,* she mused, dressed formally, boots polished to a turn, well-fitting trousers clinging to long, muscular legs, coat shaped to his broad chest and shoulders, that perfection of a neckcloth... *Well, she would give him a piece of her mind!*

"Isaac, do not think I take the question of your proposal lightly, but that hasn't been uppermost in my mind these last few moments. However," she continued, holding up a hand to stay him before he could interject comments, "I believe you shall have your answer shortly." She put her hands out to him now, as they both rose from the ground. "If you please, Cousin, do help me to my feet. Thank you."

She stood and dusted her skirts perfunctorily. The wandering bee had righted itself and drifted off slowly in search of its hive-mates. Mary dismissed the servants, thanking them for coming to her aid, her voice husky with emotion. They departed, albeit reluctantly, as if sensing more drama would be unfolding soon.

Mrs. Pepperwit waddled over. "Miss Molly, I'll make you a cup of chamomile tea. 'Twill strengthen your nerves after this terrible fright."

"Fiddle, Mrs. P., I am perfectly fine," she insisted, as her knees began to buckle. In a twinkling, Isaac had grasped her under the arms and easily set her back on her feet.

"Steady, my dear," he cautioned. He recognized the signs of shock. He had seen it on the battlefield amongst raw young recruits, and he felt deeply for her pain and disorientation. He wished he could draw all of her suffering into himself and take it away.

She looked up at him. "I'm trying so very hard to be brave, Isaac," she said in a throaty whisper, "but I am not yet feeling..." Her voice broke, then, and all of his defenses crumbled.

Isaac brushed a soft, swift kiss on her brow. "You are the dearest, bravest girl I know, Mary, and I love you so very, very much."

Mary snapped to attention, utterly taken aback with surprise, surprise that overcame even the great shock she had just undergone. "Isaac?"

He smiled and brushed her cheek lovingly, gently, with his knuckles. "I believe I've loved you since the first time I saw you at Draycott Terrace dressed like a serving wench, a great basket of wriggling worms in your hand." He grinned now. "The more fool I, for not realizing it at once."

She was overwhelmed. It was too much. Much too much. *Isaac! He loved her. Not Sophia. Her!* "Isaac...I..." She couldn't speak, thoroughly overcome with bursting emotion.

He took her hands in his and brought them to his lips. She felt the familiar, ecstatic tingle as his warm flesh touched hers. "Here I am," he said ruefully, "rushing my fences again. Have no fear, my dear Mary. I came with the express purpose of abiding by your decision, whatever it was. You must make the choice right for you. I shall understand and honor it."

The morning's horrible, bloody events receded to the back of her mind. She knew memory would return and it would be a long time before she was wholly at peace with what had occurred, but now...now, there was only Isaac, dearest Isaac and his freely offered love, the love she had desired as long as she could remember.

Mary dimpled prettily. "You shall have to kiss me, first."

Shocked, Isaac looked down at her. Then he laughed, laughed heartily and long, and drew her into his arms. His face was very close and she thought she had never known anyone so dear, so beloved. He lowered his mouth to hers and she felt the sweet, soft pressure of his lips. She sighed with happiness, melted with joy.

"Isaac?" she murmured, pulling away slightly from his kiss.

"Mmmm?" he answered, attempting to pull her closer to him.

"Isaac, yes. The answer is yes!"

"Mmmm, not good enough," he whispered against the sweet, soft corner of her delicious mouth. "Try again."

She gazed at him, perplexed. "I said I accept your offer, Isaac, I shall marry you. Yes, I have answered yes."

He kissed the tip of her nose lightly, then each eyelid in turn. "Ah, but I shall marry only for love," he told her, "your love, freely given."

"I have loved you always, Isaac, always," she blurted out honestly, her throaty voice cracking with emotion.

He smiled and tightened his hold. She felt her heart beating rapidly against her ribs and heard his heart thumping hard inside his chest. She was dizzy with excitement.

"Say it, then, my dearest darling, say it," he asked.

She looked him full in the face and passed her thumb lightly across his parted lips. He caught it in his strong white teeth and nipped it playfully.

"Ouch!" she gasped, teasing, smiling up at him.

"Say it," he whispered, as one hand dropped down to stroke the back of her thighs and moved slowly up and across her round *derrière*. He rained feather-light

kisses on her neck and nipped at her ear. She thought she would faint again as the excitement engendered by his caresses began to mount and her body temperature rose.

With what had to be—she was sure—the very last breath in her almost-breathless body, she shouted, *"I love you!"*

He barked with laughter and swung her about joyously.

"Do stop!" she pleaded. *"Isaac!* I shall faint! I'm getting dizzy!"

He stopped and kissed her again. This time, his kiss was hard and demanding, and she opened her mouth eagerly for it.

Mary did not faint after all. She was wide awake...and never had she been more alive.

The End

Dear Reader,

Perhaps you might like to know—The Story Behind The Story....
        ...of THE RELUCTANT GUARDIAN

THE RELUCTANT GUARDIAN opens with a direct quote from Mary Martin, the 18th-century gentlewoman who inspired this story. Yes, Mary was a real person, as were Isaac Rebow, Matthew Martin, Sally, Madam, Emma Davenport, Dot Scofield, Jamie Fraser, Mrs. Pepperwit, Tommy Adams, and others.

The biggest changes I made were to move the historical setting from mid-Georgian to Regency, and to alter what actually happened in real life. The incident that opens the story is true: Matthew Martin did elope in the dead of night, and all he left his daughters was the money in the harpsichord drawer. From then on, my imagination took over. Isaac Rebow was never the Martin sisters' guardian; he didn't have a mistress named Sophia. As far as I know, Dot had no brother named Bart: however, Mary and Isaac really were first cousins.

I discovered the letters of Mary Martin Rebow at the Washington State University Library in 1970, when I worked in the Archives Division. They'd been purchased at a London antiquarian shop and had lain untouched for a number of years; they'd never been reported to the National Union Catalog. The first thing I did was report them, so that they'd be available to scholars everywhere, and the second thing I did was sit down and read them. They were the letters of a young woman to the man she loved, the man she later called husband. A thoroughly charming Georgian love story, but far different from what was to become The Reluctant Guardian.

The story percolated in my head for over twenty years. When I was introduced to Regency romance, I toyed with the idea of using the real love story as a fictional starting-off point. I had wonderful characters, with unique names no one could ever make up, and a romantic historical setting. I had walked around the London of Mary and Isaac, visiting their haunts. Queen Square is still there, but Duke Street was swallowed up (WW II bombing). I even went to Essex, where Wivenhoe Park still stands and is now part of the Unversity of Essex. The Rebow name is well-known in Colchester, but, alas, the family died out in the early 19th-century. There are no descendants of Mary and Isaac, and I don't know if Alresford Hall is still extant.

In Colchester, I met the county librarian, who was also very interested in the Rebow family. He was thrilled to find that Mary's letters to Isaac still existed! He'd been looking for them for years. He told me that there was a lost, rare Constable portrait of Mary, painted at the same time Constable painted the famous landscape of Wivenhoe Park that hangs in our National Gallery, in Washington, DC. The scene where Isaac looks out of the window and sees the cows is <u>that</u> landscape. If you are interested in the true story of Mary Martin and Isaac Rebow, it is contained in the Washington State University Archives journal, The Record, Volume 32, 1971, pages 5-46, and Volume 33, 1972, pages 5-25. The WSU Archives are in Pullman, Washington 99163.

I dedicate this work of fiction to the memory of *Earle Connette*, a gentleman, a scholar, and a truly wonderful person, who encouraged me to write the story of the Mary Martin Rebow letters—the story that became THE RELUCTANT GUARDIAN.

Jo Manning
1999